HE WAS NOT THERE

ALSO BY THIS AUTHOR

California Corwin P. I. Mystery Series
The Girl in the Morgue

Stand Alone Suspense Novels
Looking Over Your Shoulder
Lion Within
Pursued by the Past
In the Tick of Time
Loose the Dogs

YOUNG ADULT FICTION:

Between the Cracks:
Ruby
June and Justin
Michelle
Chloe
Ronnie
June, Into the Light

Tamara's Teardrops:
Tattooed Teardrops
Two Teardrops
Tortured Teardrops
Vanishing Teardrops

Medical Kidnap Files:
Mito
EDS
Proxy
Toxo

These and much more at pdworkman.com

HE WAS NOT THERE

ZACHARY GOLDMAN MYSTERIES

P.D. WORKMAN

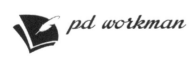

ISBN: 9781989415184

That those who have been hurt may find healing.

CHAPTER ONE

ZACHARY WAS GLAD THAT Tyrrell had called. He had needed a reason to get away from Kenzie for a while. Their relationship, which had begun more than a year ago, had gotten more complicated since Zachary had been attacked, and he needed a reason to take a break from Kenzie's ministrations. He didn't want to tell her to leave him alone and give him some space, but he wasn't sure how else to get her out of his apartment when she came over for a visit.

But his brother Tyrrell's call had given him an excuse to say that he was busy and needed to deal with a family emergency.

Not that Tyrrell had said it was an emergency. He and Heather were perfectly willing to wait until a convenient time for Zachary, but for Zachary that was a good enough excuse to tell Kenzie that he needed to take care of family stuff and would have to see her later.

"Do you want me to drive you somewhere?" Kenzie offered, still happy to do whatever he needed her to.

"I'm fine to drive."

"I know, it's just that..." she trailed off, apparently unable to find an excuse for taking care of him. He hadn't been drinking. He hadn't been having a particularly upsetting evening. She just wanted to know that everything was okay. She wanted to keep an eye on him. Zachary appreciated it, but he didn't want the attention.

"I'm fine," he repeated, getting his jacket on to signal to her that it was time to go.

Kenzie reluctantly got her coat on as well. She pulled the hood on over her dark, short curls and gave him a brief kiss with her bright-red-lipsticked lips, holding on to him more tightly and longer than was necessary for a goodbye. He gave her a squeeze of acknowledgment and headed to the door. Kenzie walked out ahead of him and watched as he locked up.

"What's going on with Tyrrell?"

"I don't know. I need to see him to find out."

"Is something wrong? Is there anything I could help with?"

"No, I don't think so. I'll let you know."

Kenzie nodded. "Okay."

They took the elevator down together, and Zachary sketched a little wave as they separated in the parking lot. "We'll talk later," he said. "Thanks for coming by."

He would have suggested that the next time, he would come by her place, just so that he had some control over the timing, but she had never invited him to her apartment, so it was out of bounds. She needed her own space and privacy. He just wished that he could have some of his back too.

As he headed to the meeting with Tyrrell, he thought about his relationship with Kenzie, the medical examiner's assistant. The relationship had transformed over the months they had known each other. Kenzie had changed from a girl who was just interested in having some fun to a woman who was really interested in him and in taking their relationship further, to one who was in his space a little too often and felt like she needed to take care of him.

It had never been like that with Bridget. He had always felt warm and rewarded when she wanted to do something for him or showed her concern. His ex-wife had more often been angry and critical when he went through a crisis, upset with him for taking too much from the relationship.

He had tried to take care of Bridget too. He had tried not to let it be a one-sided relationship, to put as much into the marriage as he took out of it, but she had never seen it that way. She had only seen him sucking the energy out of her, taking time away from her parties and social events. He'd never felt smothered by Bridget. Like with his relationship with his mother before he was put into foster care, he'd felt like he had to earn every bit of attention and every smile and kindness she might bestow upon him.

It was good that his younger brother Tyrrell was back in his life. Zachary hadn't had any contact with biological family for thirty years and it felt good to see him again. And he was going to meet Heather. He hadn't seen any of the others since the fire. He could remember the scrappy little blond tomboy Heather had been. His second sister, a couple of years older than he was, she had been one of his little surrogate mothers. One of the two big sisters who tried to keep the younger children out of trouble and out from underfoot to avoid any unnecessary problems with their mother or father. To him, they had seemed so much older and more mature at the time. He had only been ten and they had almost seemed like adults to him.

He hadn't expected to meet any of the other kids. Even Tyrrell had said that he hadn't met Heather face-to-face since they had found each other. They talked on Skype or FaceTime, but hadn't actually gotten together. What could have happened that had changed that? Was it just the natural progression of their relationship, or was there something wrong? Tyrrell had sounded concerned on the phone. Then relieved when Zachary said they could meet right away instead of trying to put it off and schedule something in the future. But maybe he was reading too much into it.

They had set up a time and place, allowing them both to meet halfway so that neither one had to drive halfway across Vermont to see each other. Zachary wasn't sure where Heather lived. Even though he was a private detective, he had never tried to find any of his siblings. They had a right to live their own lives without having to deal with him, especially since he was the reason that the family had been broken up.

Whatever reason Heather had for wanting to meet with him, Tyrrell had sounded pretty serious. Zachary pushed back the worry that it might be just to give him a piece of her mind about the problems he had caused in her life and the way he had ripped apart their family.

They had agreed to meet at a coffee shop. Clintock was a small town, so it didn't take long to find the little store. In a world that seemed to have been taken over by Starbucks, it was nice to see some independent shops were still alive and well. Zachary sat in his parked car for a few minutes, suddenly anxious about going inside. He knew Tyrrell didn't hold any resentments about what had happened to their family. But Heather was an unknown. Zachary had tried hard to please his big sisters when he was young. With his ADHD and their family problems, it had been an impossible proposition. One of them would go off on him for some stupid, impulsive mistake he had made, and he would get that knot in his stomach, that feeling that he had again come up short. And the worry that he always would.

Now she wanted him back in her life again. Why? What if he couldn't meet her expectations? He spent too much of his life with that lump in his stomach, worrying that he would never measure up to expectations. His clients, Bridget, Kenzie, the police officers that he worked with, his doctor and therapist, his surrogate fathers Lorne and Pat. They all had expectations, and he was only too aware of his failings.

The longer he stayed in the car, the harder it was going to be to actually break free of his fears and go in there and see what Tyrrell and Heather wanted, so in spite of his anxiety, he forced his body to climb out of the car, lock the doors, and walk toward the coffee shop. He clicked the lock button on his key remote a couple more times just to be sure, then stood at the door of the coffee shop, staring inside.

He saw them before they saw him. They were sitting at a table in the back. The coffee shop tables were almost deserted. People lined up at the counter to order and pick up their drinks, but they didn't stay to consume them, taking them 'to go' and carrying on with their busy lives. Tyrrell looked much the same as Zachary, but his dark hair was cut longer and shaggier than Zachary's buzz-cut. They both had dark eyes and a narrow build. Tyrrell was taller than Zachary was, not having spent as many years in a home where the food was inadequate or on meds that stunted his growth. He didn't have the hollows in his cheek that Zachary attempted to hide with a few days' growth of beard.

Zachary always lost weight before Christmas, and he hadn't been able to get back to a healthy weight before the assault. Since that incident, he'd been lucky if he could keep his weight stable. He told himself it was just a side effect of the meds, not admitting how much of his day was spent thinking about what Teddy had done to him and of other assaults in the years before he aged out of foster care. He didn't want those experiences to be a part of his life. He wanted to forget them.

Heather's appearance was quite different from Zachary's and Tyrrell's. She was blond, with a full figure. Not overweight, but a look that suggested she was a mother, having borne and nourished a few children, giving her wider hips and a silhouette that was no longer girlish, but mature. Her face looked worn and a little sad. She talked to Tyrrell earnestly, but her manner was hesitant, not animated.

She didn't look angry. Yet.

As Zachary entered the coffee shop, a two-tone electronic chime sounded, and Heather and Tyrrell looked up and turned toward the door. Tyrrell said something to Heather, probably 'there he is,' and got up to greet Zachary.

Tyrrell was always cheerful and enthusiastic when he saw Zachary, as if he really were happy to see him. Zachary's doubts always built up when he hadn't seen Tyrrell for a while, thinking his brother wouldn't really want to see him. But when he saw Tyrrell's face wreathed in smiles, and the way he reached out his hand to shake Zachary's and then pulled him in for a hug, he couldn't doubt it. Tyrrell slapped Zachary on the back and then pulled back to look at him.

"How are you, Zach? Doing okay?"

It was the first time Tyrrell had seen Zachary face-to-face since the assault, so he looked Zachary over searchingly, wanting to verify for himself that Zachary wasn't horribly mutilated.

"I'm fine," Zachary assured him. He looked past Tyrrell to Heather, who had remained sitting and didn't rush forward to be reunited with Zachary. She watched the two of them, her expression pensive.

Tyrrell turned and looked toward Heather. "Come and meet her."

They walked over to the table. Heather gazed up at Zachary and still didn't stand up to hug him or shake his hand. He sat down and she nodded to him.

"Hi."

"Hi, Heather."

Her eyes moved over him, taking everything in and finally stopping on his face. "Wow. You know, you look just the same."

"Really?" He thought of himself as almost a completely different person from who he had been before the fire. He'd only been ten years old, how could he look the same as an adult?

But he remembered recognizing Tyrrell's eyes. How they danced just the way they had when he was five. It didn't matter if the rest of him had grown up, Zachary had still seen his little brother in those eyes.

Heather nodded. Zachary fumbled for something to say. "You... grew up."

She gave a little smile. "Yeah. That's the way it works."

He didn't see it yet. He couldn't find the little girl's face he remembered in this grown-up woman.

"So, how are you? Tyrrell said that you are married with a couple of kids?"

"Yeah. They're grown up now, but I have a boy and a girl. And Grant."

"Grant is your husband?"

"Yeah."

"You're still married after the kids moved out? How many years is that?"

"Twenty-four."

"Wow. Coming up on the big one. That's really something. Not a lot of people make it that far anymore."

Of course, his perspective was slightly skewed, spending hours following unfaithful spouses during or before divorces. But lasting twenty-four years was still a big accomplishment.

"We've had our ups and downs," Heather said. "But... I never really considered leaving him over any of our issues. We just pressed on through them. You're not married?"

"No... divorced. We managed about two years. Doesn't measure up too well to your twenty-four years, does it?"

"Living with someone else can be hard." Heather's voice was toneless, she sounded as if she were far away. "If there are things that you can't come to terms with..."

Zachary nodded. "I guess... we were just too different. We wanted different things."

But it wasn't really their philosophical differences that had precipitated the divorce. The truth was far more painful than that. Zachary didn't see the need to bare his soul to Heather yet. They hardly knew each other. He had the feeling she had come to him in some kind of trouble. She needed him for something. There was no point in telling her all of his problems when she was looking for help.

Heather nodded and had a sip of her coffee. Zachary realized that he hadn't ordered, and probably should have. He had to decide whether it would make Heather more uncomfortable for him to be sitting there without a drink or for him to take a break to go get one. On balance, he thought it was probably better to stay where he was. Heather seemed like she would spook at the slightest provocation. He glanced at Tyrrell to see what he thought of the situation. Tyrrell gave him a quick nod of encouragement. But Zachary didn't know where to go with the conversation.

"So... are you in contact with any of the others? Other than Tyrrell, I mean?"

"Me and Joss have kept in touch pretty well. There were times when we couldn't, but as adults... we reconnected and have kept up with each other."

"You and Joss didn't stay together?"

"No. We were put in the same home to start out with, but... well, they said they couldn't handle both of us, and that it was interfering with their discipline to have us both there because we always got in the way. You know, if one person was getting crap, the other one was always jumping in. So they said that one of us had to go, and I was the troublemaker, so..."

"You were a troublemaker?" Zachary repeated. He could remember how Heather used to get after him when he had screwed up. He had always thought she was next to perfect. She and Joss were always trying to help their mother by taking care of the younger kids and whatever they could around the house. They were nearly adults, as far as Zachary was concerned. They couldn't have been more than twelve and fourteen when they were separated. That was awfully young to be taking care of all of the other kids. And Joss and Heather had been trying to drag up the rest of the children since they were much younger than that, probably nine or ten.

He couldn't believe that Heather would have been identified as a troublemaker. Zachary had always been a disciplinary problem, but not the girls.

"Sure," Heather gave him the corner of a grin, looking engaged for the first time. "You don't remember all the stuff I used to do? I was always getting in trouble for leading the rest of you into trouble. If everyone was into something, it was always me who had started it. I had brilliant ideas of fun things to do to entertain ourselves and they didn't always turn out well."

Zachary smiled. He did remember that Heather had been the more fun of his older sisters. She had been better at thinking up things to do and keeping the younger kids engaged and involved in a game or project. He didn't remember them ending badly because of Heather. He was so often in trouble himself, he just assumed that he had been to blame for whatever trouble they got into. "You used to make up great games. Imaginary zoos or trips. Going on an adventure. Cops and robbers."

"Yeah. We were all pretty good at pretending." Her expression grew distant again. "Maybe too good."

"What else were we going to do? It wasn't like we had electronics or the latest toys. We had ourselves, whatever we could find outside. Rocks, sticks, stuff we scavenged from other people's garbage. We had to do something."

"It was really different raising my children. They expected to have all of the things that their friends did. To be able to do all of the same things. I was always trying to get them involved in imaginary games, role playing, stuff like that, and they just wanted to watch TV or play video games. We never had that choice. We had to use our imaginations."

Zachary nodded his agreement. Tyrrell gave a bit of a nod, but he wouldn't remember much. He had only been five or six when they had been separated. He wouldn't have much memory of those lean times and how much they had lacked that other kids had. Not having the latest and greatest toys had not been their worry. They had been more concerned with getting enough to eat, and avoiding the back of one parent's hand or the other's. Or worse.

"So they moved you out how long after we were separated?" Zachary asked. "Was it right away? They never gave me an update on how either one of you was doing. I used to ask Mrs. Pratt, but she would just give me the brush-off, like she didn't even know. I knew she knew. She just didn't want to tell me."

"I don't know how long we were together. Maybe a few months or a year. Then they decided I needed to go somewhere else."

"Did you get moved a lot?"

"No, not too much. I was mostly with one family, the Astors. They weren't too bad."

Zachary nodded slowly. It was good if she'd managed to stay in one place. Not like him, jumping from one family to another so quickly that sometimes he couldn't remember where to go home after school. And institutions and group homes in between, when his behavior or anxiety was too much for a family to handle.

"I was there until I was sixteen, almost seventeen," Heather offered. "Then… mostly groups homes and shelters until I aged out. I figured I'd better get myself straightened out and either get a husband or a job, or I wasn't going to be able to last on the streets."

"Yeah." Zachary too had been driven to find a way to support himself right away. Mr. Peterson—Lorne—was the one who had suggested putting his photography skills to use in a way that would bring in some money. Art obviously didn't make anything, but private investigator work had brought in enough to pay the rent most of the time. "So what did you get into?"

"Into?" she repeated vaguely. "Oh… I didn't ever really find a job that would make me anything. I was in and out of a few relationships before I found Grant. Since then… he's a good supporter. I didn't have to work when the kids were little. Then once they were gone… he said there wasn't any reason for me to be rushing out to find a job just because they were old enough to look after themselves. So… I didn't. I just stayed at home. Kept house. Kept myself busy."

"Yeah? Good for you. I bet you were a really good mom. You were so good with us when we were kids."

"I don't think I was too bad at it. But… I don't think I ever really excelled at anything, including being a mother." She shook her head and made a face, as if he'd tried to feed her something bitter. "I didn't come here to talk about small-talk and get caught up on each other's lives."

Her words were clipped and abrupt. Zachary blinked at her. He thought that he'd been putting her at ease so that she would be able to share whatever it was she had come to him about. If it wasn't about the family and reuniting, then what was it?

Heather opened her mouth, but she seemed uncertain of herself, no longer able to speak. She looked at Tyrrell as if he might help her.

Tyrrell hesitated for a moment before venturing, "Heather saw reports of what happened with Teddy Archuro."

So had everyone else in the country. Even on the international stage. Teddy Archuro had been big news. A serial killer who, for so many years, had flown under the police radar, primarily because the men that he used and killed were illegal immigrants whose status as missing persons was never reported to the police department. No missing persons meant no investigation, and he was able to keep torturing and killing men until Zachary had investigated the missing Jose Flores. Then everything had changed.

"Uh-huh," Zachary waited for Tyrrell to finish the thought and explain why Heather wanted to contact him after the announcement of his involvement with the capture of serial killer Teddy Archuro.

Tyrrell looked at Heather to see if she would explain it to Zachary, but she said nothing, chewing on the inside of her lip.

"Heather wants to know if you would investigate an old case for her. Something that happened a long time ago."

Zachary looked at Heather. "What kind of case?"

She stared down at her coffee. Zachary again regretted that he hadn't gotten one for himself as soon as he walked into the coffee shop, but he seemed to have missed the opportunity. He waited, not pressing Heather to answer. She would get to it faster if he waited than if he tried to force her. He'd learned at least that much from his investigations and interrogations as a private detective. The hard-hitting style of the noir private eye didn't work. At least, not for him.

"It happened a long time ago," she said. "I don't know whether there is anything you can even do now. Cold cases are... I know a lot of them never get solved."

"Some of them do get solved," Zachary assured her. "Especially as new technologies come into existence. There are a lot of cases that have been solved recently solely on forensic evidence where the technology to use it just wasn't there ten or twenty years ago, but now they can go back and test the materials that they already have."

Heather nodded. "I know... I think about that... whenever I see one of those cases..."

"You never know until you try it. What kind of case was it?" Most of his high-profile cases had been murder. With Heather approaching him due to his appearance on the national news scene, he was anxious about whether it was another murder case. What kind of murder could Heather have been involved in years before?

"I saw on the news, about that serial killer, how he would... *abuse* the men he kidnapped before he killed them."

"Yes," Zachary agreed. He focused on the pulse pounding in his head. He didn't want to go back there. He didn't need to replay what had happened to him. He had been rescued, and everything that had happened between being kidnapped and being rescued was like it had happened to someone else. He didn't need to integrate it as his own memory.

"Zachary?"

He didn't even hear Heather or Tyrrell trying to call him back to earth. He just saw and heard and felt the things that had been done to him. He was in the grip of the memory, trying to pull away from what happened to his body. Trying to separate from it. He didn't want to allow it to become part of his consciousness.

"Zachary." Tyrrell's hand on his arm made Zachary jerk back instantly. He looked at Tyrrell in panic, then looked at Heather, rising an inch or two off of his seat, before he realized that he wasn't in any danger and plopped back down.

"Sorry." He swallowed. He looked at Heather. "What happened?"

"I... I was just telling you... about how... I didn't know whether..." she looked back at Tyrrell for help. He didn't offer anything, just looking from her to Zachary. "They said that he had captured you. They said it like it was just a few minutes. Was it... just a few minutes?"

It might have been only a few minutes or it might have been hours. Zachary had no way to measure the time that had passed. Teddy had given Zachary drugs so that he could act without any resistance. Zachary had been so doped up, there had been no chance of escape from the sadist who worked him over, doing whatever his twisted little brain could come up with. And yet, he'd been conscious the whole time.

"I don't know," he told Heather honestly. "It seemed like a long time."

Heather nodded, and he saw understanding in her eyes. Not just a surface emotion, but something that told him that she too understood that disassociation and time distortion. As if she, too, had been through a similar experience. He looked at her, hesitating to ask.

"What happened to you?"

CHAPTER TWO

S HE RESISTED, NOT ANSWERING his query. "That man. What did he do to you? Did he…?"

Zachary looked at Tyrrell, self-conscious. Then back at Heather. "I don't really want to talk about it, Heather. I don't… I don't even know you. My foster father wanted to know. My girlfriend wanted to know. But I can't… I don't want to talk about it to anyone."

She nodded. "Then he did, didn't he? He hurt you and you couldn't do anything to stop it."

He shrugged. She had read the news articles. She had read about the conditions of the bodies that they had discovered. She could read between the lines. She knew that he hadn't just been held as a hostage, but that Teddy had centered his time and attention on Zachary. He had exercised the power he had over Zachary to take whatever pleasure he wanted.

Heather looked away again, breaking eye contact. She swallowed and looked at the surface of her coffee.

"I was raped when I was fourteen," she said baldly. "They never figured out who it was, and I want you to find out. I want to know that he's been punished and been stopped from doing it to anyone else."

"These guys… like the guy that held me. They don't stop after one. If he assaulted you, you can bet that he assaulted other girls as well. It wasn't the first time. They don't stop unless they are behind bars."

"Yeah, I know," she admitted, still looking down. "That's why I want to put him there. If he's not already. And to make sure that he's not getting out again."

"Thirty years ago. It's not going to be easy to find him, unless you have a really good memory or some evidence. If he was thirty or forty at the time he hurt you… then he's sixty or seventy now. Hopefully, not a threat anymore."

Teddy had not been a young man. He was probably sixty. But he had still been strong and virile and able to do all kinds of unthinkable damage. He'd had plenty of experience and lots of time to experiment over the years. There was no way he would stop being a predator just because he was sixty or seventy. He would be one of the men who was always going to victimize people around him. He would always take on a new victim, as long as he had the ability.

"No. I think… unless he's lost his drive… he's going to just keep going on and on as long as they let him."

Heather nodded.

Zachary looked down at his hands, focusing on a freckle near the webbing of his first finger and thumb.

"Would you help me?" Heather prompted.

"I should," Zachary said, which he knew wasn't any kind of answer. "I don't know… how much evidence was kept? What do you remember?"

"Are you going to find him? Are you going to put him behind bars?" Heather pressed, not satisfied with his non-answer.

"I don't know. I'll start out… doing what I can to help. But I don't know how far I'll be able to get with it. I don't want to promise you results when…. there might not be anything I can do."

He took a glance in her direction. She was looking at him angrily, wanting to insist that he put her attacker behind bars. But he couldn't promise anything on a case, especially one that he hadn't been given any information on. She had undoubtedly been told before that no one could promise her anything, but that didn't stop her from wanting it. From needing it so badly.

Heather put her hands over her face and bowed, leaning her elbows on the table. "I need someone to do something about it."

"I'll try. If you'll give me the information you have now, I'll do everything I possibly can… but I don't know what to say. If there aren't some pretty good leads, I can't very well promise results. Did the police look into it at the time? Did you report it?"

Heather nodded. "Mrs. Astor took me to the police and made an official report. I had to go to the hospital, get a rape kit." She swallowed hard and tried to keep her composure. She looked at Tyrrell instead of Zachary, explaining it to him. "It was… almost worse than the rape itself. It took hours and hours… having to describe everything, them processing my clothes, my skin, every part of my body. Everything. You have no clue what it's like. When they talk about it on TV, it's like, they just do a cheek swab and clip your fingernails. But what it's like… it's like being assaulted all over again. It's like they don't even care what happened to you. They examine every inch of your body. Every… orifice."

Tyrrell nodded, his face pale. It was probably more than he wanted to know, and it was certainly more than Zachary wanted to hear, having been through a forensic exam himself much too recently. He stared away from Heather and Tyrrell, looking out one of the side windows of the coffee shop into the parking lot. He didn't have to remember anything he didn't want to. In his earlier years, he'd been able to just forget about what they did to him and go on with his life, since otherwise, there was no way he could carry on.

There was silence from both Heather and Tyrrell. Eventually he turned back toward them. Heather looked at him for an instant, the raw pain in her own eyes. How could it be so raw after so many years? Zachary cleared his throat, wishing that he at least had a drink of water in front of him, and spoke as unemotionally as he could.

"It's good that they opened an investigation and did a kit," he said brusquely. "That means that there is a cold case file somewhere with information in it that we can access, and evidence that we can have retested. You never know. With today's technology, they may be able to get a hit."

Heather nodded.

"I'll need the details of what police department it was reported to and it will probably take me a few days at least to track down the file and get it pulled from storage. Pray there were no black mold infestations. It would be good if you could come in with me to talk to them, because they'll be more likely to put the time and effort into it if they can put a face to the victim and understand that you're still waiting for justice than if it's just some annoying little PI demanding answers."

Heather gave a little smile at his words, but shook her head. "I don't know if I can do that," she said. "I'm not... very good with people and with talking about it. I haven't talked about it since it happened. I just... never told anyone else about it."

"What about your husband?"

She shook her head. "I didn't think... there wasn't any point in having to relive it and get all emotional. It wasn't like there was anything he could do. Knowing wouldn't make either of us feel any better, so I just didn't talk about it."

Zachary couldn't imagine her having a relationship with someone for so long and not talking about the things that had affected her so intimately.

Or maybe he could, since he had pushed his own memories away and had never discussed them with Bridget. But she would have been overwhelmed if he had told her everything that had ever happened to him. She was overwhelmed enough by just dealing with him on a daily basis.

For something to do, Zachary pulled out his notepad and flipped through it to find a blank page. He smoothed the paper. "What's he like? Your husband."

She eyed his pencil and paper. "He doesn't have anything to do with this. It happened long before he was ever in the picture. And he doesn't even know about it."

"I know. I'm not looking at him as a suspect or even as a witness. I'm just looking for something easy to talk about. To get warmed up before we get into anything that might be painful."

She looked doubtful. "I don't know how that's going to help. Grant is... he's a good guy. Bookkeeper. He's always been a good supporter for the family. Hasn't ever been out of work. He's changed jobs a few times, but he always has something new lined up before he gives up on the old job. He has a lot of friends. Likes to get out and do things. I don't know... what else you want to know about him? He's a good father. Loves the kids. He wasn't ever one of these dads who came home and read the paper and didn't want anyone to make any noise until he'd had his smoke and his dinner. He'd come home and want to know all about what they'd been doing that day, how things were going at school, he'd help them with homework or *ooh* and *ah* over projects that they brought home."

Zachary smiled, nodding. "He sounds like a really good guy."

"He is. Nothing like some of the dads you run into…" she didn't finish the sentence, but he assumed she was going to say 'in foster care.' There were a lot of good dads in foster care too. It was just that some of the others, the dads who didn't want anything to do with the kids, or who were violent, or who wanted too much contact of the wrong sort, ruined it for everyone. Spend time in one home with a dad like that, and it felt like he represented every other home.

"One of the foster dads I had," Zachary told her, "he was like that. He was really great. Always interested in hearing about what had happened during the day. He introduced me to photography, and even though I wasn't in the home anymore, he still helped me to develop my film over the years after that. I'm still in touch with him, even though I was only in the home for a couple of weeks. He's the only one who I would consider… a parent."

"Really?" Heather cocked her head, thinking about it. "That's really cool. I'm glad you found someone like that. There *are* some really great parents in foster care."

"It's just that those bad apples make it a miserable experience for everyone," Zachary agreed.

"Is that your Mr. Peterson?" Tyrrell asked. "Lorne?"

Zachary nodded. Of course it was. "Yeah."

"I had dinner with him and his partner," Tyrrell informed Heather. "Zachary invited me over to dinner. And Lorne and Pat are really great. You'd never guess that they weren't Zachary's foster dads for years."

"They were in the articles, weren't they? The ones about the serial killer? They were involved?"

"They weren't *involved* in anything," Zachary said quickly. "They knew one of the victims, and that's how I got the case. I offered to look into Jose's disappearance for Pat. They were really close and Pat wanted to find out what had happened to him. Didn't believe that he had just gone back home to El Salvador or was somewhere else, hiding from Immigration. They knew… that something must have happened to him for him to have disappeared suddenly like that."

"But nobody else did?"

"Other people might have doubted it. But the police didn't really think there was anything to it. And that's the trouble… because they were immigrants, no one ever took it seriously. Immigrant men disappear without a trace all the time. On purpose."

"But you were right."

"Pat was right," Zachary corrected. "I wasn't the one who thought anything. I was just following the evidence and making inquiries. He was the one who knew that something was wrong."

"Zachary really is a great investigator," Tyrrell told Heather. "He cares about people and he is good at tracking down details and noticing the things that other people don't. I was telling you about the other cases that he's solved recently—"

"I know," Heather agreed. "The paper talked about some of those cases as well. But those are all murder, right? What about something else? What about rape? Do you have any experience with that?"

Zachary looked away, swallowing. "I haven't had a lot of cases that I've investigated, no. But I've worked with other police departments and I'm good at following the clues. I have a friend who helps me with some of the forensics." He didn't tell her that Kenzie was with the medical examiner's office. That might freak Heather out. "So I have all the bases covered. Whatever I don't know, I can contract help on. I doubt there will be much I'll need to go to outside consultants on in a case like this. It sounds pretty straightforward."

"Does it?" When he looked back at her, she leveled her gaze at him. "I haven't told you anything about it."

"I just mean that you dealt with the police on it, so things are straightforward from there. We need to reexamine any data that they have, see if we can figure anything else out… identify suspects…"

"How can you do that? How can you find a suspect when they couldn't all those years ago? You can't talk to people anymore. You don't know who might have seen something or been close by. You don't know who was living in the area. You don't know anything that would help you to identify who it was in those woods all those years ago."

"I'll follow the evidence that the police have on file. I'll get your statement. You may remember more than you think you do. A lot of attacks by strangers, they aren't really strangers. It was probably someone who lived in your neighborhood. They might have seen you coming and going to school or other places. Even if you don't know who it was, the chances that it was someone who just randomly drove into the neighborhood and attacked you are pretty slim."

"Look at Elizabeth Smart. That's what happened to her."

"Even with her, they did have some contact with her father. They had been around the neighborhood and seen her before they targeted her. The police in your case would have canvassed the neighborhood. They would have talked to people they thought were suspicious. They might have talked to the perpetrator and not known it. Or they might have suspected him, but then not been able to prove it. I'll find out what I can."

She nodded slowly, studying him. He waited for her to make her decision. Finally, Heather nodded.

"Okay... I'll tell you what happened. You can talk to the cops, see what they can tell you about the investigation back then." She paused. "I don't think they did much. I never heard about any suspects and they never called me back to ask me anything else."

"They probably wouldn't have told you very much about the investigation, especially since you were a minor. And I don't know how much we'll be able to find of the original file and evidence. Sometimes there isn't a lot. We'll cross our fingers..."

"How much do you charge?" Heather asked, shifting and pulling out her purse to find her checkbook. "I assume you'll need a retainer."

Zachary shook his head and held up his hand. "Oh, no. You're family. I wouldn't charge you..."

"You're trying to make a living, aren't you? If you're working on my case, I want it to get your full attention, not just be something you're doing on the side between paying gigs."

He wanted to tell her that he would give it his full attention whether she paid him or not, but he couldn't quite say that truthfully. Not when he had done Pat's case pro bono. He needed to get a cash injection. He had plenty of small jobs, the bread and butter jobs that would pay his daily bills, but they also filled up his day. If he were going to put in the effort Heather's case deserved, he would have to put some of the others on hold for a few days or weeks.

"So how much?" Heather repeated, pen poised above her checkbook.

CHAPTER THREE

Z ACHARY'S MIND WOULDN'T LET go of Heather's story as he tried to calm himself down enough to find sleep. He tried to distract himself by thinking about other cases, mundane tasks. It was like counting sheep.

He had been sleeping better since he'd gotten home from the hospital. Not because he was on any different sleep aids. The reason, instead, was that he wanted to shut everything off. The more the stresses built up in his head, the more he just wanted to sleep to shut them off. That had never been the case before. He'd had problems getting to sleep for as long as he could remember.

But since the attack, he was sleeping more and more. He would find himself in bed halfway through the afternoon, unable to cope with the images pressing in on him. He would close his eyes to escape into the nothingness. More than once, he had slept through supper, had slept through Kenzie calling him or knocking on his door, and had wakened long after his usual pre-dawn rising to wonder what the heck had happened to the rest of the hours of the day.

Talking to Heather about her experience decades before had not calmed the beast. Focusing on someone else's experience instead of his own had not distracted him from his own distress. Instead, Heather's recollection had been added to his own; the images pressed in on him, mixing with his own experiences, adding their own weight and insistence.

He pressed his face into the pillow, seeking the darkness of sleep, but when it came it was not silent and quiet.

He dreamed he was walking in the woods. Going home from school, cutting through a green park area. He was enjoying the green of the trees and the birdsong and the rustling of squirrels in the leaves, letting the pressures of the day go. Technically, it was out of bounds, but the space called to him and he couldn't avoid it. What was wrong with walking through a public park on the way home from school? It wasn't like he was damaging property. He always just walked quietly through and didn't break branches, cut his initials into the trees, or litter.

Then he became aware of another presence in the woods with him. Not a squirrel or a bird. Something menacing. There was a presence in the woods with him. He could feel someone watching him.

He turned and looked back the way he had come, weighing whether he ought to retreat and go around the park like he was supposed to. He was past the halfway mark, so it was faster to just keep going through the park. If there were someone else there, it was probably just someone else from school, and they wouldn't want to be caught either. If he actually saw someone threatening, he could run. It wasn't that much farther. He would soon be out the other side of the park and there would be other people around who could help if he needed assistance.

He shifted the backpack on his back, running his thumbs under the shoulder straps. He looked around for any sign of anyone else around him. He looked back behind him once more to make sure he wasn't being followed. He couldn't rid himself of the feeling.

Instead of continuing in a straight line, he stepped off the worn trail and ducked behind a tree. For a minute, he just stayed there, frozen, listening for someone else's footsteps. But he couldn't hear anyone. Just the birds in the trees and the rustling of the leaves. There was another way out of the woods, a twistier path, less traveled. If someone else were in the woods with him, they would continue to follow the well-traveled path. Zachary could take the quieter path and remain unseen.

He took a few tentative steps through the grass and leaves, stopped and listened, and then took a few more, until he reached the faint trail that led through the darker, denser trees.

He had looked back so many times, not expecting the danger to come from ahead of him. And instead of avoiding trouble, he had walked right into it. A dark shape stepped out of the trees and, before he could turn and run, grabbed him.

Zachary let out a shout and jerked back, trying to pull away. But the man held him tightly.

He towered over Zachary, much taller than he was, face covered with a black balaclava that was a sharp contrast to the warm spring weather. The eyes were blue, fringed with eyelashes that were long and dark, almost feminine.

"Let go!" Zachary croaked, trying to pull away.

But the intruder didn't let go. With a glistening knife held at Zachary's throat, he pulled Zachary deeper into the woods. He looked around, making sure that they were alone and no one else who followed the trails through the park would be able to see them.

CHAPTER FOUR

Z ACHARY'S OWN SCREAM WOKE him up. He thrashed around, trying to get loose of the blankets, sure that the man was still holding on to him. He could still feel the man's weight pinning him down. His heart thudded hard and he fought back against the images of Archuro admiring his knife, laughing at Zachary's inability to get loose from him, the drugs preventing Zachary from being able to control his body properly. Archuro could see the panic in his expression and drank it in, high on Zachary's terror. He talked to him in a low, pleasant voice, talking about the things he would do to Zachary, all of the delightful tortures he had in store. He had honed his craft on the many men who had come before Zachary and looked forward to the rituals he had developed.

Zachary stumbled out of bed, needing to prove to himself that he had control over his own body and wasn't still lying in bed to be victimized again. His limbs were clumsy and his head spun, but he was able to control his body enough to stumble and crash his way into the bathroom to turn on the light and look at himself.

His face was slick with sweat, his eyes and hair wild. But the bruises and cuts that had been on his face were gone, what remained blending in with the other scars from the past.

He was not the one who had been attacked cutting through the woods on the way home from school. His experiences had been different. That was not his memory.

With shaking hands, he filled a glass with water and raised it to his lips. His mouth was as dry as a desert. Maybe a side effect of his meds, rather than the terror of the dream. His throat hurt from screaming. He wondered how long he had been yelling before he had woken himself up. He wouldn't like to be one of his own neighbors, wondering what the heck the weirdo next door was screaming about again. Maybe they thought he watched horror movies late at night.

He sat down on the lid of the toilet, breathing and trying to get his body calmed down. He was still fully dressed. He squinted at the bedroom clock, trying to read the time. Two in the morning. He should go back to bed and try to sleep more, but he didn't want to fall back into that dream. He'd been sleeping enough lately that being short on sleep one night wouldn't be a problem. He was used to being chronically short on sleep.

For a while, he just sat there, hands on his face, elbows on his knees, and sought equilibrium. He focused on other images; happier times with Kenzie, Bridget, Tyrrell, Lorne Peterson. The amazing fact that he'd met another of his siblings. That was a highlight in his life, not something to be upset about. He knew two of his siblings now. In the future, maybe there would be more. Maybe eventually, he would have contact with all of them.

They might get together for some holiday reunion and talk and share memories together. Good memories of the games they had played and other things they had done together. Not the fire and the break-up of the family.

Zachary got up, letting out a long, calming breath. He combed his hair and had another drink of water. He splashed cold water on his face and bloodshot eyes. Then he went to his computer.

He worked through reports that he hadn't completed and made sure that he got final billings out to all of the clients he had finished the work for. He wanted to clear the decks of as much as he could before diving into Heather's case, and to make sure that he had billed everyone he could so that the household bills would be covered even if Heather's case took longer than usual. He had to stay on top of the money if he wanted to stay in business. He hated accounting and hated asking people to pay up, even though he knew he was providing a valuable service and that he should expect to get paid for it. It sometimes felt like making money off of someone else's painful experience was unethical.

He did some research into cold cases and what police were solving with new technology. He was going to need to know what to look for and what to ask for as he went over Heather's case. It wouldn't get him anywhere if some file clerk just gave it a cursory scan to make sure that nothing new had popped up on the case. He needed to stay on top of it and to ask the right questions.

There were a lot of advancements in forensics. Back when Heather had been attacked, there would not have been much for the forensics guys to do when they got her evidence. They needed something to compare it against before they could provide any useful information. There weren't the same databases and computer matching abilities as there were thirty years later. Technology had blown up. As long as they had stored Heather's evidence properly, the police might be able to use it to find a DNA match to her attacker and get him put behind bars or, if he were already there, to keep him there.

Light had crept in through the windows until the whole apartment was bright, and Zachary looked at the system clock and decided it was time to take a break. He wasn't hungry, but he forced himself to go to the fridge and pick something for breakfast. His stomach just didn't appreciate food first thing in the morning, and later on, his appetite would be low because of his meds. A lot of the time he was nauseated, and that didn't help when he was supposed to be putting weight back on so that his doctor and Kenzie would stop getting on his case about how he looked like a skeleton or a scarecrow. He picked up a cup of cherry yogurt and put it on the table beside a granola bar. The kind with chocolate chips. It was his way of bribing himself to eat breakfast.

He got out a clean spoon and sat down, staring at the food, which, in spite of the sugar levels, seemed incredibly unappetizing. He removed the wrapper from the granola bar and the lid from the yogurt and sat looking at them, smelling them and waiting for his mouth to start watering in anticipation. But of course, he had no such luck. He slid his spoon into the yogurt and managed to finish it off in a few quick swallows. He took the granola bar with him to the computer, even though he was usually disciplined about not eating around the electronics. He would nibble at it while he was checking his social networks and email, and it would be gone before he knew it.

CHAPTER FIVE

A COUPLE OF HOURS later, he decided it was time to make the call to the Clintock police department, where Heather's rape case had been reported. The day shift would be in and would hopefully have had their coffees and have cleared all of the morning emergencies out of the way. He dialed the main number and prepared himself to have to tell his story to several people as they transferred him around and tried to figure out who would talk to him about getting Heather's file and evidence pulled for a new review. Police tended not to like it when people started inquiring about old cold cases. They preferred to let sleeping cases lie, or to let someone else do the footwork. He waited for the formal greeting from the duty officer, stating her name and the department and asking how she could help him.

"My sister asked me if I would call about an old case of hers to see if anything can be done to move it forward," he explained. "I'm not sure who to ask for, whether I need to talk to someone in archives, or in sex crimes, or whether there is a department that reviews cold cases regularly…"

She made an irritated noise in the back of her throat. "How old is this case?"

"Thirty years."

"Oh, good grief. It won't even be here anymore."

"I imagine it's in a warehouse somewhere," Zachary agreed. "But it is a rape, and there's no statute of limitations, right? So it stays open as a cold case indefinitely."

"I suppose so. Is there new evidence to be considered?"

"No new evidence," Zachary admitted. "But there is the old evidence to be considered. There is a lot more they can do with the forensics that they collected back then. You never know, we might just get a hit on CODIS."

"It happens," the woman allowed. "But you don't know what evidence might have been collected that long ago. Whose file is this?"

"My sister's. She's asked me to look into it and see if I can find anything out. We'll need to pull the file and the evidence before we know if there is anything that can be pursued."

"Maybe she should just let it go. It was a long time ago. She should go on and live her life."

Zachary could find nothing to say to that. He sat with his mouth open, waiting for the words to come, but he couldn't think of an appropriate answer. Would the policewoman have said the same thing if it were a murder or kidnapping? Just go on with your life and don't worry about it? Maybe she would have. Maybe she didn't understand that a violent crime could leave a black hole in the middle of a person's life, pulling everything into it, swallowing up all of the light and goodness that was created anywhere else and leaving nothing but a bare crater behind. Someone who hadn't personally experienced a crime like rape or murder... maybe she just didn't understand how it consumed a person's whole life.

"Are you still there?" the duty officer asked eventually.

"Yes."

"I guess you'd better give me her name and any other information you have. The year of the offense. If you have a file number or the name of the officer who opened it. Anything else."

Zachary dutifully gave her Heather's name and birthdate, and the date of the assault. "She didn't have the file number or the name of the officer. She was only fourteen at the time. It would have been her foster mother that had that information."

"Poor kid. Well, this will be enough to start, but it may take a while for us to find the file and evidence and get it back here. Are you in town?"

"No, but I'm in Vermont. I'll come in once you find it."

"Don't expect a lot," she warned again.

"I know. I've told Heather not to get her hopes up. But if there is anything... I have to at least try. See if I can bring her some kind of peace. If we can get the guy who did this to her behind bars, or keep him behind bars..."

"If it was investigated at the time, they would have run down all of the leads. It could have been someone who lived out of town, even out of the state. And if there is any evidence left, it might be completely degraded by now. You don't know if it will be usable."

"Yeah."

There was the tapping of keys and Zachary didn't know whether he should say goodbye and get off of the line, or wait for her to say something else.

"I am getting a hit on our archives catalog," the duty officer offered. "So we do have something at the warehouse. That's good news. That means that at least you called the right police department. You wouldn't believe the number of times when people don't even know what police department a file was opened with. We spend hours looking for a 'lost' case, only to find out that it was opened in another county. Or even another state."

"Memories are faulty," Zachary acknowledged. "Especially if it's someone like Heather, who was only a child at the time. I don't remember the details of a lot of the homes that I was in. If they move a kid to another city to get away from a bad influence, he might not even remember a year or two later."

"Mmm-hmm." Her voice was distant, as if she weren't really listening to him.

"So, you'll put in a request for that file and then let me know? And I'll come in to talk to whatever officer it's assigned to and we can work through what evidence there is and if there are any other leads to pursue?"

"Yes, that's right. *Who* exactly are you?"

Her tone made it sound like she had suddenly discovered he had told her a lie or was trying to pull something over on her.

"Uh. My name is Zachary Goldman. Heather is my sister…"

"But who are you? You're not a reporter…?"

"No. I…" he wondered if she recognized his name from the news and was trying to place it. "I'm a private investigator, actually. That's why Heather thought I might be able to help. Find a lead that hadn't been considered before."

"Oh, you're a PI. Well, that changes things."

"I don't see how. I'm just helping my sister out, like I said."

"Our department doesn't work with private investigators."

"I'm looking into it for my sister. I'll bring her along when the officer is ready, if I can, but she's traumatized. I don't know whether I'll be able to get her in. If I can't, do you need her to fill out an authorization or something to talk to the officer?"

"We'll definitely need her written authorization. And I don't know if they'll accept it if it's for a private investigator. Like I said, we don't deal with PIs."

"I'll deal with whatever forms you need me to. I'm Heather's brother." It was obviously going to be a tricky situation, and he was actually grateful that the duty officer had tipped him off to it before he had to deal with the officer who would be in charge of the file when it was brought out of storage. He wouldn't mention to them that he was a private investigator, just Heather's brother.

Zachary had been checking his social networks when an alert came up on his computer and he saw that he had an incoming video call. It was Lorne Peterson, his former foster father and probably his best friend, so he couldn't turn down the call without a good reason. If he were in the middle of something important or a conference with a client, that was one thing, but he had just been taking a break to look at his email and social networks, and Lorne had probably seen that he was online in a status line. Zachary let it ring for a minute while his mind jumped ahead, trying to script the call. He clicked to answer it.

He would have turned off the video and just done a voice call, except that the whole reason Mr. Peterson was calling using video chat was so that they could talk face-to-face. Zachary had promised that they could see each other more often that way so that he didn't have to make the two-hour drive to see

Lorne and Pat for them to see that he was okay. So he let the video load, and in a minute was looking at the round face and fringe of white hair that was so familiar and important to him. He couldn't help smiling at Mr. Peterson's cheerful smile.

"Hi."

"Zachary! Believe it or not, I actually set up the call myself this time." He gave a self-satisfied nod, as if he had conquered a difficult task. "I'll get the hang of this yet!"

"Great job." Zachary rubbed his face and scratched at his stubbly skin, looking at himself in the smaller picture in the corner of his screen. "I don't actually look as bad as this video makes me look, trust me."

"It's just good to see you. You don't have to get all dressed up for me."

"Yeah, but I could have at least combed my hair and washed my face." Zachary rubbed his slightly-bleary eyes. At least with the buzz cut, he didn't really have to do anything to take care of his hair. And he had splashed water on his face; that had to count for something.

"So tell me what's new. I can't believe how fast the time goes by. It seems like you were just here, but it's been weeks."

They had, at least, talked in that time, so Zachary didn't have to feel guilty about not having gone to visit Lorne and Pat during that time. "I saw Tyrrell yesterday. He says 'hi.'"

"Oh, I'm glad to hear that you got together. He's such a nice young man. Tell him 'hi' from me too. How is he doing?"

"Seems to be doing pretty well. He actually called me because one of my sisters wanted to meet me. Heather."

"Really? Zach, that's fantastic. How was it?"

"It was nice to see her again. She's... a lot older."

Mr. Peterson laughed. "I would guess so!"

There was movement behind him on the screen and, in a moment, Pat was leaning over Lorne's shoulder to look at Zachary. "Hi, Zachary! How's it going?" Pat was younger than Lorne. Not a young man anymore, looking more distinguished with some gray at his temples, but still vigorous and fit.

"Good, Pat. How about you?"

"Can't complain. I'll leave you two alone. I just wanted to make sure that Lorne hadn't run into any problem and that I got to say 'hi.'"

"Thanks!"

Pat withdrew again. Mr. Peterson watched him leave, smiling fondly. "Okay, where were we? Oh, your sister. Which one?"

"Heather. Second-oldest."

"Right. How did that go? Did you have a good visit?"

"Well, it wasn't really much catching up... she had T contact me so that she could talk to me about a cold case she wanted me to look into."

"Oh." Mr. Peterson's eyebrows climbed upward. "What kind of a case?"

"She was assaulted as a teenager. They never caught the guy who did it, and she's thinking that now with the technological advances, maybe they'll be able to, and she can rest a little easier knowing that he's off the streets."

"The poor girl. Do you think you'll be able to help her? It's been so long."

"I know it's been a long time, but with DNA testing and some of the other forensics they can do now, I think there's at least a good chance that they'll be able to make some kind of break on the case. It's worth looking at, anyway. And there might be other leads on the file that I can follow up on. Sometimes just a fresh pair of eyes on a case…"

"Well, I hope it works out. After this long, I'm sure she'd be glad to get a little justice. But it was a long time ago…"

"Yeah. We're all trying not to get our hopes up about everything just falling into place and being able to pin it on someone."

CHAPTER SIX

Z ACHARY GAVE IT A few days before calling the police department of Clintock again, hoping that they would call him back and let him know that the file had arrived. But there was no word, so eventually, he called again to find out if they had made any progress. Sometimes he just didn't hear from people until he started to make some noise. There was a different officer on duty on the main phone number, and he muttered under his breath while he tapped information into the computer, trying to get the system to spit out the status of the case that Zachary had requested. Not complaining about Zachary, just a steady stream of search terms, talking to the computer, and cursing the makers of the software and computer for making it so difficult to find what it was he was looking for.

"Okay… Heather Goldman, is that what you said?"

"Yes. That's right."

"Looks like there was a request to pull the file. I just have to jump over to another database to see where it is in the system…" More muttering. "Looks like we got it. It should have been assigned to an officer. Why isn't it showing up on the damn system?" The duty officer pounded the keys, frustrated and trying to beat an answer out of the computer. "There's the file in the log, so whose desk did it end up on? Just a minute. Can you hold?"

Before Zachary could answer, the man was gone and he was listening to some easy listening version of U2. Zachary rolled his eyes and put down his phone, switching it to speaker phone so he could keep himself occupied while the officer tried to track down the file. Several songs played, and he was getting sick of whatever station they had it tuned to. It had to qualify as some kind of torture to have to listen to that music for more than a minute. Zachary checked his email and went through the next few bits of spam and responses on other files. It would be ironic if he got an email from the officer who had been charged with Heather's case while the duty officer was trying to track down that information. But no such luck.

"Hello? Are you there?"

"Oh, hi." Zachary tapped the phone off of speaker mode and picked it back up. "I'm here. Were you able to track it down?"

"I was able, and he is Able."

"What?"

"It's been assigned to Detective Able. I'll put you through. Do you want his number in case you have to call back later?"

"Yes, please."

The Duty Officer read the number off to him and Zachary jotted it down. Then he was ringing through to Detective Able without another word. Zachary didn't know whether the Duty Officer had already talked to Detective Able to give him a warning that he was putting a call through or not, so he again prepared to start from the beginning.

"Able."

"Uh… hi, Detective Able. I don't know if anyone told you, but I'm Zachary Goldman and I'm calling about a file that has apparently been assigned to you. A cold case for my sister, Heather Goldman."

"Yeah, I saw that. Goldman…" He made a noise for Zachary to wait while he apparently looked through his inbox or a stack of files that had ended up on his desk. "Yeah, here it is. Heather Goldman. This is a dusty one!" Able sneezed. "Nineteen eighty-nine. Really?"

"Yes, really. She was only fourteen at the time. It would be nice if we could find something that would help her to move on."

"Who's going to find something after this long?"

Zachary hoped that he wasn't assigned too many cold cases to review, if that was his approach.

"You never know. There have been a lot of advancements in technology," Zachary started again, "There might be—"

"Technology isn't going to be able to help us much in this case." There was the sound of turning pages as Able looked over the file.

"What do you mean?"

"I mean that all I've got here is paper. Maybe there is a police sketch or something that they could age-advance, but other than that, about the only technology that's going to be used in this case is eyes on paper."

"You didn't get the physical evidence? Maybe it was transferred to your medical examiner or forensic department…?"

"No physical evidence here," Able agreed. "If they transferred evidence to another department for testing, there should at least be a sticky on the file, and I don't see anything. There is no physical evidence on this file."

"But a rape kit was done."

"No, it doesn't look like it."

"I think Heather knows whether there was a rape kit done or not. They take several hours and she has a very clear recollection of it."

"Witness recall is often faulty. She might have had to go to the hospital for some follow up and thought that they did a kit. But there wasn't anything sent back with the file."

CHAPTER SEVEN

Z ACHARY WENT TO CLINTOCK without Heather. He wasn't about to drag her all that way just to find out that they hadn't managed to find the forensic evidence that had been collected all of those years ago. She had been as traumatized with the collection of the evidence as she had been by the assault itself, and he understood better than anyone how it would feel for all of that evidence to be lost after the ordeal it had been to collect it in the first place. He'd wait until he had something concrete to tell her.

The town brought back memories. He had lived there for most of his growing-up years. The shape of the place had changed; there were new buildings and broader streets and other indications of the progress of time, but he recognized a lot of what he saw. The hospital, the skyline, though it was much more crowded now. The residential streets that he had walked or been taken over by bus or social workers or foster parents. He passed one of his old schools, and tried hard not to be sucked into the memories. He had been at a lot of different schools, and he didn't remember specifically anything that had happened at that one, but that just meant a flood of unfiltered memories rose up around him, threatening to drown him in flashbacks. He kept driving, refusing to be distracted, trying to keep them all at bay.

Because of Heather's case and the time he had spent thinking about it, memories of school bullies and foster families who had threatened or assaulted him were at the forefront, pressing for him to remember what he had worked so hard to forget. He stared at the road and reviewed his route to the police station in his mind, trying to keep everything else out. How was it going to help Heather for him to remember what had happened to him as a kid? He might be able to be sympathetic to her, but that didn't help to solve her case.

It was a little better once the school was out of sight again, and he pressed forward, finding the police station and looking for the public parking.

It was a building that he knew. He hadn't been there as Heather had, reporting the assault that had happened to her. Instead, he was pretty sure it was the station he had been taken to that first December after the fire. With the first anniversary of the fire looming large ahead of him, he had run away, and had, for a day at least, joined up with a group of older, more experienced street kids and learned some of the ropes of street life.

It was cold and he'd left home without the clothing he would need to get through the bitter nights on the street. He had worn the coat that he would wear to get from the climate-controlled house to the warm car, not the kind of gear he would need to keep warm all day and all night outside. Unfortunately, he and his partner in crime had been caught shoplifting warmer clothes, and he had been taken to the police station where his social worker had picked him up.

He could clearly remember sitting there on a bench with older criminals around him, waiting for Mrs. Pratt to pick him up, unsure where he would go or what he would do once she arrived.

As it turned out, he hadn't been able to handle it when she took him back to his foster family, and she had eventually taken him to Bonnie Brown, the children's secure care facility, where they could keep him safe for the next couple of weeks until he could get past the anniversary. It had been a relief to get away from the Christmas tree, candles, and wood-frame house and to know that he wasn't going to be caught in another fire on Christmas Eve. But unlike Scrooge's Christmas Eve visitors, those ghosts had continued to haunt him all through his life, whenever the anniversary approached again.

Zachary swallowed and had a drink of his cold coffee. He got out of the car and went to the front doors of the police station. He wasn't a child anymore. He was a grown man and no one there would have any idea of his past history. Not that they would care, even if they knew. He wasn't a master criminal. He was just a guy who'd had a troubled childhood.

He waited at the front desk and then introduced himself, explaining that he'd set up an appointment with Detective Able.

Detective Able called Zachary's name and motioned him to follow. He was an older cop, maybe riding a desk until retirement. He had dark hair with plenty of gray. He was a little too heavy, not in the same shape he'd been as a patrol officer on the streets.

"Nice to meet you," he said to Zachary, not meeting his eye or paying any attention to see if he answered or not. He led Zachary through a number of corridors to a small meeting room. It was furnished with a wood conference table and soft chairs, not the spare, sturdier furniture of an interrogation room. A room intended for meetings with families and victims, not violent offender interviews.

There was an old, yellowing folder on the table. Maybe half an inch thick, with an archival bar code on the front and Heather's name neatly printed in black felt pen on the tab. Able motioned for Zachary to have a seat on the side of the table, not the head where the folder was.

"So Heather is your sister?"

"Yes."

Able stared at him. Zachary worked his wallet out of his back pocket and produced his driver's license. He also unfolded the authorization note Heather had written and smoothed it out on the table while Able examined his license and compared the picture to Zachary's face. He'd lost weight since the picture had been taken, but it was still a good enough likeness. Able glanced at the authorization letter but didn't read it, pick it up, or make a copy. He sat down in front of the folder.

"So you remember when she was attacked? You were how old?"

"I would have been twelve."

"So you probably weren't told much."

"I was in a different foster home. We were only recently reunited, I didn't hear about it at the time."

"And what has she told you?"

"The basics. A stranger attack when she was walking home from school through a wooded area." Zachary swallowed and tried to keep his voice unemotional. "She was dragged to an isolated area and assaulted at knife point, then released. She told her foster mom and that started the whole investigation."

Able nodded. He opened the file. Zachary could see the edges of the yellowing pages, all trued up at the top and inserted into a two-prong fastener. There were brown, heat-transfer fax reports that were probably completely unreadable if they hadn't been copied onto regular paper. Some colored forms. Heather's sad story, all reduced to a small sheaf of papers. Just like Zachary's experience with Archuro, all summarized in bald, unfeeling description by someone removed from the experience. But it was good that it was all reduced to words on paper. That meant that it was recorded for anyone who needed to know the details and he could forget about it. He didn't have to think about being trapped in the dark, dirty shack, too drugged to do anything to stop a man who wanted nothing more than to control and degrade him.

"Sir…?"

Zachary caught his breath, startled. He looked at Able and tried to relax his body. This interview wasn't about him. It was about Heather. Helping her to find the man who had hurt her and to put him behind bars or somehow assure her that he wouldn't be able to hurt anyone else again.

He cleared his throat. "It doesn't look like there's a whole lot to go on there."

Able looked down at it again. "They investigated what they could. But Miss Goldman was not able to provide them with any kind of description of her attacker. Average height and build, white, wearing a mask. No identifying features. Nothing that she noticed about him. You would think that she could have at least given eye color, but maybe not. Maybe it was too dark or her eyes were shut or she was just too panicked to notice."

"So what did they do? Canvassed the neighborhood to see if anyone had seen anything? Check registered sex offenders in the area?"

"No sex offender registry until 1996. They checked anyone known to police. But without a description, there wasn't much they could do."

"What about the rape kit?"

Able looked down at the folder, fiddling with one of the corners. He flipped through a few pages as if looking it up, but Zachary knew from his body language that he already knew what he was going to tell Zachary, and it wasn't good news. Able searched for a form and held the other pages in place so they wouldn't flop back down over it.

"She was taken to the hospital and a forensic sexual assault kit was performed that day, as well as treating her injuries." He looked up at Zachary. "He beat her up pretty good. Her foster mother couldn't have helped but see that something had happened to her."

Zachary nodded. Heather hadn't told him those details, but he wasn't surprised. Rape wasn't about love or sex. It was about violence and control. Depravity.

"So what were they able to discover from the forensics at the time?"

"Not a lot. The technology wasn't where it is now. There were dark hairs recovered. Straight. They should have done blood typing, but I don't see any on the file. It was too long ago for any kind of DNA testing."

"But that can be done now, if the samples were preserved."

Able didn't look at him. Zachary waited. The duty officer had told him that there wasn't any physical evidence. He wasn't sure how they could have done a rape kit and then lost it, but it was decades before. Things went astray. Got miscataloged. It happened.

"The rape kit was destroyed," Able said finally.

"Destroyed. By accident?"

"No. It wasn't the same as it is now… They couldn't use it to develop a profile. They could only test it against suspects, compare samples. If there were no suspects, and the case wasn't going anywhere… they had a policy."

"A policy on what?"

"On retention of rape kit evidence. They were only retained for two years."

"Two years? But there's no statute of limitations on rape."

Able scratched his ear. "There's no statute of limitations on *aggravated* sexual assault. Sexual assault has a six-year limitation. But back at the beginning of eighty-nine, before your sister's case… aggravated was six years and sexual assault was three years."

"But if they destroyed the evidence at two years…"

"That was just the policy at the time. In some jurisdictions, it was as little as six months. Or if it didn't look like there was any chance of solving the case… it might be ditched within a few weeks. They never anticipated that we'd be able to do anything with it decades later. It was beyond imagination."

Zachary sat back in his chair, head spinning. After all that Heather had gone through, the rape, the kit, and the decades of emotional trauma that followed her everywhere she went, she was going to have to face the fact that all of the hard evidence in the case had been destroyed, and with it, any chance of identifying the unknown man.

He would still go through the motions of following up on every lead and trying to solve the crime, but the chances that the police who had initially investigated it had overlooked some obvious clue that was still usable thirty years later were slim to none. Without the evidence, they were up the creek.

"Sorry," Able said without looking at him. "Wish I had some better news for you. But maybe… this is a sign that it's time for her to just move on, and give up on the case ever being solved."

Like the duty officer Zachary had talked to the first day, Able didn't seem to have any comprehension of just how impossible that was. He had no doubt that Heather had tried to move on. She had gone on to get married and have a family. But she hadn't been able to leave it behind and had finally turned to Zachary for help. He hated the fact that he was going to have to tell her that it wasn't going to work.

"Well…" Able closed the file and started to heft himself up from the table. "I'll show you out."

"I still want to look at the file," Zachary said, not getting up.

"Why would you want to do that? There's nothing in there. I'm telling you. I've read through it. They did everything they could, and they weren't able to find the perp. Being able to find a stranger without any forensics is hard enough when it just happened. But decades later? There's no way. It can't be done."

Zachary nodded. "I know. But I need to do this for her."

Able stared at him, waiting for him to reconsider and come to his senses.

Zachary bit his lip. He shook his head. "I've been where she is. I know what she's going through. I have to do what I can. Maybe I can't do anything for her, but I have to try. This is all my fault. I have to try to make it right."

"Your fault?" Able questioned, not sitting back down, but towering over Zachary and making him feel ten years old all over again. "You said that you weren't even in the same home as her. So how could any of this be your fault?"

"It was because of me that she was there, in that home. It's my fault that we all got separated and had to go into foster care. Because of the stuff that I did. If I hadn't… then we would both have still been home with our biological parents, and this wouldn't have happened to her."

"I'm not exactly a fatalist, but I don't think it's that simple. I think some stuff is going to happen, no matter what, we can't stop it. If it didn't happen in that foster home when she was fourteen… then maybe in another when she was sixteen. Do you know how many women are sexually assaulted at some point in their lifetime? Yeah, kids in foster care are a big target group, girls and boys, but outside of foster care, a high percentage of women still get assaulted.

And some women are just natural targets, no matter what they might do to try to protect themselves." He shrugged his thick shoulders. "You can't put that all on yourself."

"The only reason she got in contact with me again was because she thought that maybe I might be able to help her out with this. That maybe there was someone who could understand what she had been through and who cared enough to try to get her justice."

Zachary reached for the file.

"It's a small file. It won't take that long for me to read through. I can make my own notes, right? I can make notes, just not photocopy it?"

Able stood there looking at him. "She's lucky to have you, but you're an idiot. Go ahead. Read the file. You're just putting yourself through extra emotional trauma that you don't have to. Cops have to face this stuff and deal with the emotional fallout that comes from seeing the world's depravity. You don't have to."

Zachary pulled the file over to himself and opened it up. He said nothing, just looked at the first page in the file, which was the last page chronologically, and skimmed over it.

Able paused in the doorway. "I'm just across the hall. Give me a shout if you have any questions. Check out at the front desk when you leave. Leave the file and everything in it here."

He left the conference room, shutting the door much harder than he needed to.

CHAPTER EIGHT

Z ACHARY LOOKED AT THE first page of the file after Able was gone. It was a densely handwritten form, and he knew from experience that he wasn't going to be able to get through the whole file or to absorb everything he read. He was better at reading than he had been in school, but he'd also taught himself some tricks. One of them was to use the tools at hand and to give himself lots of time to go over things repeatedly, getting another layer of knowledge each time.

Able wasn't there directly supervising him and, as far as Zachary knew, the video surveillance inside the room hadn't been turned on either, so he pulled out his phone and went to work. He opened up the two-prong fastener so that he could lay each page flat and work with one at a time instead of trying to hold the file open like Able had. He took a quick photo of each page, and the camera straightened and squared them and started processing them in the background. It wouldn't be able to interpret the handwriting, but it would be able to OCR the typewritten information so that he could search it for keywords later. And he would have all the time he needed to read and re-read each page of the file.

He skimmed each page as he took his photos, reading the form headings and phrases on the typewritten statements and reports. Incident report. Evidence logs. Who had been questioned, what streets had been canvassed. He would go through it all and make sure that no lead had been left unfollowed. Did she have classmates who knew what was going on? Had other girls been assaulted? Had there been any eyewitnesses who saw the man in the mask or someone dressed in dark colors as he had been? He could put together a profile. They could find *something* out. Even if it didn't lead anywhere, at least he could show her that he had done everything he could to help her out.

He stopped when he got to the pictures.

Long, spindly arms and legs. Unruly or uncombed blond hair pulled back into a messy ponytail. Bruises all over her body. He had cut her throat a couple of times, minor lacerations. He hadn't drugged her. He'd used force and violence to keep her under control.

Zachary laid the pictures out one at a time and snapped photos of them. Her eyes had been blocked out, and in some of the pictures, the more intimate parts of her body, but they had taken close-ups of those areas as well, showing the bruising and tearing. He felt nauseated, but went on, working his way mechanically through the stack. Maybe Kenzie would be able to tell something from the photos. Something that they now knew on a visual inspection that they wouldn't have known back then.

He was relieved when he got through the small stack of photos and got back to statements and questions. There was commentary on what Heather had been wearing at the time. Where she had been and the time of day. All pointing toward the authorities thinking that she'd gotten herself into the situation by being careless. Or worse, that she'd been asking for it. That had been the culture at the time. Victim blaming. Shaming. Rather than being kind and gentle in their questions, they would attack her with their words, trying to break her. Trying to get her to admit that it had all been her fault or that she had made it all up.

Zachary himself had known, even at a very young age, that he couldn't go to the authorities with complaints about the abuse that he received. He had known that they would blame him. Didn't he get blamed for everything else? Didn't they always tell him that it was his own fault when he got hurt? He was too impulsive, he made stupid decisions, he took risks. He never stopped to think about what he was doing or what the consequences could be.

Going to anyone to report sexual abuse would just be admitting that he wasn't big enough, strong enough, or man enough. That kind of thing didn't happen to *real* men. And Zachary, always small for his age, always skinny with twigs for arms, did not need to be told how unmanly he was.

When he got back home, he wanted nothing more than to just lie down and go to sleep again and shut out the rest of the world, especially all that he'd just seen of what had befallen Heather.

First, Heather had been attacked. Then she'd had to endure the questioning at the hands of the policemen who wanted to find out whether it had really been an attack, or whether she had somehow consented or asked for it. They should have known, looking at her bruises, just as her foster mother had known, that there was no issue of whether consent had been given. Heather had obviously been attacked. It hadn't been some kind of frat party mistake. It hadn't been a date. Even if she had arranged to meet with someone—and Zachary believed her when she said she hadn't—that person had been there only to victimize Heather.

Had her foster mother not known what kind of culture they would face if she took Heather in? Maybe she was a militant mom, wanting to change the world and make things better for her foster kids, even at their own expense. Zachary remembered then that she hadn't had a lot of foster kids. Heather said that she had two older sons and had wanted to take in a girl. So Heather wasn't one of many, as Zachary had usually been when he was placed in a new family, but just one girl, maybe their only foster. Maybe her mother hadn't known what kind of a world was out there for a teenage girl who was just trying to find her way in the world and hadn't known the kind of rape culture that they lived in.

Zachary was thinking longingly of his bed from at least ten miles away. But when he got up to his apartment door, he could see that someone had been there. There was a sticky note at eye level, beside the peephole.

I'm here. K

Kenzie. She knew better than to surprise him by being in his apartment unannounced. Even though he had given her a key, she still didn't usually go into the apartment if he weren't there. She knew that he had previously called the police on Bridget when he had thought there was an intruder in his apartment. Best not to startle him or to have the police on the scene because of a visit from his girlfriend.

Zachary pulled the note off of the door and turned the handle. Without the note, he would have noticed that the door was unlocked, and that would have set off all kinds of alarm bells. He closed and locked the door behind him and walked through the kitchen into the living room.

"Hey." He gave Kenzie a smile and held up the note. "Thanks for letting me know."

"I figured it was better not to give you a heart attack."

"Yeah. Much appreciated."

She knew how jumpy he had been since the attack. It wouldn't be hard to send him into a flashback.

"Long day?" Kenzie asked, looking him over.

Zachary rubbed his eyes with the pads of his fingers. "Yeah, a little rough."

"Come sit down." She patted the couch cushion next to him. "Get yourself a drink and come relax and tell me about it."

He went to the fridge for a soft drink and returned.

"I'm working on a new case." He elected not to tell her that it was Heather. She could be more objective if she didn't know that it was his sister. And he wasn't sure how comfortable he was sharing Heather's story with anyone without her express permission. "It's a cold case. Really cold. Thirty years ago."

"A murder?"

"Aggravated sexual assault."

She cocked her head. "Do you really think that's wise?"

"Why?"

"I just think… you've been having such a hard time since… you know… Archuro… I didn't think you'd want to be reminded about what happened to you."

Not that he'd told her anything about what Teddy had done. But she wasn't stupid.

"I'm just fine." He popped the top of his can and wiggled closer to her, cuddling up to show her that he was over what had happened with Teddy

Archuro and she didn't need to worry about dealing with a head-case. No more than usual.

"Okay. If you're sure. I wouldn't want it to set you off."

He thought about his nightmares the night before and didn't admit to her or himself that she might be right. He was over it. He was completely okay dealing with Heather's case.

"Anyway… I had to drive out to look at the police file today and see what we had to go on."

"I gather from your tone that it wasn't very much."

"No. The file is pretty small, and it looks like they pretty much blamed her for what had happened. Why was a young woman walking through the park on her own, you know? And even though she had a sexual assault kit done… the evidence was all destroyed. There's nothing left to test."

"Ouch. That's not very helpful. I had heard that a lot of kits had been destroyed. Or else stored but never tested."

"I'd understand if it was never tested. They didn't have the ability to do it back then, and they can't have every kit that was ever taken tested all at once. There has to be some kind of decision made as to priority, and then it takes time. But destroying it… I just can't fathom how they thought that was a good idea at the time. The statute of limitations wasn't even up. How could they ever prosecute anyone if they destroyed all of the evidence?"

"I guess they didn't think there was any way they'd ever be bringing anyone to trial."

"Exactly. A stranger attack, no one to try to match it against… so they just decided it was worthless." Zachary shook his head. "Tell me that wouldn't happen with today's protocols and procedures. Tell me that there are no destruction polices for hard evidence in a murder or aggravated assault."

"Most of the police departments have pretty strict retention policies now. Which causes other difficulties, like finding enough warehouse space."

Zachary sipped his cold drink, savoring the sweetness at the end of a long, hard day. Of course, a beer would be even better, but he intentionally didn't keep any alcohol in the apartment.

"So it was a wasted trip?"

"I'm still going to find out what I can. See if I can pick up on any leads or avenues they might have left unexplored. But I'm not really hopeful of finding anything like that… much less the rapist. It was just too long ago. We can't go back and question people who were in the area at the time."

"There might still be some old residents. But after thirty years, you're not going to have a whole lot of luck that way. Either people weren't there that long ago, or if they were old enough to observe anything and know that there was a problem, they are getting on in years now and aren't reliable as witnesses."

"Yeah. We might be able to find a nosy neighbor, if we're lucky, but the chances that the neighbor would have a lead that was never followed up on…"

"Not great," Kenzie agreed.

"I have some pictures. Do you want to look at them?"

Kenzie shrugged. "If you want. How bad are they?"

"She was pretty battered. But I'm sure you've seen worse."

"I probably have, but sexual assault is always a difficult one to deal with."

"Worse than murdered children?"

Kenzie just had a sip of her drink and didn't answer.

Zachary grabbed his tablet and pulled up his photo stream to look at the pictures of the file photos. He made sure they were not labeled on the front with Heather's name, then passed the tablet over to Kenzie to allow her to examine them. Kenzie put her drink down on the coffee table and slowly swiped through the photos. A couple of times she panned or zoomed the pictures, taking a closer look.

"Poor girl. He must have been pretty strong."

"That's what I figured." There had been a lot of bruising. Her arms where he had held her down. Her battered face. Her ribs and her thighs. She had fought back, but he had overwhelmed her with force.

"I think these are bite marks," Kenzie said, pointing to one of the bruises, outlining a semicircle shape. "We can compare those to the guy's teeth, if you get a suspect. Teeth do change over time, they might have drifted or he might even have had braces to straighten them later in life. He could have implants or dentures now. But if you're lucky, he's still got his permanent teeth and hasn't done anything with them, and we'll still be able to compare the positions against the bruises."

Zachary nodded eagerly. At least it was something. It wouldn't help him to find a suspect, but if he had one, they might be able to rule him in or out. "That would be good."

"If it was modern-day, they would have swabbed those for saliva, and have a DNA profile."

He was quiet while she continued to look through the pictures.

"A lot of sexual assault victims don't have any visible injuries," Kenzie said. "But it's pretty obvious in this case. Scratches and gouges and restraint injuries on her arms. Back abrasions. The genital bruising and tears. The level of violence... there shouldn't have been any doubt that this was non-consensual, even disregarding her age, which I would put at thirteen to fifteen?"

Zachary nodded. "Fourteen."

Kenzie sighed, shaking her head. "And they never found the guy?"

"No. No suspects. It was a stranger and she couldn't describe him."

"What else did they find? Did they log any fingerprints? Hairs? Plant matter and soil? Footprints?"

"They got some hairs. Dark and straight. They were destroyed along with everything else. Not much else. There is some fingerprint evidence; I have to look through it. Not sure what I'm going to find. Just partials. Nothing that they could match at the time, but the officer has agreed to run them through the system and see if they have anything now. Back then, they didn't have a properly automated system and weren't connected to other states."

Kenzie handed the tablet back to him. "I hope you can find something. Because I don't see much here that could be used to identify the perp now. Other than the bite marks. Possibly."

Zachary nodded and put the tablet on the side table.

"So," Kenzie settled against him, pulling his arm around her shoulders, "how are you doing?"

"I'm fine."

"Yeah? This hasn't bothered you at all?" She indicated the tablet. "You aren't triggered by it?"

Zachary shook his head, aware that he was not being completely truthful. While he was trying not to let Heather's experience affect his life, it had triggered nightmares and at times he had trouble untangling his experiences from hers. But Kenzie didn't need to know that. He wasn't melting down over the details of Heather's assault. He wasn't constantly fighting flashbacks. It was bothersome, yes, but probably no more than it would be for a normal person. He had a hard time judging exactly what impact it would have on Kenzie.

"Good." Kenzie snuggled close and warm against his body.

Zachary breathed slowly, trying to relax all of his muscles so that she'd know he was enjoying himself and not overreacting to her proximity.

"What do you want to do tonight?" Kenzie asked. "Have you eaten?"

"Uh… I've had some food." But mostly, he'd been thinking more about getting the documents on the file digitized and getting home to go over them, and he hadn't stopped for anything nutritious along the way. Not a real meal, like she would have expected him to have.

"*Some food* meaning a cup of coffee and something else from the gas station?" Kenzie suggested.

"Well… yeah, something like that."

She laughed. "At least you're telling me the truth. Should we order in? Pizza? Chinese? Or you want to go out?"

"I don't want to go out," he said immediately. He was glad to be home and didn't have any desire to leave again so soon. "Whatever you want to eat is fine."

"Well, let's just go with a pizza. I've been behaving myself lately, so I deserve a treat."

"Why don't you go ahead and order. And I could… find something on TV for us?"

"Sure. But no more thrillers. How about something a little more romantic tonight?"

She gave him a look that told him she wasn't just talking about the movie. He quickly analyzed whether that meant she was looking for some attention before the pizza came, or whether she would want to wait until after the movie was finished. They had only recently become intimate. They had taken their relationship slowly, and she'd been pushing for more romance before Christmas, but he hadn't been able to do anything about it then, too mired in depression.

It wasn't until he had gotten home after the serial killer case that they had actually taken the next step. Not because Zachary felt like he was ready or Kenzie had pushed harder, but because he wanted to prove that he hadn't been affected by Teddy. He'd wanted to prove it to Kenzie so that she would stop asking questions and telling him that he needed more therapy. By showing her that he was in full working order, she could stop worrying about him and they could just enjoy their relationship and the increased closeness.

"Zachary?"

He looked at Kenzie. She had her phone to her ear, and at first he wasn't sure whether she had spoken to him or to the pizza place.

She said his name again and he smiled cheerfully. "Just thinking about a movie. Let's see what's on."

She watched him like a hawk while he turned the TV on and browsed through what was available.

"How about an old classic?"

She looked at the Bogart he had selected. "A bit *too* slow for my tastes. A little bit of action is fine."

"Uh, sure." He continued to scroll through. Kenzie turned her attention back to the phone to finish the transaction, then hung up.

"Okay, dinner and a movie, and then a little action of our own."

He loved her laughing eyes and wildly curly dark hair. She was fun to be with and supportive in spite of his many shortcomings and issues. He counted himself lucky to have her as a girlfriend. He just wished sometimes for the space to decompress by himself and not to have to worry about putting on a mask for her.

CHAPTER NINE

ZACHARY AWOKE TO SOMEONE touching him. He instantly clenched every muscle in a full-body flinch, pulling back and gasping for air, trying to figure out where he was and who was threatening him. It only took a split-second to recognize his own bedroom, and another second or two to focus on Kenzie beside him.

"Oh. Sorry. You startled me."

She laid her hand back on his shoulder, warm and firm. "Your phone."

"Huh?"

"Your phone is ringing," she pointed out. "I didn't know if it was anything important or whether you would just want to let it go...?"

"Oh." Zachary rolled over away from her and felt for the phone on the side table. He managed to pick it up and fumbled for the on-screen answer button before he processed the name on the screen.

Bridget.

He couldn't exactly talk to his ex-wife with his girlfriend in bed with him. Zachary looked around for something to put on so he could at least go into the other room. Kenzie would assume that it was a confidential client call. She wouldn't know it was Bridget.

But he had already touched the answer button and he could hear Bridget's tinny voice coming out of the speaker. He hoped it wasn't loud enough for Kenzie to hear, because she seemed to be rousing herself and looking at the time. It was early, but not as early as Zachary used to wake up before the attack. Zachary scrubbed at his eyes with a fist as he hurried out of the bedroom.

He put the phone to his ear as he sat down on the couch. He grabbed one of the cozy blankets on the couch that Kenzie liked to cuddle up with and wrapped it around his waist.

"Hello?"

"Zachary? What happened, did you drop the phone? I was asking you—"

"Is everything okay?"

"Yes, everything is fine," she enunciated as if she were talking to someone who didn't know English well. "I was calling to make sure that everything was okay with you."

Zachary shook his head, wondering what it really was that she wanted to know. She didn't just call him to ask him how he was without a reason. There was always something. Some ulterior motive or favor. Or because she knew that he really was in bad shape. But he wasn't. He was doing very well for himself.

"Yeah, sure. Everything is good with me."

"Everything? Because I was worried, you know, about how you were doing after that horrible case. I can't imagine how difficult that must have been for you."

If anyone could understand what he had been through, it was Bridget. Because she too had been kidnapped. She hadn't been tortured, but she had not been given the necessities of life, and when he had finally found her, she had been at death's door. She knew what it was like to suffer at the hands of someone who was not in their right mind.

"It wasn't fun," Zachary agreed, "but I'm over it. Everything is back to normal and I've got plenty of cases to take care of, so everything is moving forward at a pretty brisk pace."

"Okay. As long as you're sure. I don't want you pretending to me that everything is perfectly okay when it isn't."

That hadn't been the way it was when they were married. She could afford to say it now when they weren't living in the same house and she didn't have to deal with his depression and anxiety and flashbacks. She just dealt with the public Zachary, the one who was doing his best to show everybody else that he was perfectly competent.

When they had been together, it had been different. She railed at him to quit acting like such a loser and man up. She had hated the cases that he 'wasted his time' on—surveillance of cheating couples, insurance work, accident reconstruction, skip tracing, all of the things that brought in money on a regular basis. He couldn't afford to do nothing while he waited around for the 'right' job, but that was what she had wanted him to do. Just take the cases that really sounded like they were important, that he could get good money. The real money.

She no longer had to see the way that he lived. It was ironic that he didn't get any of the really big jobs that had gotten his name on TV until after they had broken up. She had never gotten to be a part of that lifestyle. She would have liked it. The name recognition. The people who saw him at the store and stopped and stared for a minute, trying to figure out where they knew him from, and then were too awkward to approach him to talk to him about it. She would have loved that.

But being a big name wasn't necessarily good for a private investigator. He didn't want people to recognize him when he was out on surveillance or reconnaissance.

"It must have been hard for you," Bridget pressed.

"Yes, but I'm fine now."

"Okay." She sounded uncertain, which wasn't like Bridget. "That's good, then."

He waited but she didn't seem to have anything else to say. "Did you need something?"

"No. No, that was all, really. I just wanted to make sure that you were taking care of yourself."

"Okay. Talk to you later, then."

He hung up. For a few minutes, he just sat there, blinking his bleary eyes and trying to finish waking up. He wanted to go back to sleep, but he knew he should be working on client files, not lazing around in bed. It was early, but Bridget knew his usual schedule and would have assumed that he'd been up for a couple of hours already.

A movement caught his eye and he realized that Kenzie was standing there looking at him. Her hair was tousled from sleep. He wasn't sure how long she had been there, great detective that he was.

"Was that bloody Bridget?" Kenzie demanded, clearly pissed.

Not sure how much she had heard or guessed from his body language, Zachary decided it was best not to lie.

"Uh… yes."

"What is she calling you about? She'd better not be trying to get you to do another job for her!"

"No. Just checking to see how I am."

"Checking to see how you are? Bull."

"That's what she said."

"Really?" Her tone was suspicious. "Have you been over there lately? Are you tracking her again?"

Zachary's face heated. He shook his head. "No. I haven't even been near her neighborhood. And I'm not tracking her. I'm behaving myself."

It sounded juvenile, but she was the one treating him like a teenager. He hadn't done anything. Just answered a call from his ex-wife. She might have been sick or in need of his help. He couldn't just ignore her.

"You need to tell her to take a hike," Kenzie told him. "Block her calls. She's got Gordon now. She doesn't need to be trying to reel you back in."

Zachary stood up, gathering the blanket around him. "She's not getting anyone back."

She paused, considering whether to go on with her tirade or to back off. "Yeah?" She asked in a softer voice.

"Who's here with me? You or her?"

"Me."

"Then she's not getting me, is she?"

Kenzie gave a little smile. "No."

In the beginning, Kenzie had been entertained by the post-divorce animosity from Bridget. Far from feeling threatened, Kenzie had even asked

Bridget to check in on Zachary once when he was very low and she was worried for his safety but couldn't get there herself.

But Kenzie's amusement had faded as Bridget's anger toward Zachary waned and she had asked him to take on a case for her. Kenzie had not been impressed by Zachary's immediate agreement and his hopes that it signaled a healing of the rift between them and maybe, just maybe, there was still hope of them getting back together again.

Kenzie no longer thought Bridget was one bit funny.

"Do you have work today?" Zachary looked at his phone, trying to remember what day of the week it was.

"No, I'm free all day. But you'll have work to do. This new case."

"Old case," Zachary corrected. "If you're not in a hurry, then why don't we go back to bed and see if we can forget about Bridget calling?"

Kenzie gave him a warm smile.

CHAPTER TEN

THE FRIDGE WHIRRED TO life as Zachary looked inside it, then closed the door without taking anything out. Zachary stood in the kitchen and looked at the time again. The day was getting away from him, marching on before he'd managed to get anything done. Kenzie was in the shower and had been in there for much longer than her normal splash-and-dash. He didn't know whether to put on coffee and toast, or to wait until she got out of the bathroom, or if it were too late to worry about breakfast and he should just use the quiet time to blast through a few emails.

Eventually, he turned on the coffee maker and drifted over to his desk and booted up the computer.

By the time Kenzie got out of the shower, the whole apartment was feeling humid and sticky. Zachary turned his head as she left the bathroom to get dressed, but she didn't say anything to him or poke her head in, so he just left her to get ready for the day on her own. She didn't need him hovering over her while she dressed.

Eventually, she made her way out, crossed behind him into the kitchen, and returned with a mug of coffee. She sat down on the couch. He could feel her watching him. He looked in her direction.

"What's up?"

"Can we talk for a minute?"

Up until then, Zachary had been feeling pretty good about himself. But a serious talk meant that he had done something wrong. And if he were to judge by the length of her shower, it wasn't a minor detail.

Was she still upset about Bridget's call? He shouldn't have answered it. He should have left the room to talk to her. He should have just done like Kenzie said and told her to shove off.

"I'm sorry."

She quirked an eyebrow at him. "Sorry for what?"

It was a foster mom's favorite trick to find out if he really understood what it was that he had done wrong. Foster dads were almost always happy if he just said he was sorry. There might still be a punishment, but they were happy to just dispense with arguments and lectures and get on with it. Women were different.

"I'm sorry about Bridget's call. I shouldn't have taken it, you're right. I should just block her."

"Oh." She waved the subject away as if it were nothing. "That's not what I wanted to talk about."

He shifted to find a comfortable position. He swallowed and tried to force himself to sit absolutely still and not fidget.

"Zachary... I'm not even sure how to say this."

It sounded like the beginning of a breakup talk. How could she be breaking up with him when they had just started sleeping together? Was that the culmination of their relationship, and now that she'd reached the peak, she was on her way out the door?

"Just... say what you're thinking," he encouraged, hoping he wouldn't regret it.

She still didn't speak right away, looking for the words. She eventually started haltingly. "When we're *together*... something happens to you. You go away. You're going through the motions, but your head... you just aren't there. You check out."

Zachary looked at her, trying to think of an argument to counter what she said. Bridget had never said that. Bridget had always said the opposite—that he was excessive in lovemaking. Immoderate.

He just sat there with his mouth open, unable to marshal any defenses.

"I'm sorry," Kenzie shook her head and took a drink of the coffee. It had been sitting on the burner throughout her marathon shower, and she winced, but drank it anyway.

"No... that's my fault, not yours. I... I'll try to do better."

"Do you even know you're doing it? What are you feeling when that happens?"

He shook his head, trying to make sense of what she said. He had done everything he could to convince her that he was okay, that he wasn't damaged. He didn't pull away when she touched him or cuddled. He never told her no, or that he was too tired or too anxious. He initiated intimacy, just as he had that morning. But it still wasn't enough for her. She still thought that there was something missing.

Him. He wasn't there.

When he thought back to what had happened that morning, he could remember everything they had said and done, up to a point. And then, as she had said, it was like he had left the room. While one part of his brain stayed behind to keep everything running, the part that was really him left. He was vaguely aware of what had happened after that point, but it was behind a heavy veil. He had no longer been a participant.

Zachary stared down at his hands, embarrassed, his skin warming as he tried to figure out what to say and how to fix it.

"I guess I feel… overwhelmed. I don't know."

"I feel like you don't want to be with me. Like you're thinking of Bridget or someone else and I'm not even there."

"No! No, I don't want to be with anyone else. I wasn't thinking of Bridget."

Her eyes were intense as she studied his face. He hoped she could see the truth there. He hadn't ever used Kenzie as a surrogate. He was with her because he wanted to be with her, not someone else.

"Then what's going on?" There was a long, awkward pause. "Do you know what dissociation is?"

"Yes, of course."

But he hadn't thought of it that way before. He had flashbacks. He had anxiety attacks. But he hadn't felt separate from what he was doing. Not until Teddy had drugged him to be free to do what he pleased. Since then… it had returned a number of times, without his really being aware of it.

"Have you ever had a psychiatrist diagnose you with dissociation?" Kenzie asked.

"No."

"If you're having dissociative episodes, you need to talk to someone about it. You've experienced a trauma and your brain and your body are trying to deal with it."

He lifted his hands helplessly. She knew that he saw several different doctors and a therapist and was also going to support groups sporadically. He didn't know what more she expected him to do to fix himself.

"Have you talked to anyone about being kidnapped? I'm not saying you have to tell me about it, but… you need to work through it. It *was* traumatic and you *haven't* fully recovered."

"I don't want to talk about it."

"Do you want to keep dissociating every time we make love? Because I'd kind of like it if you were around for that part."

"I will be," he promised. "I'll work on it. I'll try harder."

She sighed and had another sip of her coffee.

CHAPTER ELEVEN

ACHARY BROUGHT UP THE documents contained in Heather's police file on the screen of his computer so that he could focus on them and gather everything he could from what had been recorded thirty years before. He tried to forget that it was Heather, his big sister, and just to concentrate on the details in the reports.

It had been a warm spring day. She was cutting through the park on her way home from school in the afternoon, something the students were not supposed to do. Zachary didn't find any explanation as to why it was out of bounds, whether there had been attacks there before or whether students had misbehaved, littering or breaking tree branches, or if there was another problem like drug dealing or prostitution going on in the shadows of the trees. Whatever the reason, Heather had known the rule against going through the park and had chosen to disobey it.

Zachary could remember a conversation he'd had with a psychologist when he first went to the Petersons. The psychologist had wanted to know why Zachary had disobeyed the rules at his school. The upshot of the conversation was that Zachary often disobeyed the rules when they were a barrier to what he wanted. He felt the rules were unfair, or that the adults didn't really understand the situation, or that he was an exception to the rule for one reason or another, and went ahead and did what he wanted to.

Of course, everyone did that at some time or another, justifying speeding because they were late, taking towels from hotels or hospitals because they felt they had been overcharged, or breaking curfew because they really wanted to attend a concert or party. But Zachary had broken rules with serious consequences, first and foremost the fire on Christmas Eve. The psychologist wanted to curb his impulsive rule-breaking to prevent further catastrophes.

Like Zachary, Heather had been quick to bend or break a rule that she felt unfair, and had done so that day in cutting through the park. According to the police report, she had been provocatively dressed, in short-shorts and a halter top. He didn't know if she had gone to school in an outfit like that. From what he remembered of the various schools he had gone to around that time, the students were not allowed to wear anything above the knee or that bared the shoulders or showed cleavage. Students who showed up in inappropriate dress were sent to the home economics room to alter their clothing, outfitted from the lost and found, or sent home to change. Maybe she had changed into a cooler outfit after school let out, wanting to be comfortable in the summer heat.

It had been a daylight attack. Because the park was off limits for the students, it had been isolated and it had been easy for the perp to grab her and drag her off where no one would see or hear her, a knife at her throat to quell any protests.

Zachary couldn't find any indication that the police had identified the exact spot she had been assaulted. There were no footprints taken or notes made of litter that might have been nearby that could have been analyzed in case he had dropped something and left his fingerprints behind. And of course they hadn't been looking for DNA. It would seem that they had simply noted the park as the place of the crime and had not made a direct examination of the scene.

There were notes that Heather was distressed and didn't want to talk, and that her foster mother had insisted a report be filed despite Heather's protests.

She had changed her clothes after the attack, but there was no indication that the police had asked for the clothes she had been wearing at the time or gone to her house to retrieve them. She had been interrogated for some hours before the police were convinced that it had, in fact, been rape and that she hadn't just gone for a tumble with some boyfriend and was trying to cover the fact up so she wouldn't be in trouble at home.

Zachary looked at the pictures of her and couldn't believe that the police could entertain the idea it was anything other than an aggravated sexual assault.

After that determination had been made, they had sent Heather to the hospital for treatment and the collection of the forensic sexual assault kit. Heather's foster mother had not taken her to the hospital for any treatment before taking her to the police station. While Zachary was glad she was so determined that the assault be properly reported and documented with the police, he wondered at the heart of a mother who was more concerned about the police report than the possibility of broken bones, concussion, internal bleeding, or any other injuries her foster daughter might have been suffering. Was she more concerned about establishing that the child had not been assaulted in her own house than she was in having her treated?

He took a break from the forms, putting his hands over his aching eyes. He knew he had been sitting at his desk staring at the screen without blinking for much too long. Kenzie had once suggested that he should set a timer to remind himself to get up and walk around and rest his eyes every fifteen or twenty minutes, but Zachary didn't like being pulled away from a job once he was focused on it. If he had been interrupted every fifteen minutes, he'd have to reestablish his focus over and over again, and that just wasn't the way his brain worked. He could hyperfocus for long periods of time, but if he were interrupted, it was hard to get back into it. He wouldn't have been nearly as effective.

He got up and poured himself a cup of coffee, even though it had been sitting on the warming burner for some hours. He put a cold cloth over his eyes for a minute or two and attempted to get some hydrating eyedrops into them, which was always a challenge because his eyes were determined to blink to avoid the drops no matter how he positioned the bottle or tried to keep his lids pinned open with his other hand.

He returned to the file, took a deep breath, and dove back in again. After the initial report, there had been some investigation. As Able had said, they called on the sexual predators that they knew, which would have been only a very small percentage of those who were actually living in the area. The police would only know of those with multiple convictions, those who were on parole, or who had warnings out on them that they were expected to reoffend. People who hadn't been caught for some time or since moving into the neighborhood would be unidentifiable. Zachary studied the names and descriptions of the various sexual predators they had talked to, memorizing their names and trying to see whether any of them could actually be ruled out.

Heather's vague description of a man who was of average height and build eliminated only a couple of them. There were a few with ironclad alibis— namely the ones who had been in court or jail at the time of the assault. The others' whereabouts were harder to verify. They had been with friends, home alone, or at the bar. The police had nothing that would rule them out, but also no reason to suspect them other than that they were known sex offenders. All of them had, of course, claimed to be reformed. The police had tentatively eliminated those who had a preference for boys or for prepubescent girls, since Heather was too well-developed for someone looking for a child's physique.

That still left way too many options. They hadn't been able to narrow the pool down to two or three solid suspects. And, of course, the perpetrator might not have been a known sex offender. He might have been someone who was just trawling the area at random, who had never been convicted before, or who had moved into the area without their knowing about it.

There was no mention in the file of similar assaults in the area, so the man had apparently not established a recognizable pattern. Maybe Heather had been his first victim. Zachary doubted it, but it was possible. Offenders usually worked up to an attack like that. The rapist first behaved inappropriately with girls he knew personally. He groped strangers or was caught peeping. He had questionable encounters at parties and bars, until he reached the point where he had to do something bigger and more audacious to satisfy his drive. Then there were a couple of bumbling, abortive attempts before he managed to close the deal.

The attack on Heather felt experienced. Maybe even someone that the school was aware of, hence the prohibition on walking through the woods. It hadn't been his first attempt, Zachary was sure of that.

Before making the call, Zachary reviewed the list of notes and questions he had made as he reviewed the file. He called Tyrrell's number first.

"Zachary! Hey, how's it going?"

"Good. Everything is fine. Uh, I wasn't sure…"

"Mmm…?"

"Whether I should contact Heather directly, or whether I should go through you. Because she went to you initially, she might not be comfortable talking to me directly."

"No, you should call her. The whole reason that she thought you might be a good person to investigate it is because of what you went through. She drew her own conclusions from what was in the news. She and I talk sometimes, but she never discussed anything personal like that with me."

Zachary knew there was a question behind Tyrrell's words. Zachary hadn't told him, or Kenzie, or the nagging reporters what had happened during his imprisonment by Archuro. The police had carefully worded any of their releases or interviews with the press to leave the question open, trying to give Zachary his privacy, but when word had spread about the details of what the man had done to his other victims before finally killing them, people easily drew a line to Zachary and made the assumption that he had been a victim of similar depravity. Tyrrell would never ask him directly, but Zachary knew the question was there every time Tyrrell mentioned the kidnapping.

"Great," he said, without giving Tyrrell any more details than he already had. "I'll call her, then."

"Sounds good. And you and I should get together for supper again before too long… maybe take in a game."

Zachary nodded automatically. "Sure, that sounds like a good idea," he agreed. But he didn't suggest a date.

"Okay… I'll call you, then. We'll talk about it another time."

CHAPTER TWELVE

Z ACHARY WAS MORE NERVOUS about calling Heather's number. It wasn't going to be an easy call, and he wondered if he should meet her in person to make sure that she was okay and didn't go off the rails. If it had been Zachary, he was pretty sure he would have gone off the rails. He couldn't imagine how devastating it would be if he got a call from the police saying that because of some glitch or technicality they would not be able to prosecute Archuro for what he had done.

But in the end, he was too much of a chicken to go to her house and see her face-to-face. Maybe it would be easier for her if she could just hang up and go cry into her pillow.

He dialed the number and it rang a number of times before Heather picked up. She probably didn't recognize his number, being so new to her. Her answer was tentative. "Hello?"

"Heather, it's Zachary." There was no response, and he tried again. "Zachary, your brother."

"Uh… hi. I guess I wasn't really expecting to hear from you."

"Would there be a better time for me to call?"

"No. Best to just get it over with, I guess, like ripping off a bandage. You didn't find anything?"

"I'm not actually done yet, but I don't have a lot of leads. I just wondered if I could ask you a few questions."

"Uh, yeah. Okay."

"You changed when you got home. You were in different clothes when you went to the police station. Did you take the clothes to the police? Or did they go to your house to pick them up?"

"No. They never asked for them. I never gave those clothes to them."

"Did you keep them?"

He couldn't think of a reason why she would keep such a morbid reminder, but he had to ask.

"No. Why would I?"

"I can't think of any reason you would. I was just hoping… that you might have something with the perp's DNA on it."

"Does that mean they couldn't use what was in the rape kit? I thought that kind of thing took weeks to analyze it."

Zachary tried to keep his voice steady. "Unfortunately, the kit was destroyed. It was a long time ago, and at the time, they didn't keep evidence like that indefinitely."

He thought that had a nice sound to it. Not that they had destroyed it in two years because that was their policy, or that they destroyed evidence when they didn't think there was ever any hope of catching the guilty party. Just that it had been a long time ago, and that during that time, the decision had been made to destroy the rape kit.

"Oh." Heather's voice was low and rough. "I was hoping they'd be able to do something with it now and maybe catch the guy."

"I know. Me too. You don't have anything else from that day? A necklace, something that he might have touched or rubbed against? Maybe something that you discovered afterward that you hadn't mentioned to the police?"

"No. I threw out anything that reminded me of what happened. I didn't want to think about it."

Zachary could relate to that. He too had tried to get rid of anything that reminded him of Archuro. He tried to avoid any possible memory triggers. When he couldn't do that, he disassociated. In time, he would forget it completely, if he worked at it hard enough.

"I have some other questions that might be hard for you to answer."

She was silent for a few seconds. He heard her draw in her breath and let it out in a long whistle. "Okay. I'll... I'll try."

He tried to start off easy, with questions that wouldn't be too personal or triggering.

"The park was out of bounds for students. Why? What had happened in the past that made them institute that rule?"

"I don't know... it was the rule for as long as I went to that school."

"Was it because of something that the students had done—vandalism or being rowdy and disturbing other people—or was it because of something that had happened to students?"

She considered. She cleared her throat. "I thought it was because of the students. But I don't know if anyone told me that."

"Did you ever run into other people when you cut through there? Students or not?"

"Yeah. It wasn't completely isolated. There were usually people coming and going. I would see one or two people each day."

"So did you start to recognize some of the ones you saw regularly? Somebody who walked their dog at the same time every day? Joggers? Other kids who broke the rule?"

"I guess so. Yeah."

"Can you give me the descriptions of the ones you remember?"

"Zachary… that was thirty years ago. I don't remember."

"You don't have to do it right now. Take some time to think about it. You might be able to recall some of the people you saw there regularly."

"Do you even remember all of the kids you were in foster care with?" she challenged.

"Uh… no."

"If you can't even remember the faces of everyone that you lived with, how can you expect me to remember people that I didn't even talk to, I just saw them in the park now and then?"

"I know it's a long shot. But if there isn't any physical evidence and the police can't give me any leads, then we need to go by what you remember. Your brain might have stored some of those people. If you were walking through that park every day, those images might have ended up in your long-term memory."

"I can't remember them," she said flatly.

"Would you consider being hypnotized?"

"What?"

"Hypnotism might help you to access some of those memories. Even though you can't remember them consciously."

"I'm not letting anyone mess with my brain and implant false memories. No way."

"I can get someone who is a professional. Someone who has been properly trained so that that won't happen."

"No. There are more things about the brain that scientists still don't understand than there are things they do. There's no way I'm taking the chance of having some satanic ritual being planted in my brain."

Even though Zachary knew it was probably the only way she'd ever be able to remember what she had seen way back then, he had to agree. He wouldn't have done it either. It was too risky. He already had too much horrific stuff in his head.

"Okay. I get it. If you change your mind or you remember something that you didn't before, just let me know. I don't want to bug you about it, so just give me a call, okay? If you don't want to talk about it, you can text or email me."

"Okay." She sounded relieved that he hadn't pushed it any further. "Is that everything?"

"Sorry, not yet."

She sighed.

"Do you remember hearing about anyone else who was assaulted around that time, either before or after you? Even if the circumstances were different. Anything at school or in the neighborhood or in the news?"

"Probably." Heather made a humming noise as she considered. "I don't know. There was a girl at school. Maybe a couple. Not like me, but date rape.

The boys always laughing and saying they must have been asking for it. Saying that they were sluts."

"Yeah. Do you remember who any of the girls or the boys were?"

"I might… I can look in my yearbook and see if I can put some names to them. But I can't promise you results."

"No. Whatever you can remember is fine. Don't try to force it. Looking at the yearbook is a good idea. How about before that? Or in the neighborhood? Any reports of assaults or rape?"

She didn't answer. He gave it a minute.

"Someone who the girls said was a pervert? A Peeping Tom or someone who looked down their shirts?" he suggested.

Heather gave a grunt. "How about every man in the neighborhood. Seriously, I couldn't count the number of times I got leered at, whistled at, or had some jerk making comments about my body. I was fourteen years old!" she said in outrage. "I've raised a fourteen-year-old girl! They aren't sluts if they wear halter tops. They aren't asking for it. And if a girl is promiscuous—and I wasn't—then it's probably because she's been abused."

"Yeah."

"What did you ask? Oh, about men in the neighborhood who made comments or groped me."

Zachary didn't correct her, but waited to see what she thought.

"It's been so long," Heather said. "And I've tried not to think about it. I've tried not to think of anything that happened around then, or anything that might trigger memories of… the rape."

"I know," Zachary agreed in a low voice.

"I'm glad I had Tyrrell call you."

Zachary smiled, feeling warm toward Heather for her words. "Why?"

"I needed someone who could understand. I couldn't just go to a private investigator or to one of the Clintock cops. I had to have someone who was on my side and understood what I was talking about."

They were both silent for a minute.

"What happened to you in foster care, Zachary? I told you about me. I was with that first family, and then with the Astors for most of the time. But that wasn't what it was like for you."

"No. I was with a lot of different families. I got moved every few months, usually. And I couldn't manage being with a family around Christmas, so I usually went to Bonnie Brown, or ended up in hospital. And then… somewhere else when I got out. Some new program or therapeutic home or institution."

"So you never really had a family. Anyone who really felt like a parent."

"I had Mr. Peterson. Tyrrell told you about him."

"Yeah. He was really impressed that someone would keep in touch for all of those years, and how close the two of you are. But you were only with him in foster care for a few months?"

"A few weeks. But that's not what mattered."

"I guess not. And Bonnie Brown…" Heather trailed off, hesitating. "I never had to go there. But I know what their reputation was like. That's where they sent the intractable kids that foster families couldn't manage. It couldn't have been much fun there."

"I didn't go there because it was fun. I went because… it didn't feel like a home, where something awful could happen and the whole thing could go up in smoke in a few minutes. It was sturdy. Concrete. I wasn't ever very good with rules, but I felt better knowing what the rules and routine were and that they didn't change. There were guards, so any violence… didn't usually last long. Though some of the guards… if they thought I was being insolent and not showing the proper respect… if I stepped over the line…" Zachary gripped the arms of his chair, steadying himself and holding himself stiff and still, as if by doing so he could physically prevent himself from sliding into a flashback of Berens or one of the other guards whaling the hell out of him.

"Zachary," Heather crooned. "Oh, my baby Zach. I'm so sorry."

It was a different kind of flashback. Zachary remembering his little mother. How she held and comforted him when he was hurt or in trouble with their parents. How he felt warm and safe in her arms, protected even though she too was so young that she would not have been able to save him from a beating. She was only a couple of years his senior, but there was a vast difference between a frightened eight-year-old boy and a fiercely protective ten-year-old mama bear.

He felt warm and tingly and found tears brimming in his eyes. He had not heard that voice for thirty years, but it was so tender and familiar, it filled him all the way up.

"I'm okay," he told her hoarsely. "Thanks."

"So many different families. You must have had a lot of bad stuff happen."

"Like you said… I did my best to just forget about it. Move on and pretend that nothing had happened."

"Could you tell me everybody that ever touched you?"

He cleared his throat. "No."

"I'll do my best to remember names, or what I can… but the culture at the time… there weren't the same boundaries as there are now. It's better now, I think, even though people complain about political correctness and about having to get explicit consent. I think it's better if people are more cautious about what they say and do, even if it is only because they are afraid of getting publicly shamed."

"Yeah."

"Back then, people just did what they liked, and you weren't supposed to complain about it. If you did, they shamed *you*."

"It's better now," Zachary agreed.

"If we just had the DNA," Heather grumbled. "I can't believe they would just destroy all of that evidence. After what I had to go through, they could at least have saved it. There were so many changes in science and technology, couldn't they have guessed that in the future we'd have better ways to analyze it?"

"I guess they just didn't have the foresight. And there were shorter statutes of limitation. Sometimes really short."

"Is that everything you wanted to know? I'll think about it and get back to you."

"Did you keep a diary? Something that might help you to remember? Or do you have a photo album? Anything?"

"If I had anything like that as a foster kid—and I don't think I did—I lost it when I was on the street. There just wasn't any way to keep many personal possessions."

CHAPTER THIRTEEN

H IS NEXT CALL WAS to Able. He didn't really want to talk to the cop again, and knew that Able wouldn't really want to have anything to do with him. The cop had made it clear that he didn't think Zachary was going to find anything helpful in the file and that he considered it a waste of his time to have to hold Zachary's hand through the process.

It wasn't Zachary's fault that Able had been assigned to the file. He was actually glad that it hadn't been assigned to some rookie just learning the ropes. Able had the policing history to know how things had been handled back when Heather was assaulted. He knew about the laws and about how the forensic evidence had been handled. He knew the kind of police work that had been done at the time and he knew what the culture had been. Those were all insights that he was able to share with Zachary, so that neither of them had to go look them up or to speculate on what the atmosphere had been at the time.

"You again?" Able complained when he picked up the phone. Probably not the way he had been trained to deal with the public. But Zachary preferred his openness to someone who would smile and pretend to be helpful when he just wanted Zachary to get lost.

"I have a few questions for you," Zachary said, ignoring the sentiment and barreling along.

"Yeah, what?"

"I don't have any experience on what it was like policing back then, about all of the legwork that you guys had to do. So all of this might sound annoying, but I just want to get a clear picture."

"Okay. What?"

"You interviewed the people that you knew were sex offenders at the time. Checked alibis the best you could, tried to rule out anyone that you could."

"That's the way it was done, yeah. That's police work. No shortcuts then like there are now with DNA that can lead you straight to the perp. It was all legwork and police procedure."

"What about other sexual assaults that might have taken place in town that were unsolved? Would you have done a survey of other cases? Tried to match up anything that was consistent between them?"

"Yeah, of course. But it wasn't like it is now, with everything automated and computerized. You talked to people, called other precincts, checked newspaper articles. There wasn't any internet or centralized database where the computer would do all of the work and spit it out for you. Lots of time on the phones, lots of time talking to people."

"And I didn't see a report of any canvass of the neighborhood. Would they have gone door-to-door asking if people had seen anything or thought that they knew anything about it?"

"Normally, yeah. But if there wasn't anything on the file… it might have been that they didn't think it would be productive. She was in an isolated area, there weren't a lot of neighbors around working in their gardens or looking out the windows. Canvassing hundreds of neighbors in the hopes of finding one person who might have seen a man leaving the park at that time… I can see why they would decide that it wasn't worth the manpower."

"What about rumors about anyone in the neighborhood? Creepers that might not have any record, but that people were suspicious of. Or people who had been convicted of peeping or… I don't know, some kind of harassment. Somebody that everyone thought was just 'off.'"

"If there were rumors, we would have followed them up. Sure. There was plenty of paperwork in that file of people who police had talked to. But there wasn't anyone that stood out, one person that they had reason to suspect more than anyone else."

"Were there any other unsolved sexual assaults around that time?"

"I'm sure there were."

"Is there any way to match them up now? To pull out any other cases of sexual assaults that year…?"

"That's asking a lot. It's not digitized, so every file would have to be pulled and gone through manually. All of the details are not on the computer. Just the very basics."

"Could we start with a general list and gradually whittle it down?"

"Like I say, a lot of man hours for something that isn't likely to provide results. Do you really think that you're going to find the perpetrator thirty years later? When you don't even have any physical evidence?"

"It happens. People do it."

"It happens in cases that were not investigated properly. Where there were holes in the information. I'm not seeing that in this case. Everything seems to have been properly followed up on at the time."

"Except for the physical evidence being destroyed."

"Yes, aside from that. But there's nothing we can to to reverse that and bring the evidence back now."

"Could you look into it? Just see if you can pull a list of the unsolved sexual assaults from that year?"

"I'll see if I have the time."

Getting together for dinner with both Kenzie and his siblings was not something that Zachary had come up with on his own. Kenzie had met Tyrrell already, and Zachary couldn't keep from her for long that he had met one of his older sisters as well.

"That's fantastic," Kenzie said, gushing a little. "I'm glad that you're getting a chance to meet everyone. What was she like?"

Zachary paused as he thought about it. Not because he didn't want to tell Kenzie about Heather, but because he was having trouble sorting out for himself what kind of person she was and how he felt about meeting her again.

"She's changed. I guess that shouldn't surprise me. I've changed too. It's been a long time, and we were just kids at the time. We've been through all kinds of stuff since then."

"I would guess so. She's had a rough life?"

"Yeah... but not the same way as me. She was mostly with one foster family. She and Joss were together to start with, but they got separated. When we were little kids, before the fire, Heather was... sort of a tomboy, I guess. A bit mischievous. Daring. Joss was the oldest, so she was the perfectionist and the one who tried to keep us all in line. Heather was supposed to help take care of us too, and she did, but sometimes she got us into trouble."

"And she's not quite the same as she was back then? She's matured, married, had kids of her own?"

"Yeah. But she's not... she is so introverted and shy now. Doesn't want to rock the boat... afraid to speak up for herself."

Their show had returned from a commercial break on the TV, and Kenzie eyed it, but didn't unmute it.

"Is that because she was abused by her foster family?"

"I don't know. Not that she's said. She was the victim of an aggravated sexual assault when she was fourteen, and maybe that's what changed her."

"Something like that could have a profound effect on a person," Kenzie agreed. She picked up her glass of water and watched Zachary over the rim as she sipped it. She didn't bring up Archuro, but she didn't have to. Zachary already knew she was thinking it. Of course he was affected by the attack, but it hadn't changed his personality. He was still the same person as he had been before. The change in Heather was jarring to him.

"I'd really like to meet them," Kenzie said after putting her glass back down on the coffee table by her knee. She cuddled up against Zachary.

He forced his muscles to relax and put his arm around her, focusing on the warmth of her body and how good it felt to have her close.

"Maybe we could get together sometime."

"When?"

"I don't know about doing it right away. Heather might need some time to get used to the idea... we just barely met."

"Why? If she's interested in reuniting with her family, why wouldn't she want to go out to dinner with you and meet your girlfriend? And I'd like to see Tyrrell again too. He's a nice guy."

Tyrrell was like a less-damaged version of Zachary. He hadn't had to live with the same abuse as Zachary had and he hadn't had to deal with the guilt that Zachary did, knowing that he was the one who had set the fire that night that resulted in the breakdown of his family.

Kenzie's eyes narrowed and the corner or her mouth lifted. "Is that jealousy I see? I'm not interested in him *romantically*, Zach. I'd like to get to know your family better. That's all."

It occurred to Zachary that he hadn't met any of Kenzie's family. He knew about them; she had two parents, both living, divorced, and she was an only child. But it had never occurred to him to ask if he could meet her parents. But maybe now that they were so close to each other, he should be considering it. Sooner or later, her family was going to want to meet him and find out what kind of a guy she was with.

"I'll ask them," Zachary said finally. "But like I said... Heather is pretty shy. I don't know whether she'll want to do it."

But Heather had agreed. Fairly quickly, and without any apparent reservations. Maybe she was only careful of men. So they arranged a place, a Chinese restaurant that each of them could get to in under an hour's drive. It was quiet, but not too quiet. A good place to talk without feeling awkward or having people eavesdrop on the conversation.

Kenzie and Heather seemed to click pretty well from the start, talking to each other comfortably and able to maintain small-talk seemingly without effort, in a way that Zachary had never been able to. Both women ordered wine, and there was a noticeable relaxation of the lines around Heather's eyes.

Zachary hadn't told Kenzie that the cold case he was investigating was Heather's, but it hadn't taken Kenzie any time to figure it out, and Heather seemed willing to talk about it with her. Zachary expected Heather probably didn't have a lot of chances to talk about it with sympathetic female friends. It didn't seem like she had much of a support network.

"What was probably hardest was raising my daughter," Heather was confiding in Kenzie. "It's so hard to raise a daughter to be cautious and to make her understand how dangerous it can be out there without sounding like a hysterical nut job or else making her too scared to do anything."

"Teaching her to take precautions," Kenzie contributed, nodding.

"Men don't understand," Heather's glance flicked to each of her brothers before going back to Kenzie. "They don't know the lengths that women have to go to to try to avoid being victimized. Grant was totally clueless about the dangers; he always thought I was being too strict with Nicole when I would get after her for thinking she could dress provocatively without any consequences or for being late and not keeping me informed about where she was."

"I would expect him to be more understanding, knowing what you had been through," Kenzie commented.

Heather splashed more wine into her glass from the bottle on the table. "I never told him about it."

Zachary paused with his fork held right in front of his mouth, remembering she had mentioned that before. "You didn't tell your husband anything about the assault?"

"I didn't talk about it with anyone. After the trauma of having to tell my mom and what happened at the police station and the hospital... I completely shut down. I can barely even remember the next ten months."

Zachary put his fork down. He looked at Kenzie for her reaction. He could see that, like he, she was struck by this comment. She looked back at him with wide eyes. Neither said anything. Tyrrell was murmuring something to Heather about being sorry for what she had gone through. Heather looked back at Kenzie and caught her expression.

"What?"

"Did you get pregnant?"

Heather looked unsure of how to answer. She looked at the three of them and fiddled anxiously with her wine glass. Finally, she gave a little nod and answered quietly. "Yes."

At first, Zachary just saw red. He was furious with the rapist and in spite of Zachary's normally nonviolent demeanor, had the man been in front of him at that moment, Zachary didn't know what he would have done. Not only had the scumbag raped Heather, but he'd gotten her pregnant, so she had to go through that physical ordeal for months, and then all of the feelings of guilt and heartbreak that she must have suffered through in giving the baby up.

Kenzie put her hand over Zachary's on the table. He struggled to get his rage under control and to mask it, so that Heather wouldn't have to deal with his anger on top of everything else. He had a sip of his soft drink and looked away for a minute. He looked back at Heather, more calm.

"You gave the baby up for adoption?" he asked.

He knew the ages of her children with Grant. She had obviously not made the choice to raise the baby conceived by the assault.

"Yes. What else was I going to do? I was fourteen. It wasn't like it is now when they practically pin a medal on a teenager for having a baby. Mom said she'd never give me permissions to have an abortion, and I didn't know that I could go ahead and have one anyway. So I did what they told me to."

Zachary sat back, his dinner forgotten, his head buzzing with the possibilities. The conversation went on around him, but he didn't hear anything else that was said.

"Do you know who adopted the baby?"

Everyone stopped talking and looked at him. Zachary realized that he had spoken out of turn and interrupted the conversation which had continued to go on without him, his question no longer seeming relevant. His face heated a little in his embarrassment, but he looked at Heather, waiting for an answer.

"No. How would I? They just took it away. Took *him* away. The birth-mother didn't get any input back then. I could tell them I wanted a Christian home or something like that, and they would consider it, but it didn't really matter what I said. They would just go ahead and do what they wanted. I didn't have any rights."

"You did, but they wouldn't tell you that."

"No. They didn't. They just overrode everything I said, decided what they wanted done with me. I didn't have anyone on my side telling me I could have made a different choice. I don't know that I could have, but it would have been nice to know I had other options."

"You didn't get put in a home?"

"No. The Astors 'let' me stay with them. Told the school I had mono. They acted like it was my fault I got pregnant. Like they didn't know that I'd been assaulted." Her voice shook with outrage. "It wasn't my fault."

"No, of course it wasn't," Kenzie agreed, rubbing Heather's shoulder soothingly. "It's horrible that you had to go through that. I hope the world has improved since then. That they aren't so ignorant and narrow-minded."

"There are still plenty of ignorant people around," Tyrrell contributed.

"Who would know what family the baby went to?" Zachary persisted, not to be distracted from the track he was on. "Did your foster parents? Your social worker?"

"I don't know." Heather shook her head. "Why does it matter? It was supposed to be a secret, no one was supposed to know. That's how it worked back then. They didn't have open adoptions."

"It matters because the baby carries his DNA."

CHAPTER FOURTEEN

T HERE WAS SILENCE AROUND the table. Everyone stared at Zachary. He
shifted uncomfortably and leaned forward, resting his elbows on the table.

"Half of that baby's DNA is Heather's, and half is *his*. If we can get
the baby's DNA, we might be able to get a match on the system."

"I don't know if the technology is that far advanced," Kenzie disagreed. "I
see where you're going with this, but I don't think they'd be able to do anything
like that. The database isn't set up that way. You need the perpetrator's DNA,
not his child's"

"Why not? If they can test a child and test a man and prove whether he is
the father, why can't they do that in this case? Why can't they prove who the
rapist is by proving who the father is?"

"I don't know. You have to have a sample to test against. You can't just run
the baby's DNA against everyone in CODIS to find a paternity match."

"Why not?"

She shook her head. "It's not set up to do that!"

"It doesn't matter anyway," Heather said. "Because there's no way to figure
out who adopted that baby."

"They do it all the time. They have TV shows where they reunite biological
families. People put posts up on Facebook with their birth information on it.
There are times you can get the records unsealed. There are databases to register
in if you want to be connected with a child or parent."

"Or you could hire a private investigator," Tyrrell said wryly.

Zachary had never been asked to trace an adopted child, but he knew a lot
of ways to track down people who changed their names and didn't want to be
found. He'd done all kinds of tracing in his career. He was sure he could track
Heather's baby down, given enough time.

Heather's eyes were wide. She shook her head. "I don't want you doing that,
Zachary. Don't look for him."

"But this could work. It could find the slimeball who hurt you."

"Kenzie's right, they aren't going to search CODIS to look for the father.
Even if they did, they'd only get a hit if he was in the system. He probably isn't.
You said it was a long shot and not to get my hopes up."

He stared at her, not understanding her sudden reluctance. Just when he hit on something that might help them to track her attacker down, she backed out of it? If she wanted to find him, then she needed to be open to all channels. Unless she had entered into the prospect knowing it was a wild goose chase and hoping to get some closure by running into a nice solid dead end. Maybe she didn't really want to find the guy; she was just hoping for some kind of confirmation that there was nothing more they could do.

Heather looked away, her eyes brimming with tears. Zachary forced himself to look down at his plate and take another bite of the Chinese food. It was good food, but he just didn't have the appetite, and had no interest in it with his brain zooming off down the paths that he could take to find his quarry. He took a deep breath, and managed to force down a few more bites while letting Heather relax and hoping Kenzie would start the conversation up again. He glanced over at Tyrrell to see what he thought. Tyrrell gave him a tiny shake of the head, which Zachary interpreted as 'just let it be for now.'

Maybe when Heather had had a chance to think about it, she would change her mind. He had sprung it on her too suddenly, and she needed time to catch up and mull over the idea. Once she'd had a few days to consider, she would change her mind.

He put down his fork, unable to eat anything else. Kenzie looked over at him, but didn't make any comment. She and Tyrrell both knew that he didn't have much appetite because of his meds, and could only force himself to eat so much.

Heather wiped at her eyes. "I'm sorry. I'm being such a spoilsport. We got together to visit and have a good time, and I'm crying all over everything."

Zachary raised his brows and shook his head. "You're allowed to have feelings about it. How could you not? It's unhealthy to just stuff them."

He caught Kenzie's amused glint.

"Or so I'm told," he added.

"I know, but this isn't the place. I'm out in public. I should be a grown-up and stay in control of myself."

"Is that what they told you?"

She got a faraway look. Zachary poked at his food, pretending he was still eating, and waited for a response. After a minute, Heather nodded. "Yeah... I guess that's where I got that from. They hated me being emotional. After the attack... I cried about everything. I cried at school, at home over dinner, when I got up in the morning... the least thing would set me off."

"You went through a very traumatic experience," Kenzie said. "And not only that, but you were hormonal as well. It's much harder to control your emotions when you're pregnant."

It was Zachary who looked at her this time.

"Or so I've heard," Kenzie said.

Heather gave a little laugh. "Yeah, I remember with my other kids… I was just a wreck. I would go into the bedroom to set up the nursery for the baby, and just lose it. Blubbering all over everything. Because of something… I don't know, a teddy bear or a cloud, and I'd just be off to the races. Grant would come home and find me with bloodshot eyes and a red blotchy face and have no idea what to do. He'd think that he'd done something wrong, but of course, he hadn't. It was just hormones."

"And you think your foster parents should have freaked out over them? Told you not to have feelings? To button them up and get them under control?"

"No." Heather picked up a napkin and wiped her nose with it. "I never told my daughter that. Not that she was pregnant, but when she was hormonal as a teenager. I never told her that she was wrong to feel something or that she shouldn't let other people see it."

"When she does get pregnant, and calls you for advice and breaks down blubbering over the phone? Or when you take her out to a nice dinner that she doesn't have to make and she bursts into tears at the restaurant, are you going to tell her it's time to grow up and not show her emotions in front of other people? Are you going to tell her that she's embarrassing you with her tears?"

Heather shook her head again. "No. I would never do that."

"You went through a lot more than just being pregnant," Tyrrell contributed. "You went through a very traumatic experience, and then you were pregnant on top of it. You felt alone and abandoned."

Heather gulped. She picked up her glass of wine and drained it. "Yeah. No one had the right to treat me that way."

Zachary stared at his plate, lost in thought.

CHAPTER FIFTEEN

ZACHARY STARTED HIS DAY with a number of phone calls and web searches as he tried to figure out his next step, which fully depended on Heather and what she decided. If she didn't want him to search for her baby... well, he still could, he didn't need her permission—but he didn't think he would. If she didn't want him to, if she really wanted him to just drop the case, he'd do what she wanted him to. He didn't want to wreck his relationship with his sister by not heeding her wishes.

But he really wanted to find that baby. He was the key to everything. With him, they might have a chance of finding the rapist. Without him, Zachary didn't see many other options. He could go back to Heather's old neighborhood and canvass homes, see if he could find anyone who had lived there thirty years before, but even if he found someone who had lived there that long, the chances that they'd have anything that could help him to break the case were doubtful.

He would search through the file again for any other leads that had been missed, but he wasn't hopeful that he'd be able to find any other avenues of investigation, other than talking a news magazine show into investigating it and blasting it all over TV. If they got some publicity, maybe they would have a chance of finding a witness that the police hadn't found. But even that was a long shot.

Still, he wanted to have all of his ducks in a row for when Heather came back with her answer, if she changed her mind. He would be all ready to put his plan into action.

He made a call to Mr. Peterson. Not a Skype call, because he didn't think that Lorne would be at his computer. Zachary also didn't want Lorne to see his face, when he still wasn't looking any better and would attract more comments about how he needed to be taking care of himself and eating properly. He would preempt a video call from Mr. Peterson by making it clear he wanted to keep in touch, even if he were having issues.

"Zachary! Hey, I'm glad you called!"

"How are you doing?"

"You know me. Still above ground. We're as happy as clams."

Zachary chuckled. "Just what makes clams happy, anyway?"

"Warm water, I assume," Lorne laughed. "So how about you, what makes you happy?"

"I had dinner with Tyrrell, Heather, and Kenzie last night."

"All three of them together. How did that go?"

"Really well. I wasn't sure about how Heather would handle it, but she and Kenzie got along."

"Your Kenzie is pretty good at putting people at ease. I'm not surprised."

"I'm still trying to get a handle on Heather… she's so different from how I remember her. But every now and then, I see the old Heather, for just a second."

"A lot has happened since you knew her. And a lot has happened to you. The two of you are coming from two completely different backgrounds, even if you started out in the same place."

"Yeah, I know."

"It's good that you're getting together and getting to know each other. You'll find each other again."

"Yeah." Zachary hesitated, not sure what he could or should share with his foster father. He didn't want to break any confidences, but he wanted to talk to Lorne about Heather. "We were talking about her case last night and she said she never even told her husband about it. They've been married for twenty-four years and she's never talked to him about it."

"Wow." Mr. Peterson thought about it. "It sounds like maybe she's tried to suppress it. To pretend it never happened."

"Yeah, I think so."

"Sort of like you're doing."

"I didn't say that," Zachary said quickly.

"You don't have to. I already know."

Zachary didn't know what to say to that. He cleared his throat and looked for a segue into another topic that would be more comfortable.

"You should be talking about it to your therapist, even if you don't want to talk to anyone else about it," Mr. Peterson advised.

"That's what everyone keeps telling me."

"We want the best for you. We want you to be healthy and happy."

"I'm doing okay." Zachary looked back at his computer. "I just thought I'd call you in between a little computer work, but I should probably be getting back at it."

"You don't need to run away. I won't harass you about it."

"It's not that. I just have a lot to do."

"We can talk for a couple more minutes. Nothing is going to blow up if you take a ten-minute call."

Zachary conceded. "How's Pat?"

"He's doing well."

But Zachary sensed a hesitation before the answer. It felt incomplete, as if there were something else that Mr. Peterson wanted to say, but had stopped himself from saying. Why? Because he wanted to protect Pat's privacy, or because there was something he didn't want to get Zachary involved in? Was it bad?

"Is he… I guess he's probably still having trouble with Jose's death," Zachary suggested.

"It takes time to process a thing like that. Not just losing someone close to you, but having them taken away so suddenly and in such a violent way. We know that Jose's last few days on earth… were not happy ones. It's not like when someone goes peacefully in their sleep, or even unexpectedly with a brain aneurysm or car accident. It's… it's very hard to work through, and Pat was closer to Jose than I was. It's hit him harder."

"Is there anything I can do?"

There was a long pause as Mr. Peterson considered it. "I don't think so, Zach. I try to talk to him about it, but we just keep going in circles. Because there's no way to explain why it happened or say it was for the better or that something good will come of it. It's just something that we have to accept."

"Is he getting any counseling? That cop, Dougan, he said that he could recommend some victim services and support groups or therapists."

"He's gone to a couple of meetings. I think that's good. But it's still very raw, and I don't know if rehashing it with this group is any better than going in circles with me. Too early to tell. I just have to be more patient and see what comes of it."

Zachary knew that it hadn't been a long time since Jose's death, but it seemed like his murder and Zachary's experience with Archuro had happened in another lifetime. And that was how he wanted it to be. He wanted it to be far away, somewhere he didn't have to think about it.

"They say time heals…"

"Yes. I'm sure that it will help. It will be less painful over time. You know Pat; it's not like him to let things get him down. He's always so cheerful, trying to make everyone else feel better."

"Well… give him a hug for me. Tell him that I'm thinking about him." Zachary stopped short of saying, "Tell him I'm here if he wants to talk," because he didn't want Pat or anyone else talking to him about what had happened.

"I will. Thanks for that, Zachary. Things will get better, I'm sure."

"Well… let me know if they don't. If you're worried about him…"

"I know you could help out with some advice and direction. I don't think that things are going to get to a crisis point, but if they do… you'll be the first one I talk to."

"Okay. Sounds good." Zachary felt a little buoyed up by the possibility that his own struggles with loss and depression might help someone else, especially someone who was so deserving as Pat was. Zachary wasn't usually the go-to guy for emotional support, but he definitely had the experience if they wanted to talk to someone about depression and mental health services.

"Okay. I'll let you go get back to your computer work. But call me anytime. Tell Tyrrell and Heather and Kenzie 'hi' for me, when you see them again."

After saying his goodbyes, Zachary ended the call and looked back at his computer. He didn't really have anything else to do while he waited for Heather to make her decision. Not on her case, anyway. As usual, there was a big pile of skip traces and other work for him to do. If it took any length of time for Heather to get back to him, he could take up a few smaller cases. There were a number of people who were looking for surveillance of employees or cheating spouses, and those kinds of jobs rarely went over a few days.

But he'd just wait a little while and see if Heather changed her mind.

The next call that he got was from Rhys's grandmother, Vera. Rhys Salter was a black teenager that Zachary had met on a previous case and liked to keep in touch with. He felt a little responsible for Rhys's mother having been sent to prison as a result of his investigation and he had a connection with the boy, who had selective mutism. They seemed to hit it off in spite of their differences in age, race, and backgrounds. Rhys had been institutionalized for some time as a child after his grandfather's murder. Institutionalization was an experience Zachary shared with Rhys that not many other people did.

"Mr. Goldman, it's Vera Salter."

"Mrs. Salter," Zachary prompted formally, trying to nudge her out of calling him Mr. Goldman again. They had been on a first name basis, but it had been a while since they had talked. Zachary never went by Mr. Goldman.

"Oh, it's Vera!" she insisted immediately. "Zachary."

"That's better. How are things going?"

"Well, they could always be worse. I have to remember what we were going through last year around this time," Zachary could almost hear her shake her head. "It was a very difficult time, with Robin suffering so badly with her cancer… a very difficult time."

"Are things not going well with Rhys? Or is it your health?"

"I'm okay. But I do think our Rhys could use a little extra support. He can be so isolated, I worry about him, about how he has no one to talk to. I mean, there's only so much you can tell an ancient old gramma like me."

Zachary liked that she said 'talk' for Rhys's communication, even though he rarely spoke more than a word or two in an entire conversation. He used gestures and text and pictures on his phone to communicate his meaning. A conversation with him could be exhausting, but it was also like playing a game or solving a puzzle. Zachary found a certain amount of satisfaction in being able to communicate with Rhys, even though most of it was non-spoken.

"Should I set something up with him? You had said that you didn't want me doing that…"

"I said you could still see the boy, but I would like it to be here. With all of the stuff about you in the media, I don't want him getting teased for being homosexual or something. I just want to protect him."

"That's fine with me. I don't want to cause him any grief. He has enough to deal with without having that on his plate too."

"Yes, that's exactly what I mean. You know how cruel teenagers can be. Even though it seems like everyone or his dog is LGB-whatever these days. I don't want him getting bullied or beaten up for his friendship with you."

Zachary nodded his silent agreement. "So shall I set something up with him next week?"

"Well…" she sounded suddenly hesitant.

Zachary frowned. She was the one who had contacted him saying that Rhys needed someone to visit with him. Why was she suddenly waffling about it?

"You don't think you could find some time today, do you?"

"Oh. Sure. I can pop by after school today. Would that work?"

"That would be wonderful. And you would be welcome to stay for supper. Is there anything you can't eat?"

"You know me. I don't eat a lot, but anything goes." Growing up in a home where they sometimes didn't have enough to eat and then in foster care where he had been faced with all different kinds of food, good and bad, and institutional food at Bonnie Brown and in the hospital, Zachary had learned to eat whatever was put in front of him. Which had served him well when Bridget had taken him to fancy events where they had all manner of fish eggs and sea creatures.

"Great," Vera declared. "We'll see you after school, then."

CHAPTER SIXTEEN

Z ACHARY WAS GLAD TO have somewhere to go later in the day when Heather still hadn't called him back and he couldn't face the pile of skip traces in his inbox anymore. He enjoyed visiting with Rhys and with his grandmother but hadn't seen either of them for some time. It had been too long. He had neglected the relationship. But he had felt put out the last time Vera had called, in the middle of the serial murder investigation, because she didn't like the way that Zachary was being presented in the media. He had been shy of calling again after that, even when life was getting back to normal again.

He made sure he gave Rhys enough time to get home after school before he showed up on the doorstep and rang the bell. Vera was there quickly, greeting him like an old friend and inviting him into the spotless living room. Roast chicken and other food smells emanated from the kitchen, making Zachary hungry in spite of his usual nausea and lack of appetite.

"Why don't you go on in to see Rhys, and I'll call you boys when dinner is ready," Vera suggested.

"Sounds good," Zachary agreed. He headed to Rhys's room.

Rhys's room looked like the typical teen boy's room. Definitely not up to Vera's standards for the rest of the house, but she had apparently accepted the fact and simply cleared out the worst of the detritus or closed the door when he was not home. Rhys was lying on the bed with his phone. Texting or playing a game, Zachary wasn't sure which. Usually when Rhys texted, he communicated in images rather than words, though he did throw in a word or two here and there, the same as in a face-to-face conversation.

Zachary knocked on the open door to warn Rhys he was there.

Rhys looked up from his phone and smiled. He sat up and gestured for Zachary to enter.

"Hey, Rhys. How's it going? I'm sorry I haven't been around much lately."

Rhys reached for his hand and gave it a strong shake, clapping Zachary on the shoulder with the other hand. He released his grip and drew his hands apart in a questioning gesture, then pointed to Zachary. *How about you?*

"I'm doing alright," Zachary said, shrugging off the question. He was more concerned with how Rhys was faring. He looked for a place to sit down, but

Rhys didn't have a chair and sitting on the floor was not going to allow them to communicate properly, besides which it was covered with shoes, sports equipment, books, and whatever else Rhys could fit in his room. Rhys motioned to his bed for Zachary to sit.

He hesitated. He didn't want Rhys to feel uncomfortable or like he was invading his privacy. He remembered how he had felt as a teenager when a house parent or social worker would sit down on his bed to talk to him. He always felt threatened, his space invaded, and he always worried about what the next step would be. Whether they wanted to be on his bed just to test out how close they could get to him, if they could desensitize him to inappropriate contact. Rhys widened his eyes and pointed again to the end of his bed insistently.

"You sure?" Zachary asked. "We could go out to the living room or something."

Rhys pointed again. Zachary sat down and tried to look comfortable.

"So, what's been going on with you lately? How is school?"

Rhys indicated a backpack on the floor, the size of a small boulder and probably just as heavy. Rhys rolled his eyes and shook his head.

"That's a lot of work," Zachary observed. "Can you really get through that much?"

Rhys shook his head. Then he shrugged and indicated his phone.

Zachary hazarded a guess at his meaning. "Not when you're spending too much time online talking with friends?"

Rhys pointed a finger at him, making a shooting-a-gun motion. *Exactly*.

"I don't imagine Grandma thinks much of that. She doesn't threaten to take away your phone?"

Rhys nodded and gave a grin. He bent over to look under the bed, clinging to it upside-down and eventually coming back up for air with a small laptop in his hand. He showed it to Zachary. It had a sticker with the school's name and logo on it, along with a warning that it was for homework only and that any student-installed programs would be deleted.

"Nice. And I'm sure you only use it for homework, like it says."

Rhys grinned again.

"I don't imagine you can do your homework without a computer and online access these days. Back in the stone ages, we didn't even have computers."

Rhys shook his head in silent disbelief.

"So, other than getting a crap-load of schoolwork, how is it going?"

Rhys pressed his lips together in a slight grimace and shrugged. *Okay*.

"You involved in any after-school sports?"

Despite the various bits and pieces of sports equipment scattered around on the floor, Rhys shook his head. He didn't seem saddened by the fact that he wasn't on any of the school teams. It was something that had never particularly bothered Zachary either. He had been more concerned with survival than with being on a team. He had been small and awkward and always was one of the last to be picked for anything when his gym classes had been forced to split into teams. Rhys was a lot taller than Zachary had been, already an inch or two taller than Zachary's adult height. Zachary suspected from the way that he walked and moved that he had at least basic skills in the sports that he played. He had a certain grace in the way he moved.

"Any girlfriends?" Zachary didn't have any doubt that there would be girls interested in Rhys. He wasn't bad looking, was black in a population that was largely white, and his mutism gave him the sympathetic appeal of a lost puppy. There would definitely be girls who wanted to make him feel better.

Rhys shook his head and made a straight line gesture with both hands. *No way*.

"That's probably a good thing," Zachary said. "If there's one thing more distracting than social media, it's girls."

Rhys nodded and laughed silently. Zachary cast around for something else to comment on or another safe topic of conversation. Rhys reached over and touched his wrist, a signal that Rhys had something else to say and wanted Zachary to focus on the message. Zachary watched carefully, meeting Rhys's eyes briefly and waiting.

Rhys pointed at Zachary, and spread his hands wide. A typical *how are you?* But made significantly slow and with plenty of eye contact and an eyebrow that stayed raised, demanding more than just a quick social *fine*.

Zachary hadn't seen Rhys since Archuro's arrest. It had been in the news and Rhys had doubtless seen online chatter that Vera might not even have been aware of, speculation on what had happened that the police weren't talking about. What had happened during the time that Archuro held Zachary, before the police were able to track them down and effect an arrest and rescue. Like Zachary's other close friends and family members, Rhys wanted to know how Zachary was *really* doing following the traumatic events.

"I am doing okay. Really. It was all pretty crazy, but I'm managing. Moving on and working on other cases."

Rhys cocked his head, considering. He didn't seem to have anything else to say, but waited, looking for more.

"It was hard," Zachary said, "but I'd rather not even think about it. I want to put it behind me."

Rhys still didn't seem satisfied with this. He considered Zachary for a few more long seconds. Zachary couldn't think of what else to say to him.

Rhys lifted his phone and powered the screen on. He tapped around for a minute, and then turned the face toward Zachary.

He saw a picture of himself. One that he had seen a few times, since it had been plastered all over news sites for days after the ordeal had ended. It was a picture of Zachary as he left the hospital—earlier than the hospital or any of his friends had wanted him to—and it clearly showed the bruises on his face.

The bruises were not from Archuro, but from a group of neo-Nazis who had attacked him earlier in the investigation. But no one reading the article would know that. In the picture, Zachary's eyes were dark shadows, his face almost skull-like in appearance. He was wearing his own clothes, which he had asked Lorne to bring to the hospital, but they hung loosely on his frame.

He looked awkward and uncomfortable, and if Rhys had seen the accompanying video footage, he would have seen how gingerly Zachary had been moving. No one could see the damage that Teddy had inflicted, but it was there, under Zachary's intentionally loose clothing and deep beneath the surface.

Zachary touched Rhys's hand holding the phone, as if to steady his hand from shaking so that he could see the picture more clearly. But that wasn't the reason he felt the need to touch Rhys.

"I know it looks bad," he said. "But I look better now, don't I?"

Rhys's gaze was piercing, looking not just at Zachary's healed face and his lean body, still not quite up to what the doctor had set as a target weight. Rhys looked much more deeply into Zachary's face, seeking the truth.

Zachary looked away, avoiding the close scrutiny. "I'm doing okay," he promised.

Rhys tapped some more on his phone, and turned it around again to show Zachary a gif of a cartoon character sinking underwater, his fingers held up in a three-two-one count with a bye-bye wave before disappearing below the surface. Certainly apropos of how Zachary sometimes felt.

"Not right now. If I need to... I'll get help. If it gets that bad, I'll check myself in."

Rhys gave him one more keen look, then nodded. As he slid his phone into his pocket, he raised his eyebrows and made a kissing sound. Zachary knew it was an inquiry into Kenzie and how things were going with her, and couldn't prevent the blush that rose to his cheeks. Rhys laughed in delight, the sound giving Zachary an unexpected rush of joy in response. He scratched his nose to hide the grin he couldn't suppress.

"Kenzie is good. I'll have to bring her by to see you again one day."

Rhys made a louder kissing sound, both eyebrows up.

"None of your business!" Zachary's cheeks grew even hotter.

Rhys mimed two hands joining, and then burping a baby on his shoulder.

"Getting married and having a baby? That might be rushing things a bit!"

Rhys indicated heads at descending heights.

"Lots of babies?" Zachary laughed. "You'd better talk to Kenzie about that." He smiled, relaxed. It was nice to think of his relationship with Kenzie and to wonder if it might someday lead to marriage and children. That was still a long way off, and he needed to sort out the issue of remaining present and not dissociating when they were together. But maybe someday...

He hoped that Kenzie wanted children. Bridget had not. She had told him that from the beginning, but he had assumed she would change her mind. Kenzie had never offered her thoughts on the matter, and it seemed like asking her would be presuming too much. Their relationship was stable, and they were seeing each other exclusively—at least, he assumed that they both were—but he didn't want to scare her off by getting too serious and talking about having babies together. While he badly wanted children of his own, he worried Kenzie might have doubts about his fitness as a father.

He looked back at Rhys, who was waiting for Zachary's attention to return. Seeing that Zachary was once again focused on him, Rhys continued the burping-a-baby mime, followed by acting out throwing up and then gingerly handling a stinky diaper.

Zachary shrugged widely. "You have babies, you have to be prepared to deal with all of the messy stuff," he agreed. He'd cared for and changed younger siblings. It had never bothered him. It made him feel grown up and responsible.

Rhys gagged.

"Then you'd better not mess around," Zachary advised.

Rhys crossed his arms in an X, then pushed them forward and out in a definitive *no way*.

Vera called them to the dinner table.

CHAPTER SEVENTEEN

H E WAS MORE RELAXED when he got home. For once, he felt like he could enjoy the evening instead of needing to crawl straight into bed. Maybe it had been thinking about the future of his relationship with Kenzie, or maybe just seeing Rhys and reminding himself that things could be a lot worse.

He surfed his social media and TV for a while, sent an email note to Kenzie to pass on the greetings from Rhys and to thank her for being so supportive. That was one of the things that he found much easier to say in an email than face-to-face. It could be hard to get the words out when the person was right in front of him and emotions were running high. He could empathize with Rhys in that respect.

Gradually, the night noises of the building started to bother him. It was too quiet, even with the TV left on, and each of the creaks and groans of the building or footsteps in the distance made him flinch or tense further. He decided it was time for a sleeping pill and bed so that he could shut it all out.

He fell asleep quickly, but had restless dreams, his brain obviously processing his concerns with Heather's case and his discussions with Rhys. He dreamed of finding Heather's baby, not a grown man but still an infant, and trying to get Heather to take him. Heather refused, and the baby was sobbing and squirming and threw up on his shirt. Heather still wouldn't take the baby, even to let Zachary get cleaned up, claiming that he'd gotten himself into the mess, it was up to him to get himself out.

The baby became a toddler, crying Zachary's name and pinching his arm. It was his baby brother Vincent, who he hadn't seen since the day of the fire. Zachary tried to kiss his cheek and settle him down, but Vinny continued to call his name and pinch him, jab his finger into the center of Zachary's chest and to slap him on the cheek. He couldn't figure out what was bothering Vinny.

Zachary's eyes opened and he was abruptly awake. He tried to clutch at Vinny, to hold him close and not lose him to the dream, but his arms were empty and he was left puffing, out of breath, trying to reorient himself in time and space.

"Zachary." It wasn't Vinny's voice, but Kenzie's, coming from the dark shadow beside him. He startled violently.

"What? Kenzie?" He sat up, trying to blink her into focus. "What are you doing here? Is everything okay?"

"Oh, thank goodness." She was sniffling.

Zachary fumbled around until he managed to find the lamp on the bedside table and turn it on. Her eyes were shadowed, but he could see tears on her face.

"Kenzie!" He hugged her, trying to comfort her, even though he didn't know what was wrong. She must have had bad news, and she'd needed someone to talk to, so she came to him. "What is it? What's wrong?"

She wiped her tears on his t-shirt, giving a shuddering sob as she tried to stop and talk to him. She swore. "I thought you'd done something. I got your email and it scared me, and when I tried to call you, there was no answer. Then you wouldn't wake up… I was afraid…"

"What?" He squeezed her and then pulled back so that he could see her face. "How did my email scare you? I just wanted to send you a note…"

She wiped her face again. He hoped she wasn't planning to blow her nose on his shirt too. "It sounded like a goodbye. I thought… you'd decided…"

He shook his head. "No!" Zachary was baffled. He grabbed his phone and pulled it off of the charge cord to look at the email he had sent Kenzie, which he could immediately see that she had written several replies to in a row. Without stopping to read them, he opened the original message. His eyes raced over the lines, and he stopped, lowering the phone to look at her.

"I was just being nice!"

"'Thanks for being such a good friend and supporting me all this time'?" Kenzie returned, "That doesn't sound like 'thanks and so long' to you? You scared the hell out of me!"

Zachary allowed a chuckle. "I just wanted you to know how much I appreciate you." He swallowed, trying to keep the lump in his throat from turning into tears. He had a feeling she wouldn't let him wipe *his* tears on *her* shirt. "It wasn't goodbye. I just… it's hard to say out loud, so I thought…"

"Sheesh, Zach." She snuffled, the mucus thick in her throat. "If you're going to say something like that in an email, you'd better at least answer your phone."

He looked at the call log, embarrassed. "I was just asleep. This new one doesn't vibrate very loudly, I didn't hear it."

She leaned with her face against his chest, cuddled up, her body relaxing. He liked the way it felt to hold her close and comfort her. Like when he used to comfort Tyrrell or one of the other littles.

He stroked Kenzie's hair, thinking back to before he had awakened. "I was having a dream. About Vinny."

"Vinny?" She didn't look up at him and her voice was muffled against his body.

"One of my little brothers. Younger than T. I was dreaming about him right before I woke up."

"Yeah? A good dream or a bad one?"

"Good." He held her, rocking slightly. "Except for when he started pinching me."

Kenzie laughed. "Sorry about that. You were hard to wake up. I was worried that you had overdosed, I didn't know whether to keep trying to wake you up or to call for an ambulance."

"I didn't overdose. I took one pill. I just didn't want to wake up from that dream."

"Okay."

He shifted so that they could both lie down together, pulling her legs up onto the bed and spooning against her. Kenzie sighed, warm and soft in his arms. He kissed the top of her head. "I'm sorry for scaring you. I never meant to do that."

"It's okay. It's not like you said 'this is the end' or 'if you're reading this I must be dead.' It just hit me the wrong way, with the trouble you've been having lately… when you said 'thank you for always supporting me,' I just immediately thought it was goodbye. It's not your fault."

"Still. I'm sorry. Next time I'll say 'thank you and I'm not going to kill myself.'"

"Yeah, that would be better," she agreed, her body shaking slightly with a silent laugh.

Zachary fell back asleep holding her.

In the morning, he was awake early, like he used to be, and didn't know what to do with himself. He wasn't sure whether he should try to get more sleep, because he'd been sleeping so much recently, or whether he should get up and attack his day, assuming that he was finished sleeping and ready for the day.

What would it be like to have a body that only slept when he needed to sleep and woke up when he'd had enough sleep, instead of trying to analyze it and force his body into some kind of reasonable facsimile of a circadian rhythm? He tossed and turned for a while, but then decided he didn't want to keep Kenzie awake and got out of bed.

"I'll just be a few minutes," Kenzie murmured.

"It's still early. Go back to sleep."

There was no response. She was probably already fast asleep again. Zachary went to his computer and checked his email, again feeling guilty as he deleted Kenzie's increasingly frantic replies to his email. He never would have guessed in a million years that she would misinterpret his intent and panic over something like that. Communication and relationships were complex systems. Miss one signal, and it could throw everything off the rails.

He was glad that Kenzie had just come over and had not panicked and called the police or stayed awake all night worrying about him. And he was glad she had been able to get to sleep after she had found out that he was okay. They would both laugh about it again when she got up. It was a work day, so she wouldn't be in bed too late. But it was still too early for decent people to be out of bed.

He checked social networks and his business emails, routing and sorting what had come in overnight.

There was an email from Heather telling him to call her.

If he hadn't gone to sleep so early, he would have been able to connect with her the night before, and wouldn't have to wait for an answer. But he couldn't call her back so early in the morning and would have to wait until the sun was up and the birds were chirping before calling to see if she had changed her mind about finding the baby.

CHAPTER EIGHTEEN

E VENTUALLY, HE HEARD KENZIE stirring. When she got up to use the bathroom, he put the coffee on and checked the cupboards and fridge to see if he had any breakfast foods that might appeal to her. There were some bagels in the freezer, so he took a couple of them out and put them in the toaster oven. She had a quick shower, and then was out, had changed into a spare set of clothes that she kept at his apartment, and joined him in the kitchen.

"Sorry about busting in on you last night."

"No, it's okay. If something had happened, then I would want you to be able to get in." He paused, thinking about what he had just said. What he meant was if some accident befell him. He would want to know that Kenzie was able to get in. But he would not want her coming to the apartment and discovering his body if he intentionally overdosed. It wasn't something he had ever thought about before, and it made him stop buttering the bagels to consider it for a moment. "If something happened to me, I mean," he said. "Not if I…"

"If you intentionally overdosed. Or did something else. That's probably something you should think about, Zachary, because I'm the one who is going to have to deal with it if you do something like that."

Zachary shook his head and resumed buttering the bagels. "I'm not going to do anything. I'm not suicidal right now. You don't need to worry about it."

"I *always* worry about it. Just because you're feeling good right now, that doesn't mean you're not going to have a setback next week. I'm always watching you for signs. Hoping that you'd tell me if you started to feel worse. Worrying because you won't talk about what happened with Archuro. And even when you're acting cheerful, I worry that it's that last little energy boost people get when they've made the decision to kill themselves."

"I've never understood that," Zachary confessed. "I never had that."

She took the bagel that he had buttered and put it on a plate, and then the plate on the table. She got a jar of jam out of the fridge. "Have you ever actually…" she stopped, mouth closing, unable to go on. She looked at the bagel he was buttering, then looked at his face. "Of course you have. I've seen the scars on your arms. You're telling me that when you made that decision, you didn't get a mood elevation?"

"Nope. I've heard that it can be one of the red flags. If you know someone who is depressed and they have an abrupt mood change for the better, that it might actually be an indicator that they are going to make an attempt. But I never had that. I felt kind of ripped off about that."

"That you didn't feel better?"

"Yeah. They say you'll feel better after you make that choice, so that's what you think. But for me, it never happened."

"Huh. Then maybe I can stop worrying when your mood picks up."

He nodded his agreement. He'd never realized before that she worried when he started to feel better. She must feel like she was on tenterhooks all the time. He sat down at the table with her and the second bagel. He watched her eat hers, not really hungry. She looked at him and raised an eyebrow. He took a small bite of the bagel.

"So, what are your plans for the day?" Kenzie asked.

Zachary looked at his watch. "After you go, I'm going to give Heather a call. She emailed me last night to call her back, but I figured it was too early to call her yet. I don't want to wake her up."

"You're probably right. She should be up any time now. Though she doesn't work, so who knows what kind of a schedule she keeps."

"Do you know what she's calling about? Did she say if she thought of something? Remembered a name or another clue?"

"No. Probably not. I want her to have changed her mind about tracing the baby, because I think that's the one thing that could really help. But she really didn't want to the other night. I don't know if that's just because she was afraid and it was too sudden…"

Kenzie nodded and sipped her coffee. "Let me know how it goes. I'm interested in if she'll go for it. I don't know of any cases where they've done that kind of DNA matching for a criminal case."

Zachary leaned toward her. "They have, actually. I've been doing a bunch of research so that I'll be ready if she decides to go ahead, and there are a number of cases where a DNA search has pulled up familial matches, and they've been able to use it as a starting point to identify suspects and build a case. They still need a direct DNA match eventually, but it's a lot easier if you just have one or two suspects to follow around and retrieve their used coffee cups or cigarette butts to make a match. Then once you know you've got the guy, you can start building a case."

"They've used familial matches?"

"Sure," Zachary nodded vigorously. "They do a search on CODIS and find out that they've got the guy's brother in prison. Or there have even been cases where they have used GENEmatch, a public database, to find several relatives of the perp, and then have used genealogical research to find out the relationships between those people to find out who is related to all of them."

Kenzie pursed her lips, thinking about it. "That's pretty smart."

"Yeah. The technology is really amazing."

"I knew DNA profiling was maturing, but I really had no idea we were to that point."

When Kenzie headed off to work, Zachary sat down with his computer notes in front of him and dialed Heather's number. He was worried that he would wake her up or that there would be no answer, but in a few rings, she picked up.

"Hi, Zachary."

"I got your email. You wanted to talk about something?"

"I just wanted to thank you for all of your work on this case. I'm sorry that there wasn't enough evidence to lead anywhere..."

Zachary immediately heard Kenzie's 'thank you and goodbye,' and understood why she had been so worried about his email. It did sound like a terminal statement.

"You're welcome. I'm not done, though. I can still canvass the neighborhood, try to make contact with the policeman who initially investigated it, maybe even call your old foster parents to see if they have any insight—"

"No."

"No?" Zachary echoed back, even though he had understood her statement perfectly.

"No. You can't contact the Astors. I don't want you to talk to them."

"They might have a recollection of other assaults that could be related, there might have been certain men they were suspicious of, but there was never any evidence to go on so it didn't make it to the police file... they might not have said anything to you because they didn't want to upset you."

"No. I mean it."

"Okay... well... like I said. There are neighbors. The cops who investigated it."

"I think I made a mistake in asking you to look at the file. I thought that I was ready to know more and to put this guy away, but I was wrong. I can't sleep at night. I just keep dreaming about the assault. I can't think about anything else. Grant wants to know what's wrong. I just want to let it go. Put it back to bed."

Zachary thought about holding Kenzie until she fell back asleep. About doing the same with his siblings when they had cried and had trouble sleeping. The dream of Vinny throwing up the night before and Rhys's miming of Zachary having to take care of baby messes.

"Heather." He interrupted her apologetic goodbyes, cutting right across her. "Maybe there's another way. Did you keep anything from your hospital stay? A memento of the baby?"

"Why would I keep a memento when I was supposed to forget about him?"

"Maybe you didn't want to completely forget. Did you take care of him at the hospital before they took him? Did you hold him and feed him?"

"Why?" she demanded, her voice irritated.

"It's just that… if you have anything that the baby wore or spit up on… we might be able to retrieve his DNA from it."

Heather gave a sharp intake of breath. She didn't answer the question, breathing in his ear and considering the question.

CHAPTER NINETEEN

H E ARRIVED AT HEATHER'S house a couple of hours later. Zachary wasn't sure what kind of shape he was going to find Heather in when he got there. Would she be angry at him? Would she break down? Would she be emotionless behind a mask? She had to be going through all kinds of turmoil he could only imagine.

He looked at her house for a moment before getting out of the car. A nondescript single-family bungalow in a nondescript, middle class neighborhood. A community where the adults came and went to work every day, the children came and went to school, each family with two cars in a heated garage, a basketball net mounted on the outside so the children could play in the driveway close to mom's watchful eye, and everyone pretended that they were happy with their lives.

Maybe some of them were.

But for Heather, it was all just a masquerade. She pretended to live a normal, happy life while inside she was broken and bleeding. Years ago, not only had she been brutally assaulted, but the people who should have protected, comforted, and avenged her had failed to show any empathy for what she had gone through.

Eventually, he got out of the car and made his way up the sidewalk. He thought that she would open the door as he walked up to the house, having been watching for his arrival, but she didn't. Nor did she open within seconds of his ringing the doorbell. Instead, Zachary was left standing on the front steps, waiting as the seconds ticked by, listening for her footsteps or some other sound from inside. He finally rang the bell again, and knocked hard for good measure. Maybe the doorbell didn't work. Maybe she had been downstairs or had been flushing the toilet or some other sound had drowned it out.

He began to worry that something had happened to her during the time he had taken to get to her house. Had the despair gotten to be too much for her and she had done herself harm? Or had she gone into a dissociative fugue, unaware of the world around her, maybe even wandering off to end up on the street somewhere with no recollection of who she was or where she had come from? All sorts of scenarios ran through his mind.

"Heather?" He pounded on the door again. "Heather, are you there? I want to make sure you're okay. Heather!"

Finally, he heard the sound of the locks being turned and the door made a little suctioning sound as the handle was turned, but it was still a few seconds before she gathered up her courage to open the door completely.

Her eyes were red and swollen, but her expression gave away nothing. She had been hiding behind a mask for decades, and that mask was firmly in place. She wasn't going to let him see her distress. Maybe she felt she had already revealed too much to him. It hurt him to see his big sister in such bad shape. He wanted to give her a hug and comfort her, but he didn't know her well enough. He didn't know how she might respond.

"Do you want to do this?" he asked. "I'm sorry for pushing. If you've changed your mind, I'll leave."

She looked at him for a long moment, emotionless. Then she shook her head, stepped back, and motioned him in.

The house was as quiet as a mausoleum. Zachary imagined it when her children had still lived there, playing and fighting when they were home, coming and going to school, bringing friends home and playing loud music. All of the chaos covering up what Heather was feeling and giving her a sense of normality. Since they had gone, did she feel the silence pressing in on her every day when Grant went to work?

Or was it only oppressive to Zachary and his imagination, and she was actually quite happy with her quiet existence? She could have turned on music or the TV. She could have had friends over, coffee, sewing parties, book club, whatever it was she was into. She could have found a job, or volunteered at the school or some other facility. She didn't have to stay home all day listening to the silence and reliving her assault, her confinement, and handing over the baby she had never planned and couldn't care for.

She didn't stop in the living room, but Zachary paused, not sure what he should do. She must expect him to stop and sit down there on the couch and wait for her return once she had calmed herself or retrieved whatever she had kept all of those years. But Heather looked back at him for an instant, clearly indicating that she expected him to follow.

All the way to the master bedroom. Zachary looked around uncomfortably, feeling like he was intruding on an intimate place. Like the rest of the house, the bedroom was tidy, neat as a pin, immaculately decorated with every picture straight, not a wrinkle in the bedspread, and each pillow artistically placed. It looked like a show home, not somewhere someone actually lived. What did she do with herself all day? He could picture her out in the garage sitting at a potter's wheel as she formed one perfect clay pot after another, opera playing quietly in the background. She must have somewhere she could escape to. Some activity that gave her a sense of peace in the silent, artificial shell.

"Sit down," Heather advised.

Like in Rhys's room, there was no chair. Nowhere to sit besides the bed. And again he felt that feeling of intruding on her space, of being somewhere he wasn't supposed to be. He had pushed past her defenses and into a private place, a violation. When he didn't move, she motioned to the bed.

Eventually, Zachary sat at the end, barely perched on the bed, his feet on the floor, in a position of readiness. He imagined her husband coming home and wondering what the hell this man was doing in his bedroom. Or maybe he and Heather slept separately, Grant in a spare room or a man cave, to give each other their own space. Maybe Grant snored, so they used it as an excuse for their distance, and they lived separate lives, side-by-side in the fake happy home.

Heather went to the closet. She glanced at Zachary. Not nervous about him being there, just checking to make sure that he was settled, that he was watching her. She didn't attempt any conversation. It wasn't the time for small-talk. He was surprised, as he watched her slow, robotic movements, that she wasn't crying anymore. He had expected the tears to start again.

She reached into the closet and pulled out a box. Everything in the closet matched. It wasn't filled with odds and ends of cardboard boxes like Zachary's closet. Instead, they were all in graduated sizes with matching decorative print exteriors. Small flowers on a medium smoky blue background. All the same, lined up on the upper shelves, the whole closet furnished with wire shelves and rods of enamel white.

She placed the one box, larger than a shoebox, but maybe the size of one that would be used for snow boots, and removed the lid.

It was a time capsule of her childhood. There was a bedraggled teddy bear, no bigger than her hand, the backpack that had served her as she had moved between group homes and shelters before she aged out of foster care, a worn shirt that might have had a rock band logo on it, folded so that he couldn't see it. A couple of other trinkets and bits of costume jewelry that looked like Cracker Jack prizes.

"I don't believe it," he said, looking at the teddy bear, "it's George the Bunny."

He couldn't remember why it had been George the Bunny. One of the younger kids must have named it. Maybe Tyrrell. Zachary had never imagined any of their possessions escaping the fire. Heather had slept with George the Bunny clutched to her every night, even as a twelve-year-old, and she must have been holding on to him tightly when the firefighters had rescued her that fateful night.

Heather smoothed one of the bear's round ears with her index finger. "Bunnies have long ears, Zachy," she said softly. He heard the echo of her words over the intervening years. He must have been the one who had named the bear decades before. He hadn't remembered that.

"Joss held on to Mindy and got her out of the house," Heather said. "I held on to my teddy bear. That tells you what kind of mother instinct I have. Rescuing my bear instead of my sister."

"Joss already had Mindy. You couldn't both take her. And the boys were in the other bedroom."

"It was so hot and there was so much smoke. I wanted to go out the door, but it was hot. When we used to have safety presentations at school, and the emergency responders would come and hand out coloring books, they always said to feel the door and if it's hot, you're not supposed to open it. You're supposed to stay low and go out another way."

Zachary breathed shallowly. He stared at the bear, focusing on not sliding back into the memories. His experience hadn't been the same as hers. He hadn't been in a bedroom, away from the fire. He'd been right in the midst of the blaze.

Heather must have noticed a shift in his body language, because she reached over and grabbed his hand, squeezing it. Trying to hold him in the present.

"I was so relieved when they brought you out. You had been screaming, waking everybody up and telling us to get out of the house. We couldn't get the window open, but the firefighters broke it and got us out. Mom and Dad were out. The firemen brought out everybody except you. I couldn't hear you screaming anymore and I thought you were dead." She swallowed. Her eyes were distant, focused on the memories of that day. "I was so relieved when one of them finally brought you out. We couldn't see you. They took you straight to the ambulance stretcher and the paramedics, so we never got to see if you were okay. But I knew they wouldn't be working on you and giving you oxygen if you were dead."

Zachary nodded. He hadn't seen any of them that night. When the fireman had carried him out of the burning living room, his eyes had been shut, blinded by the smoke, and after they laid him down and started to treat him, he had been surrounded by a wall of people and had never seen his family watching from a distance. He hadn't seen any of them again until the day that he opened Mr. Peterson's door and saw Tyrrell on the doorstep.

"Tyrrell said that you have scars," Heather said. "The social worker told us you were okay. She never said how badly you were burned. You don't have scars on your face."

He had scars on his face, but no burn scars from that fire. Nothing that was too grotesque. "I covered my face," he explained. "Tried to protect it and to breathe..."

With reluctance, he took off his jacket, pushed his sleeves back and displayed his arms to her, turning them to show her the worst of the burn scars on his arms.

"On my legs too, and some on my back."

She studied them, integrating their experiences. She had escaped with George the Bunny and no injuries, and he had been burned badly enough to require skin grafts and still have scars. But most of the time he didn't even think of the burns. Thanks to plenty of PT, there had been no permanent physical disability. The emotional scars ran much deeper.

He saw Heather's eyes shift to his scarred wrists, and he pulled his jacket back on. She made no comment. Zachary looked back at the box from the closet, wondering why she had brought him there. He didn't see any mementos of the baby she had borne.

Heather turned back to it. She gently lifted George the bunny out of the box and laid him on the bed. She lifted out the backpack and felt inside its various pockets. On the third attempt, she grasped something and pulled it out. She opened her hand and displayed it to Zachary. A pacifier in a zipped plastic bag. It was so small he wondered whether it was for a preemie baby. There was a little Donald Duck painted on the front.

She had kept it all those years. He knew how hard it was to hang on to personal items in foster care and group homes. He had kept his camera strapped around his neck all the time, even when he was sleeping. He still lost specialty lenses, even when nobody else in the home had a camera to put them on. Somehow Heather had kept the small memento all of those years, hiding it and guarding it carefully. If any other children had found her hanging on to a baby soother, she would have been teased mercilessly about it. Worse than for a teddy bear.

Zachary didn't take it from her. He wanted it to be her own decision and her own initiative. She could take her time. She'd been pushed around enough by everyone else who had ever touched the case.

CHAPTER TWENTY

HEATHER SAT DOWN ON the bed beside him. She didn't look at him, but stared down at the pacifier held in her lap.

"I don't really know why I kept it. Everyone kept telling me that I needed to make a clean break. I had to have the baby, but then I had to give him up. I couldn't raise him. A fourteen-year-old didn't have the resources to keep a baby back then. I would have been on the street. They said that I shouldn't look at him, or hold him, or name him. The doctor would just pass him to the nurses, and they would take him to the nursery, and that would be the end of that. The adoptive parents would get him when he was released from the hospital."

"Things were different back then. But you had other ideas?"

Heather nodded. "I thought at the beginning that I was just going to do what they said. But in the delivery room, after he was born... I couldn't. I couldn't hear him cry and not hold him. I had to see him, to touch him and know that he was real and that he existed. I was so young, Zachary, and I knew I couldn't raise him, but I wanted to see him."

Zachary nodded. He put his hand on her back, then rubbed it when she didn't object to his touch. "None of it was your fault. Not getting attacked and not getting pregnant. And not having to give him up for adoption."

"I told them to give him to me, even though Mrs. Astor said no, and the doctor listened to me." She shook her head. "I'm lucky he did. I've heard of other cases where they wouldn't listen to anything the teen mom said. Like she didn't matter. Like she didn't even exist. But he overrode Mrs. Astor and told the nurses to let me hold him when he was cleaned up."

They were both silent for a few minutes. Zachary let her decide where she wanted to go with the conversation.

"Do you remember what it was like, Zachary? When Vinny was born? Or Mindy? You remember what it's like to look into a brand-new baby's face and hold him in your arms?"

Zachary nodded. They had all been responsible for the children younger than they were. They had taken as much of the load as they had been able to, feeding and changing the babies, taking them for walks in the afternoon after school, going to the park. Trying to keep all of the children out of the house as much as possible. There had still been too much of a burden on their mother. Six children were just too many, especially with their poverty, and when you threw into the mix a child who couldn't moderate his behavior, who was always getting into trouble at school and raising havoc at home… no woman could have been expected to handle it.

"Yes," he whispered to Heather. "New and innocent and… like angels from heaven." He didn't believe in God or heaven. Not really. But he couldn't think of any other way to describe the awe that he felt on holding one of his newborn siblings. He ached to have children of his own and to feel that again. To be responsible for them and to be a good father and raise them to a happier life than he had enjoyed.

Heather looked at him briefly, and nodded. "And he was. Even with everything that came before… I didn't blame him. He was innocent. I imagined him growing up and the things he would do with his life and how lovely he would be."

There was another period of silence.

"I held him as much as I could for the next couple of days. I gave him bottles and changed his diapers and just held him and rocked him and told him how perfect he was. I didn't nurse him. I was afraid it would hurt too much when they had to take him away. They gave me drugs to help to dry up my milk. Then it was time for me to go home and for him to go to his. But I kept this." She looked down at the soother. "Nobody knew. I hid it. I never let anybody see."

Zachary nodded. She looked at him for a moment, pushed her hand into the backpack again, and pulled out another little bag with teeny tiny flannel mittens in it.

"And these." She smoothed the plastic over the mittens, flattening them out. "I was always afraid that someone would find them and take them. So for a long time, I kept them inside my bra." She gave a laugh at Zachary's expression. "In the bag. But that way… I knew no one could see them or get them while I was away from the house. The binky was too awkward to keep with me all the time. I kept it in my school bag, but if I was somewhere else… I couldn't always carry a backpack with me."

Zachary looked down at the two treasures. "That's amazing. I can't believe you managed to hang on to them and keep them a secret for that long. And… were they always in the plastic bag? Did you ever take them out to touch them or wash them or anything?"

"No. I just kept them in the bags. Like they had to be kept in mint condition."

Zachary wondered how many skin cells the baby would have needed to shed inside the mittens for a lab to pull enough DNA to test and how long he would have had to have them on. The soother was a better prospect. It would be coated in the baby's saliva.

"Would you be okay about giving the binky to the police to test for DNA?"

"Would I get it back?"

"I don't know. Maybe not."

She looked at it for a long time. Finally, she sighed and nodded. "Yes. I guess." She swallowed. "Let me take a couple of pictures of it, at least."

"Sure. Of course. And you should probably be the one to hand it to the police. To preserve the chain of evidence. You're the one who can testify that it was in your baby's mouth. That you're the only one who has ever had it in your possession."

"I don't want to talk to the police."

"I'll set up a meeting with Able. He won't accuse you of anything. He's not going to treat you like a suspect. He's not one of the officers who initially investigated it. They're long gone."

"I thought you would do it."

"I'll come with you. I'll do the talking. Everything except actually handing it over."

She drew back. "Maybe. I'll have to think about it. I don't know."

"You've held on to it for thirty years. You can think about it for a few more days."

"Yeah."

"This could catch him, Heather. I've been reading about other cases that have been solved with DNA testing recently, and this could really work."

She raised her eyes to him. "Do you really think so?"

"Yeah. We can't go very far on physical descriptions or people's memories three decades later. But if there is surviving DNA that they can test and search, the chances of getting some kind of hit are really good. A stranger assault way back then, there wasn't much they could do. With your rape kit being destroyed, I didn't think there was any chance at all of finding a stranger. But with this, it's a definite possibility."

"Okay. Give me some more time. I'll think about it. Try to prepare myself."

"Good. I know it can't be easy for you. I know... I wouldn't want to have to relive any of my experiences. And I wouldn't want to have to face the police about them. But if this could end up putting the guy behind bars... it would be good for you to know that he wasn't out there anymore. That someone actually was punished for it."

"Yeah." She touched his face gently, looking into his eyes. She ran her finger down his stubbly chin. He should have shaved before going to see her. Made himself more presentable. "It's so good to see you again, Zachary. I never thought I'd see you again. When they separated us, I thought that was the end of it. That social worker always said she'd let us visit each other, but the longer it went... I knew she never intended to. She thought it was better if we just went on and lived our new lives and didn't think about the past."

"As if that was possible."

She put both of her hands on his face, framing it, staring at his face as if she might never see it again. She ran her fingers over his features like a blind person. Normally, having someone that close to him, intruding on his space would have made him anxious and uncomfortable. But he didn't feel that way with Heather. He took advantage of her closeness to examine her face as well, looking for signs of the little girl he had known. She had a sprinkling of freckles over her nose and cheeks that were familiar. He remembered how freckled she would get in the summer, remembered her blond hair pulled back into tatty pigtails and pictured her laughing, caught up in a game with her siblings. It had been a long time since he had seen that girl.

"It really is me," he told her.

"Yes. I can see." She released his face and sat back again, holding the baby things in her lap. "I don't know how they could have given us up. I know that the social worker said it was voluntary, that they hadn't apprehended us. She said that Mom just couldn't take care of us anymore, but they'd try to change her mind. Maybe after she'd had some time to get some rest, some of us would be able to go back home. But I never thought that was going to happen. I couldn't understand why she gave us up in the first place. I know... it was hard, and she... I don't think she liked being a mom. But I never thought she'd just give us away, like unwanted kittens."

"It was my fault."

"No, it wasn't. The fire might have hurried her decision along, but I think it would have happened sooner or later anyway."

"She said that I was incorrigible. That I was the worst and she would never be our mother again."

Heather frowned. "She didn't. The social worker never said anything like that. Why would she tell you something like that?"

"It wasn't Mrs. Pratt who told me. It was Mom. She told me to my face. At the hospital."

Heather gaped. Her eyes and her mouth were round circles. "How could that happen? The social worker took her to the hospital and let her say that to your face?"

"I think... she thought that when Mom saw me there, when she saw me, she would realize I was just... a hurt little kid and that she would want to take care of me. But she didn't. She said she would never take us back again, especially not me."

"You didn't set that fire on purpose."

He shrugged helplessly. "No. But I did cause it. She's right about that. And if she'd taken us back, who knows what other crap I would have pulled. The house could have burned down with everyone in it. I could have been responsible for all of your deaths, not just for the family being split up."

She put her arm around his shoulders and squeezed him tightly. "You're not the reason the family split up."

"I started the fire and the fire split up the family."

"It would have happened sooner or later anyway. After that night... how much longer do you think they would have stayed together, even without the fire? Do you think Mom and Dad would have made up and been able to be a happy family after that? Tyrrell doesn't remember how it was, but I know you do. You remember how they would fight. Not just arguing, not just yelling, but hitting and shoving each other around. I thought they'd kill each other one day. It's probably a good thing that they broke up when they did, because I don't think they would both have survived otherwise."

Zachary had seen enough domestic abuse and infidelity cases since then to agree. Couples who fought didn't just stop hitting each other one day. They didn't quit until one of them was killed or had the sense to get out of the situation. Too often, it ended up tragically with one partner or one or all of the children in the morgue. Whenever he heard of one of those cases in the media where one of the parents had killed the children, he thought about his family, and about how lucky he was to have been pulled out of such an explosive and abusive home before it had happened to them.

Or on his darker days, how unlucky.

Zachary gave Heather's knee a squeeze. She used to have such knobby little knees and stick-thin legs. But she'd grown into a woman. "You take whatever time you need to make a decision. And maybe... it might be time to tell your husband about what happened. I think he'd want to know and you need the support."

"Did you tell Kenzie what happened with that sicko serial killer?"

She knew before he shook his head that he hadn't. She'd known it when she had met Kenzie. Probably as soon as she had met Zachary.

"And have you told her about everything that happened when you were a kid?" Heather persisted.

"I don't think I could remember everything that happened when I was a kid."

"Have you told her any of it?"

"She knows generalities. About what happened to the family and me being in foster care. Some of what that was like."

"And did you tell her about any of the sexual abuse?"

Zachary's throat was dry. He swallowed. "No."

"Exactly. Then don't be a hypocrite and tell me I should tell Grant."

He nodded in agreement. It was easy to look at someone else's life and say what they should do, and to repeat what he had heard other people say to him so many times. She should talk openly to her husband, get counseling, go into some kind of support group.

All of the things that Kenzie and Mr. Peterson said would help Zachary to heal.

It was easy to give advice. Not so easy to follow it.

CHAPTER TWENTY-ONE

H E WENT HOME EMPTY-handed and without Heather's agreement to turn the pacifier over to Able. He thought that she would agree in time, but he understood her not wanting to face another cop over her rape. The cops who had further traumatized her during the investigation had made sure of that.

His phone buzzed and he looked down at it. Kenzie. He answered it hands-free, staring out at the highway ahead of him.

"I'm on my way back. Should be about half an hour. Are you off?"

"Just cleaning up," she confirmed. "You did get out to see Heather, then?"

"Yeah. And after I left there, I went back to the scene... the neighborhood she lived in. The park is still there. Looks like most of the original homes are still there, though a few have been knocked down and replaced. I didn't canvass any homes, but it looks mostly like younger families now, not the people who would have been there thirty years ago. I asked at the library about the old newspapers, and they have an archives room. I didn't have enough time to go through it today, but maybe... I can look through the papers and see if there were any other assaults reported around the same time. Heather said that hers never made it to the paper, so maybe there won't be. Maybe they didn't report on stuff like that."

He was just running through a stream-of-consciousness report of what had happened that day, trying to clarify and order everything in his own mind. He stopped, giving Kenzie a chance to contribute.

"That's good. But...? Did Heather change her mind about tracking the baby down?"

"Oh! I didn't catch you up... we went another direction. I asked her whether she had anything from the baby, anything that might have spit-up or any of the baby's DNA on it."

"And...?"

"She has a pacifier and little mittens. That she's kept in plastic bags all this time and never told anyone about."

"Are you getting them tested?" Kenzie's tone went up, excited about the new lead.

"Maybe. She doesn't want to go to the police herself, but I don't want to break the chain of evidence. So she's going to think about it. I think she will. I'm pretty sure."

"That's great! The pacifier especially should have enough DNA on it to test. Maybe there is a way to catch this guy after all."

"We might just get lucky."

Checking the gas gauge as he reentered city limits, Zachary decided he'd better fill up. There was an independent gas station nearby that often priced its gas a few cents cheaper than its competitors, so he thought he might as well go there rather than the station nearer his house.

He and Bridget used to gas up there all the time. It was close to their old apartment. He pulled up to a free pump, his mind flooded with memories. Was it silly to have romantic memories of filling the car with gas? Those first few months after they were married had been happy. They did lots of things together. Went to a lot of events, which required filling up the tank pretty often.

There was a yellow VW parked at one of the other pumps, which set his heart racing. It looked just like Bridget's car. The owner was inside the convenience store, so he allowed himself to fantasize for a moment that it was Bridget's car and they were both there together again. It was hard to stay focused on filling his own car with the yellow VW there.

His brain immediately went back to the days after the divorce when he had been tracking her movements. It wasn't creepy, it wasn't to threaten her or to show up places where she was. It was just... comforting to know where she was and what she was up to. Even as he pumped his gas, it was difficult to tamp down his impulse to meander past the yellow VW and see if he could unobtrusively slide a tracker under her bumper. He could crouch down to tie a shoe, make sure that no one was looking, and put it into place. Then once again, he'd be able to follow her on his phone and to know where she was at all times.

And she would find it again, and she would get a restraining order. And he could end up in jail.

He looked away from the car to the numbers on his pump as the tank was nearing full.

He looked back at the convenience store as a blond woman walked out and headed toward the yellow VW.

It *was* Bridget. He had to blink his eyes several times and shake his head before he was convinced that it really was her and not a flashback or hallucination. It really was her car. It really was Bridget.

He should have been thrilled at the unplanned sighting, but Bridget seemed pale. Maybe it was just the fluorescent lighting underneath the canopy. She opened her door and then stood there for a moment, her hand going to her pelvic area as if she were bloated or in pain. That was all it took for a kaleidoscope of memories to flood back of Bridget before and in the early days after her diagnosis. Before their relationship had blown apart and he had been excised from her life. As if she needed to surgically remove him before the cancer.

He stared at her, and as if his gaze were so intense that she could feel it, she turned and looked at him. Zachary swallowed. He immediately looked for an excuse to be there, a way to explain to him why he was in the same place as she was. Bridget slammed the door of the VW closed and marched over to him, her eyes blazing.

"Zachary. What are you doing here?"

He looked at the gas pump, where the numbers had quit moving. "I was out of town. I was just filling up. I remembered it was cheaper here."

She looked at the gas pump. It was obvious that his tank had been low. He wasn't just pretending that he needed gas while he stalked her. "Are you following me?"

"No. I haven't done that for—" he choked, his voice betraying his emotion, "—it's been months. I swear."

"If you put anything on my car, I'll find it! I'll go straight to a mechanic and have him put it up on a lift, and he'll find whatever you put on there!"

"I didn't. I was just filling up. I didn't realize it was your car until you came out."

"Excuse me," Bridget used a loud voice to address the potential witnesses, who were in their own worlds gassing up their cars or picking up snacks. She pointed at the VW. "Has this man been near my car? Did anyone see him walk up to my car or touch it or look in the windows?"

They looked around at each other, not liking being pulled into some kind of dispute. But everyone shook their heads, looking at Bridget with wide eyes.

"I've just been here, I didn't get close to it," Zachary insisted.

"Don't try telling me you wouldn't rather be over there, touching my car, looking through my stuff, putting a bug on it." Bridget's voice was harsh as she turned back to him.

Zachary shook his head, unable to find his voice. He was electrified by her proximity, his heart racing at being so close to her. Was it possible that she could stand there, just inches away from him, and not feel the chemistry between them? Kenzie insisted that the vitriol Bridget aimed at him was proof that she was still attracted to him, that it was just camouflage for what she was really feeling.

Being so close to her, Zachary just wanted to hold her and comfort her, to tell her that he was sorry and that they could get back together again. It was a complete betrayal of the relationship he had with Kenzie, but he couldn't help the desire he felt whenever he was close to Bridget. He wanted to recapture those first happy days together.

Bridget stopped talking. She just stood there looking at him, breathing heavily. Her paleness was more than just the bluish lighting of the gas station.

Her eyes rolled up as if she were going to faint and he released the gas nozzle and reached out for her, trying to catch her before she could collapse to the ground. She recovered and slapped his hands away, not letting him touch her.

"What is it?" Zachary asked. "Are you okay? Bridge?"

"Don't touch me. I don't need your help."

His heart was beating so fast he was only a hair's breadth away from a panic attack. But he had to hold it together for her. Despite her words, he was sure that she needed him. She was clearly sick.

Was the cancer back? He remembered how she had been in the days before and immediately after the diagnosis, before she had started treatment. Pale, nauseated, making frequent trips to the bathroom. They had both mistaken the early signs for pregnancy.

Zachary had been overjoyed at a positive home pregnancy test.

She had not been.

Not overjoyed and not pregnant.

"I didn't follow you here. I didn't know you were here. That it was your car here. Bridget, you're sick. Let me help. Does Gordon know…?"

He reached toward her again, wanting to escort her back to her car, to settle her in and make sure she was safe to get home. Maybe he should call Gordon to pick her up, to avoid her having to drive when she was sick.

"Just leave me alone, Zachary. Don't touch me. And if I see you near me or my car again…!" She didn't voice the threat. "I'm going to get it checked out, and if you have put some kind of tracker or bug on it, I swear, I'll have you in court for stalking."

"I didn't. I haven't been anywhere near it." He gestured at the people who had spoken up for him, the people who had agreed he hadn't been close to the car.

"Maybe you didn't now. Maybe it was earlier in the week, and you followed your tracker here so you could just *happen* to be where I was. I'm going to have it checked out."

"Is it back?" He had to know. "Your cancer? Please tell if it is."

Her look softened only slightly. "No. It's not. Now just stay away from me and leave me alone."

CHAPTER TWENTY-TWO

K ENZIE WAS AT THE apartment went he got there, as they had agreed. Zachary had forgotten between the time that they talked and the time that he got home that she was coming. He brushed it off irritably as ADHD distraction. He'd just had his mind on the case. Of course she was there.

Kenzie greeted him with a brief hug and kiss, then studied his face. "What is it?"

"What? Nothing."

She touched the worry lines between his eyes. "Something is bothering you."

"Just thinking about the case."

"What is it? You sounded happy on the phone with the way things were progressing."

"I am. I'm glad that we might have a way to find the guy who hurt Heather. Really glad." He didn't want to tell her about running into Bridget at the gas station, and about his concerns with her health. What if Bridget were lying and the cancer was back? Or she didn't know that it was back yet? He knew Kenzie wouldn't like him worrying about it, but how could he not be upset when his ex-wife was in danger of her life? "No, I'm just worried about her."

"About Heather?"

Zachary brought his thoughts back to the conversation. "Heather. Yes."

"What are you worried about?"

They wandered together into the living room and sat down. Zachary looked around. Kenzie had ordered in, but he wasn't hungry. His insides were still twisting around as he worried about Bridget.

"Just... I don't know. Heather is dealing with something really traumatic... but she doesn't have a support system. Her husband doesn't even know about it. When she came to the door... it took a really long time and I was worried that she might have done something. And then, it was obvious she had been crying, but she didn't show any emotion. The whole time I was there... she was keeping so much bottled up. I kept waiting for her to start crying, but she just withdrew. Put up a wall."

Kenzie nodded, a hint of a smile on her face.

"I know I'm a hypocrite for thinking she'd be better off if she would talk about it and get some support," Zachary admitted. "She told me that."

"Yeah. You see what it's like now to deal with someone who is holding so much inside, and you just can't... reach them."

"Uh-huh. I'm sorry for being that way, but... it's just... when we were kids, the attitude was just to forget it and go on. It was best to just put bad experiences behind you."

"Are you talking about the fire," she asked carefully, "or something else?"

He wasn't going to talk about Teddy.

"About everything. As a foster kid, they know you're damaged. They know you're not going to like things about the home they put you in. That you're going to have trouble adjusting to a new school. That there are going to be personality clashes, especially with other foster kids or 'troubled' youth. And the attitude is—or at least, was—just shut up and deal with it. They don't want to hear the complaints. The family is doing the best they can to deal with your physical needs, and they know it's never going to be perfect. If you're going through a rocky patch... you just push through. Whatever kind of crap you might have to deal with... you just try to survive."

"I can understand that for little things. You're not going to have all the toys and clothes other kids have, and you're going to have to get used to new foods and rules and bedtimes. But for the more serious stuff... they wouldn't tell you to just shut up, would they?"

"If they don't listen to you about the little stuff, why would you talk to them about the big stuff? You don't have..." Zachary searched for a way to put it into words, "you don't have any trust. They haven't given you any reason to think that they would fix it. If they can't fix little things, and they don't believe you or they blame you for things when you complain... you know they'd just do the same about other stuff. Look at the way Heather was treated when she was attacked. The cops told her it was her fault. Her parents and social worker told her that she had to give the baby up and never think about him again. They all knew she'd been raped. But it was inconvenient for them. They told her to just forget about it and move on. So that's what we learned to do."

Kenzie stroked his arm with the tip of her finger as she thought about it. "That makes me so sad, Zachary. For her and for all of you. You know, you see these movies on TV about foster care... about those inspiring cases where they took in a foster child and made him part of the family and everything worked out so wonderfully. Like Anne of Green Gables or The Blind Side. But what you've told me about your experiences, and what I've gathered from what Tyrrell and Heather have said... it's far from a fairy-tale ending."

Zachary nodded. He caught her hand and held it for a minute against his face, so warm and strong. She wanted to be there for him. And he didn't want to shut her out. Not really.

"Everybody has stuff happen in foster care. People know they can get away with abuse because you've been trained not to complain."

She looked at him and he tried not to look away. "You want to talk about it?"

"No. But maybe I do need to."

It was three long days before Heather called. Zachary worked hard on other jobs to try to forget about her case, and to forget about the rest of the mess broiling in the back of his brain. He slept a lot, sometimes even in the middle of the day, and was irritable when anyone woke him up, though he refused to tell them that he'd been sleeping. He didn't want anyone to know how much of his day he was spending just avoiding life.

He'd been dozing in front of his computer, trying to decide whether to lie down on the couch and actually get an hour of sleep, when the phone vibrating jolted him back into consciousness. He pulled it out, already scowling about whoever was waking him up, when he saw by the caller ID that it was Heather.

"Hey, Feathers."

There was a sharp intake of breath and then she laughed. "Do you know how long it's been since I heard that name, Zachy? Oh, my. I forgot!"

He smiled at the real pleasure in her voice. They'd had good times together. He wanted her to remember that. She had been a fun big sister. He wished he could still see some of that carefree bluster in her.

She gave another laugh and continued. "So I called to say… go ahead and set something up with the cop. I'll give him the baby's binky to test."

"Great. I'll give him a call. Is there a specific time that you want to meet? Or a time that doesn't work for you?"

"No, I can do it pretty much any time. There's no one here to tell me when I can or can't do anything."

"Okay. I'll let you know when I've got it set up. And don't worry, it's going to be okay. It's not going to be like it was back then."

"I'm tough," she said breezily, as if she had no concerns about it. Apparently, it was easier for her to mask her feelings over the phone. "Whatever. I don't care what he says."

CHAPTER TWENTY-THREE

Z ACHARY HAD A MEETING set up with Able and was on his way to meet the two of them within half an hour. The highway driving didn't bother him. He always found it meditative, easy to get into a zen state. He'd had several therapists who had suggested meditation as a way to deal with his PTSD and ADHD, but none of them had ever suggested highway driving as a way to get into that mindset.

He met with Heather in the foyer of the police station. She was noticeably jittery, her eyes flicking around, trying to take everything in, hands tapping at the sides of her legs and worry lines between her eyebrows. He tried to be supportive and reassuring without treating her like a child or making promises he couldn't keep.

"It shouldn't take too long. Able is an old hand at this. He wants to solve the case, he just hasn't had any evidence to go on. He'll be happy to get DNA to test."

Heather nodded. Her eyes were so wide that he could see the whites all around her iris. He tapped the thumb and fingertips of one hand together, trying not to get wound up by her anxiety.

"It's lucky that you kept those things from the baby. Not lucky, I mean. Smart. You couldn't have known back then that they would ever be useful in the assault case, but you kept them, and you made sure they were safe, and that's why we can move this case forward."

"I just... wanted something to remember him by. I didn't want to be forced by the social worker and everybody else. I wanted to make the decision myself."

"Would you still have given him up if you'd had the choice? If it had been all up to you and you knew that you could have supports?"

She looked at him for a minute, the frown lines getting deeper, then they smoothed out. "No, probably not. I was just a kid myself. I wasn't ready to be a mom. I was trying to keep myself alive. Being in charge of another person would have been too much for me. I was just trying to make it from one day to the next."

"Yeah. But it still would have been nice if they had let you make that decision."

Heather grunted in agreement.

Zachary saw Able approaching. Able looked around the lobby and gave Zachary a wave. "This way, folks."

He led them again to a meeting room. A different one from where he had met Zachary before, he thought. Smaller. But maybe that was just Zachary's anxiety and having more people in the room than when they had met the first time.

"This is Heather Goldman, my sister," Zachary introduced. "Heather, this is Detective Able."

Heather nodded. She folded her arms, not putting her hand out to shake. She looked thin and cold and Zachary could almost see her as she had been back then, a gawky adolescent, hurt and scared to death by what had happened to her and what was going to happen next. She probably hadn't known the ordeal she was going to go through, but she knew enough to recognize that it wasn't going to be good.

"Why don't you have a seat," Able suggested. He pulled out one of the chairs and sat down himself, not waiting to see if they would. Heather paused for a moment, then pulled out the next chair and sat down. Zachary pulled out the chair around the corner on her right and sat down with her. He gave her leg a reassuring pat and looked at her face to see if she wanted to say anything.

"We've come across some evidence that the police didn't have at the time of the original investigation," he told Able.

Able raised his eyebrows. He scratched the back of his neck and waited for more information. He hadn't brought the file with him. Zachary had said that they had something to show him, not that they wanted to look at the file again.

"What they didn't know at the time of the investigation was that Heather got pregnant by her attacker," Zachary said, enunciating the words quickly and getting them out of the way. Like ripping off a bandage. "She had the baby and gave him up for adoption."

Able tapped on the table with the end of a pen. "That's very interesting. Even if they'd known it at the time, though, there wouldn't have been anything they could do with it. Paternity tests wouldn't be available for a number of years, and even then, they would need a sample to compare it against."

"But now they can."

"Do you know the location and identity of the baby you gave up?" Able directed his question at Heather.

But Zachary had promised her that she wouldn't have to talk, and he jumped in to make good on his word. "She doesn't know where he is and was never told who adopted him. But when I asked her if she had kept anything from when she was in hospital with the baby, she did."

Zachary nodded to Heather, and she carefully put the baby pacifier in the plastic bag down on the table. Able stared at it, fascinated.

"A soother. The baby used this?"

"Yes," Zachary agreed. "He used it for several days and it wasn't washed. She put it into the plastic bag and she kept it hidden until now. It hasn't been taken out of the bag."

Able looked at Heather. "If we match it to something, you might have to testify in court. Could you testify to that? That the baby was the only one who used it and that you kept it protected from the time you took it out of his mouth until now?"

Heather nodded. "I never took it out of the bag. And no one else has ever touched it. Just me and the baby."

"Well, there's no telling how much the DNA might have degraded and if it will still be usable, but we can try."

Zachary breathed out a long sigh of relief. "You'll have the lab test it and run it through CODIS and any other databases the police department has access to? You'll find out if the father has ever been convicted of a crime?"

Able nodded. "Best if I have a swab of the mother too. Will you give a sample?"

Heather nodded without the hesitation Zachary had seen in her previously. "Thank you," she said softly.

"Don't thank me. You're the one who is doing this. It never even occurred to me that there might be a baby or DNA that hadn't been destroyed. I'm going to ask you some questions. This is for the record, it's just procedure. Don't take them personally, okay?"

Heather nodded. She looked at Zachary with dread in her eyes. Under the table, he caught her hand and held it tightly.

"Are you one hundred percent sure that your attacker was the baby's father?"

She breathed out. "Yes."

"Was there anyone else that you had sexual contact with?"

"No."

"Before or after the assault. Anyone at all."

"No."

"Did you have a boyfriend at school?"

"No."

"Anyone that you messed around with? Kissed under the bleachers or in a lonely hallway?"

"No."

"What about in your foster home? Did Mr. Astor ever molest you?"

She shook her head. Zachary could see her withdrawing, shriveling up into herself. He squeezed her hand again.

"Never? He didn't come into your room at night? He didn't touch you? Ever?"

"No."

He studied her, looking for the truth. "There were other boys in the home. Two older boys."

"Yes."

"What about them? Did you go out with either of them? Experiment? Did either one of them show you unwanted attention?"

"No." She held tightly to Zachary's hand. He could see her breathing, rapid and shallow. The little freckles stood out on a sheet-white face.

"And there was no one else who you were intimate with? No one at all?"

She shook her head.

"So you're one hundred percent sure that this baby was conceived in the assault."

"Yes," she whispered.

"What day was he born?"

Heather gave his date of birth. Able's lips moved as he calculated the weeks between the two dates.

"A couple of weeks preterm."

"Yes."

"And his weight?"

"Six pounds."

Able was checking all of the boxes. If the baby were weeks premature and weighed ten pounds, that would be a problem.

"Whose names were on the birth certificate?"

"Mine. And unknown."

"If I tracked down the Astors or your social worker, they would tell me that you didn't have any boyfriends?"

Heather looked terrified. "You're not going to call them?"

"If we end up prosecuting the case, these questions are going to come up. They're going to want to question your foster family and the social worker. And anyone else they deem appropriate. They'll want as many first-hand witnesses as possible."

"I didn't have a boyfriend."

"They would corroborate that?"

Heather nodded. "I haven't seen them in years, though," she said. "I don't know where they are."

"You leave that to me. If necessary, we can track them down. First, we'll see if we can get a hit on this sample."

She blinked, looking at it. "I just want to be able to move on."

"Have you had counseling? We have victim services. I can give you some numbers."

"I couldn't talk to anyone about it."

"But you have now. You're stronger than you think."

Heather looked up at him in surprise.

He met her gaze. "You *are* strong. You look at what you went through. If you want, I can bring the file in here and show you the pictures. The little girl that went through that hell was tougher than any of the cops who questioned her. Tougher than the foster mom or the social worker. Strong enough to stand up for herself and tell what happened to her. And to carry a baby and bring it into the world."

Heather swallowed. "And to give him away."

He nodded. "And to give him away. You have carried a heavy burden for decades. By yourself, without telling anyone about it. And you're strong enough to share that burden with someone now and lighten the load a little."

CHAPTER TWENTY-FOUR

Heather's step seemed a little lighter when they left the police station. Zachary didn't know if she was going to call any of the numbers that Able had given her, but she had accepted them, folding them carefully and putting them into her purse. She was quiet as Zachary walked her to her car, a dark blue four-door. She stopped with her door open before getting in.

"Thanks."

"He's right, you know. You're strong."

"Strong enough to let it go?"

"I think so."

"What about you?"

Zachary didn't answer. His hand was on her car door, and she stroked the scar on one of his wrists that showed with his sleeve riding up a couple of inches.

"You're strong too."

Zachary didn't believe it. He was a train wreck. Bridget had taunted him for being a coward, for running away from conflict, for having a panic attack when faced with his worst fears. Group home leaders and professionals who had been tasked with caring for him had bullied him relentlessly for his dysfunctional ADHD and PTSD behaviors.

Even those who tried to help him; Mr. Peterson, Kenzie, Mario Bowman, they pitied him for his weakness and tried to protect him from the stresses of the world because they knew he couldn't handle it himself.

He forced a smile and nodded at Heather. "Sure."

She looked at him for another minute, then climbed into her car. "He said it would be a couple of weeks for the lab to do their work."

"Yup."

"And you'll come in with me when he calls?"

"Of course."

Zachary had, without Kenzie or anyone else in his support network knowing, been skipping his appointments with his therapist ever since getting back after breaking the Teddy Archuro serial killer case. He would call his therapist's office a day or two before an appointment or even the day of, and announce that he wouldn't be able to attend due to some work or family emergency. They would dutifully reschedule, and he'd have a couple more weeks before he had to do it again.

After all of the talks with Kenzie and Heather, he decided it was time to tough it out and actually go to his appointment. So he sat in the upholstered chair in front of Dr. Boyle's desk and waited for her to begin the session. She wrote down the date at the top of the page at the front of his file, then flipped back to look at the last session notes. She flipped through a few pages, frowning.

"Has it actually been that long since you've been in, or are we missing some session notes?"

Zachary cleared his throat. "It's been quite a while," he admitted. "I've rescheduled... a few times."

"A few? What's been going on?"

He sat there looking down at his hands. If he wanted to get help, then he needed to be truthful with her. He knew all of the things he would tell Heather. He would tell her that she needed to be fully open and honest if she wanted to get the benefits of the therapy session. That there was no way for the doctor to know what she had been through if she didn't explain it. But he wasn't sure how to start.

"Zachary? How about you tell me what's happened with you since the last time you were in for a session?"

"I had a case."

"A case of what?" She didn't look up from the file.

"A missing person case. Someone I was supposed to track down."

"Oh. Of course. And how did that go? Did you find him?"

"I was..." Zachary was a little baffled that she didn't seem to be aware of anything that had been reported in the media. "You didn't see any of it on TV or the internet? About the serial killer they arrested?"

She looked up, frowning. "Yes, I heard the buzz about that, of course."

"That was my case. That's what it turned into. The missing man was one of his victims."

"You broke *that* case?" Dr. Boyle looked astonished.

"They didn't even know there was a serial killer before I started. I was the one who had to convince them that they were looking for someone who had been killing gay illegal immigrants for years."

"And you tracked down who it was."

"I sort of... walked into his net. Not the best way to track a killer."

"No," she studied him, "probably not the best." She swiveled her chair toward her computer. "Do you mind? My recollection of the articles that I saw is really vague. I don't know how I didn't connect that you were involved in the case."

She brought up a browser window and tapped in her search. Her screen immediately filled up with hits, and she opened one of the top links, the comprehensive story by one of the big national syndicates. Zachary saw Teddy Archuro's handsome face. She scrolled down too fast to actually be reading the article, but maybe skimming the headings as she moved down the page. She paused at a picture of Zachary, the one Rhys had of Zachary leaving the hospital. She stared at it for a long minute.

"I never would have even recognized you. I'm sorry, I never clued in that this was you." She was silent as she read the next portion of the report. Then she clicked to minimize the browser and turned to him, her expression grave.

"If I'd realized... I would have made sure my office manager knew not to reschedule you."

Zachary shifted uncomfortably. "Sorry."

"You should have been in here for extra sessions, not skipping out."

"I just didn't feel like I could handle it. I wasn't ready."

"Well, now it's time to pay the piper." She sat back in her chair, giving him her full attention. "Let's talk."

Zachary awoke to the ringing of his phone. He had given up on leaving it on vibrate, sleeping through too many important client calls. He had selected the loudest, most annoying ring he could find, and kept the sound on whenever he was at home. When he left the house, he could turn it back to vibrate so that he could drive or meet with clients without interruption, but when he was at home, he needed to know when people were calling him.

He picked it up and looked at the face. Heather.

"Hi, Feathers."

She gave a little laugh, not so surprised by this greeting as she had been the first time. "Hi, Zachy. How are you doing?"

"Fine. What's up?" He tried to figure out what day it was and to count back to when they had given Able the DNA sample. He was pretty sure that it was too soon to have any results back yet, even if they had put a rush on it.

"I told Grant."

"Told him what?"

"Everything. Well..." she trailed off a little. "I couldn't tell him everything at once, that's just too much, but I told him the main points. About... the assault and the baby, and giving him away. And about you, and opening up the case again. And the DNA."

"That's a lot. How did he handle it?"

"Really well." Her voice was warm. He could hear the relief in it. In spite of everything that they had all told her, she had still been afraid that he would reject her when he heard the truth. He would consider her damaged goods, or think it was her fault, or would be angry at her for keeping it a secret for so many years. But that hadn't happened and Zachary was grateful to the man that he'd never met. He'd shown Heather the respect that she deserved, and that would go a long way to helping Heather to talk more about the details and to start the healing process.

"I'm glad. That's really good."

"And you know… he actually wasn't that surprised. I always thought I'd done a pretty good job of hiding my past and acting like nothing had happened. But he'd suspected for a long time. He said he knew that someone had hurt me that way. He knew that I had issues that I'd been trying to cover up all these years."

"Didn't he ever ask you about it?"

"Well… little things, now and then. He never pushed hard, and I was never ready to tell him anything about it, so he'd just let it go."

"Patient guy."

She laughed. "Yeah, he is. Waiting all this time, through pregnancy and kids and being empty-nesters, before I finally told him what had happened."

"I'm glad you did it. You sound… less burdened."

"Yeah. That's how I feel, too. Lighter. It's been really hard all of these years, to wear a mask the whole time. Or at least the whole time that I was with other people. Being here alone in the house, sometimes I could let go, and cry or scream into a pillow. I didn't even always know what was bothering me. Just that everything was too much. That I was unhappy all the time, even though nobody was doing anything to make me feel that way and I could choose to do whatever I wanted to… I just couldn't find anything that would make me happy. I didn't have anything I wanted to do. Except maybe sleep. Grant and the kids used to joke about how I needed afternoon naps more than the kids did. I would just…"

"Hibernate," Zachary contributed. "Shut it all out and not have to think about anything."

"Yeah. Exactly."

They were both quiet for a bit.

"How about you, Zachary?"

"What?"

"How are you doing with everything? When I came to you, it was because of that guy. Because I knew that you had gone through what I had gone through, so you would be able to understand. I'm just wondering… how you're managing."

He sighed and stared off into space. Heather was one of the people who wouldn't accept that he was just fine and had gotten over his experience with Teddy Archuro. She knew that even if he were doing everything he could for his mental health, it was going to take time, and that his mind would need time to heal just like his body did. And it would take longer.

"I went back to my therapist. I couldn't tell her much, but she knows now, and she's modified up my schedule, so that I'm seeing her more often. I'm still… not really ready to talk about what happened."

"Yeah. That's okay. You don't need to rush it. Work around the edges."

"Uh-huh. Are you seeing someone?"

"Yeah. I called some of the numbers that Able gave me. So I've got a therapist, and a doctor who has put me on a few meds to see if they will help with my focus and depression, and I'm going to a couple of support group meetings a week now, while I try to sort it out."

"That sounds like a lot. It must keep you busy."

"Not really. But I'm trying to get out to other places too. Going for walks. I might do some volunteering. I've never really worked, so I don't know if I'll get a job, but I can at least help out at a shelter or soup kitchen. Do something for other people. Think about other people who are going through troubles too, instead of just myself. It might help."

He thought about her sleeping the days away, like he had been, blocking out the memories, not just for days but for decades. He didn't want to live that way. He didn't like it when he couldn't sleep, either. It seemed like there should be a happy medium somewhere between not getting any sleep and having to sleep all the time, but he couldn't seem to find it.

"I could teach you some stuff about skip tracing and some other basic detective work. If that's something you'd be interested in."

"Really? You think I'd be any good at that?"

"There's a lot of stuff that you can just do on your computer. Finding people, doing background, scouting out surveillance locations, that kind of thing. It wouldn't be anything dangerous. It's not like on TV. I don't carry a gun and end up in firefights with suspects. I don't even own a gun."

"No, but you have gotten yourself into some trouble," she pointed out.

"Well… that's not stuff you'd have to do, though. Kenzie says these things wouldn't happen to me if I just thought things through and made better decisions." He paused. "Just like every school teacher and foster mother always told me. Being a private investigator doesn't mean that you have to put yourself in harm's way. And you don't even have to have a license to do a lot of the stuff that I do. If you're interested…"

"Yes!" She surprised him with her vehemence. "I'd love to learn about what you do. I don't know if I'd like it or not, but since you're offering… yeah, I'd like to give it a try."

CHAPTER TWENTY-FIVE

K ENZIE HAD BEEN WORKING long hours for a couple of weeks, staying late and putting in so much overtime that a lot of the time she didn't even have time to talk to Zachary on the phone. Surprisingly, that was okay with him. He felt like he needed some time to himself and that he hadn't had any since he had returned home from the Archuro investigation. Kenzie had been there too much, attentive, watching him, trying to keep him on track, and it had been suffocating him. It was good that she had to pull back and focus on her work more.

Dr. Boyle said that Zachary needed to talk to Kenzie and get things sorted out with her, but he was content that for a couple of weeks anyway, he had a good excuse not to. She had too much on her plate as it was. She didn't need a needy, damaged boyfriend trying to split her attention.

But she had put away the big case that she and the rest of the medical examiner's office had been working on, and had arranged for a celebratory dinner at their favorite buffet. She claimed she was going to take a full week off and just sleep the whole time. That sounded like paradise to Zachary, but he knew she wouldn't actually do it, and that even if he tried to sleep for a solid week, he would still have to get up and think about his life and deal with his career and relationships and face the world. There wasn't any way he could just turn off for a week or two.

Back at the apartment after dinner, Kenzie waved away Zachary's suggestion of a movie and popcorn.

"I want to spend some time with you," she insisted. "It's been crazy hectic and you're important. I know it hasn't felt like it lately, and I want to make up for it."

"We would be watching together. We could cuddle. I could rub your feet."

Kenzie shook her head and gave his hand a little tug to urge him toward the bedroom. "Real time. Not screen time. Just you and me. That foot rub is not a bad idea. And maybe a back rub. Maybe a full-body massage. And whatever else we need to do to get totally relaxed." She grinned and waggled her eyebrows at him in a Groucho Marx impression.

Zachary followed her without objection, but his mind was going a mile a minute. Kenzie sat down on the edge of the bed, and patted the center of it. "Come on. Come here. Let's just enjoy each other's company."

He did as he was told. Kenzie kissed him, pushed him down, and embraced, putting her weight on him. Zachary put his hands on her shoulders, stopping her. Kenzie rolled onto her side and looked at him, curious but not upset. Looking at him to see what he wanted.

Zachary swallowed. He looked past her, but then realized he was shutting her out and tried to focus on her face. He looked at the bridge of her nose rather than into her eyes. "I've had a few appointments with my therapist."

She cocked her head. "Yeah... but you've been doing that forever, haven't you? For at least the last year."

"No." He pressed his lips together, biting them inside and trying not to feel like the little boy who had been caught shoplifting. "I've been skipping out. Avoiding it. Ever since... you know."

She leaned back onto one of the pillows, fluffed it up and repositioned it, and continued to look at him. She was relaxed. Not jumping all over him. He'd been expecting a Bridget-scale explosion, demanding to know why he hadn't been going to his appointments and how he could have lied to her and told her that he was. He wasn't sure he had ever lied to Kenzie about it straight out, but he had certainly obfuscated and never intended for her to know that he was skipping them.

"And now you've started going again," Kenzie prompted.

"Yeah. I'm sorry..."

"No. Go on. I'm glad you started going back to him."

"Her."

"What?"

"Her. My therapist is a woman."

"Why did I think it was a man?"

He shrugged uneasily. "I might have let you think that."

"Why? Did you think I would be jealous? Or think it was inappropriate?"

"I don't know. I just didn't want you to think I was spending time with another woman, I guess. Or telling another woman things about myself and our relationship."

She shook her head, smiling and bemused. "I don't know why you think that would bother me."

"Just being silly, I guess... Bridget might have minded."

"Might have, or did?"

"I don't know. I wasn't really seeing anyone while I was with her. Just whoever I needed to see to get my meds. Bridget never liked me talking to other women..."

"She's one crazy broad."

"She's not crazy," Zachary protested. "If anyone was crazy… it was obviously me."

Kenzie chuckled. "Well, I'm not going to argue with that part. You're kind of veering off topic though. You're seeing your therapist again. That's where this started. So tell me about that."

Zachary hesitated. He shifted around on the bed, trying to find a position where he was comfortable and didn't feel vulnerable. It was difficult talking about intimacy when he was on the bed with her and feeling so exposed.

"I talked a little about us, and about dissociation…"

"Good." She nodded. "I'm glad you talked about that. What did she have to say?"

He felt a little more confident going on. "She talked about grounding and anchoring. Ways to help me to stay present when I have a flashback or something starts bothering me. And she said that we—you and I—should try to find things that are less triggering, and get gradually more comfortable before… moving into things that are more triggering."

"Okay."

"The trouble is…" Zachary gave a helpless shrug and his face heated. "Pretty much anything is triggering right now, so I don't know what to do about that."

"We could talk about it."

"Isn't that what we're doing?"

"No… I don't mean talking about it as a concept. I mean, talking about it in the moment. Talk about how it feels. When she's talking about anchoring, is she talking about noticing concrete things in your environment? Five things you see, five things you hear, stuff like that?"

Zachary shouldn't have been surprised that she would know the technique, but he was. He nodded and rubbed his short whiskers. Kenzie was in the medical profession, so why would he be surprised? She was the one who had brought up his dissociation, so she had probably researched it on her own, looking for ways to help him or fix their relationship.

"Yeah. That's what she was saying."

"So you can talk to me about what you're seeing and feeling, right? That will help you not to dissociate. And if something bothers you too much, I'll know right away and can back off. It's not that different from telling your partner when something feels good or you want them to do something differently, is it?"

Zachary's scalp prickled as his embarrassment grew. He gave a quick nod.

"I'm cool with talking. Are you?" Kenzie asked.

"Uh… maybe. I'll try."

"Okay." She reached out and cupped the side of his face in her hand, and ran her thumb down his jawline. "Since we're talking about what feels good and what doesn't, why don't you go shave so I don't get whisker burns all over the place? That will give you a few minutes to calm down, and then we can start over."

Zachary agreed and retreated to the bathroom. He was glad to shut the door and to be able to breathe in his own space for a few minutes. He didn't understand why his throat was so tight and the tears were so close to the surface. He cupped both hands over his eyes for a few minutes, breathing deeply and trying to calm his roller coaster emotions. There was nothing to be upset about. Kenzie had been perfectly understanding and agreeable. She hadn't criticized him for skipping his appointments or for bringing up his therapy right when she had been ready to engage. There had been no yelling, no recriminations. Maybe that was why he felt so raw and exposed. He'd fully expected an explosion, and she'd reacted with a calm and informed attitude. It was more than he could have expected.

He ran the tap and first splashed cold water on his eyes and face to head off any tears, then ran the hot water to prepare for a shave.

She was right, and after Zachary had finished the ritual of shaving, he was feeling a lot more calm and relaxed. He went back to the bedroom and found her on the bed with a housecoat wrapped around her, reading something on her phone. She put it down, smiling at him. "That looks better. And I love the smell of the shaving cream. Come here."

He slid in beside her and she wrapped her arms around him and buried her face in the soft skin below his ear, breathing the smell of the shaving cream in deeply and making him break out in goosebumps.

"Hey!"

She snuffled against the sensitive skin, laughing. "Does this bother you?"

"No. It tickles!"

Her body pressed up against his, warm and soft. He held her close, closing his eyes. She started to kiss him.

"Just let me hold you for a minute," Zachary whispered.

She stopped and snuggled in his arms, molding her body against his. "That feels good, huh?"

"Yeah."

He wasn't sure how far he was going to be able to get before he started to flash back or dissociate. In the weeks immediately following the encounter with Teddy, he had been unable to tolerate her touch or even to let her see his body. Knowing how uncomfortable he was, she hadn't asked him, once he had been able to let his guard down, about the pink, healing scars on his body. She hadn't asked him exactly what Teddy had said or done to him.

Zachary had worked hard to overcome any negative reactions to her advances, which resulted in the natural progression of their physical relationship, but at the expense of Zachary's mental participation.

It was going to take time to fix his problems.

CHAPTER TWENTY-SIX

Zachary?" Heather's voice was in his ear before he could even greet her on the phone. "Detective Able called to say that they got the DNA results back and we should go in. Would you come?"

"Sure, of course," Zachary agreed. He looked over the paperwork on his desk. He had been planning on doing surveillance for a few days, but if he had to put it off for one more day, it wouldn't hurt anything. He took out his phone and looked at the calendar to assure himself that he hadn't forgotten about any appointments. "Today?"

"Yeah. I know it's a long way to come just to go with me to the police station, but I don't think that I can do it by myself."

"It's not that far. I don't mind a little drive. I'll head over right away. You want me to meet you there?"

"Yes."

"I'll call you when I hit city limits, then we should both get there about the same time. Okay?"

"Okay." Her voice was a little calmer with a plan in place. "And do you mind if Grant is there? He wanted to come along too."

Zachary frowned at the phone. He wasn't sure why she needed him there if her husband was going along. She wasn't exactly going to be alone. But he didn't know very much about Grant. Maybe Heather would find it harder with him there, instead of easier. Maybe he was the kind who asked too many questions, or was too boisterous, or something else that sucked the energy from her or made it harder for her to deal with the policeman. Maybe it was because of Grant that she needed Zachary there, as some kind of a buffer or to handle the questions when she couldn't think of what she needed to say. In which case, he'd better be prepared with his questions and not let himself be distracted by her husband.

"Of course. Bring whoever you want. It's good that he wants to be involved."

"Yeah. It's just kind of weird. He hasn't had anything to do with it before."

"It will be okay," he assured her.

"I hope so."

They arrived at the police station at just about the same time. Heather's husband had driven her. Zachary eyed him as the two of them got out of the car. Grant was tall and had probably been lean in his earlier years when he and Heather had first met and gotten married. He had put on some weight in his later years, around his neck and stomach, but still moved like a younger man. He was outgoing, immediately approaching Zachary and putting out his hand in greeting. "You must be Zachary. It's wonderful to meet someone from Heather's family! I knew that she had siblings, but I never really thought that I would get the chance to meet any of them."

Zachary looked at Heather. Didn't he know that she'd been in contact with Tyrrell for some time? Or that she was in contact with their eldest sister, Joss? Didn't he think that sooner or later he would meet them in person?

But Heather didn't speak up. Maybe she hadn't shared those things with him yet. There had been a lot to tell him, and the information about the progress on the cold case was obviously more urgent than a few Skype calls she had while he was at work during the day.

"Good to meet you, Grant," Zachary said, taking Grant's hand and giving him a friendly nod as they shook hands.

"You don't look like her at all," Grant marveled, studying Zachary's face. "I thought I would at least be able to see a bit of a family connection, but the two of you couldn't be less like each other."

Zachary looked at Heather. "Well, we could be," he pointed out. "We have the same skin color."

Grant laughed quite a bit more loudly than Zachary thought was warranted. If their parents had been mixed-race, the children could have a variety of skin colors. Or if they were foster or adopted siblings... but they weren't, and Grant was probably right. With two white parents, he and Heather couldn't have been much more different. Heather was blond and fair, Zachary was dark-haired, his face lean and hollow where Heather's was filled in. Not round, but pleasant. And she had those pretty freckles that he remembered from their early summers.

"Zachary and I are a lot more alike than you would think," Heather said, touching Zachary's arm fleetingly as they moved toward the police station together. Zachary smiled and nodded. It wasn't what was outside that counted. It was what was inside, their shared experience and genetics, the personalities that had been shaped in their early years.

Able didn't keep them waiting very long. He seemed surprised to see one more person joining the meeting, and nodded to Grant. "Mr.... er..."

"Garrity," Grant offered, and Zachary realized that he'd been introducing Heather as Heather Goldman the whole time, and had never even asked her if she went by her married name.

"Mr. Garrity. Nice to meet you. Follow me."

He led them to a meeting room and they all sat down, the room seeming closer and more claustrophobic than ever.

Able didn't have the file with him, just a single sheet of paper, and Zachary couldn't read it from where he sat. Able settled into his chair with a noisy sigh, and wriggled around to get comfortable, something Zachary didn't remember him doing on previous occasions. Why was he so uncomfortable?

"It turns out," Able said, his eyes down, "that in Vermont, the police are prohibited from using partial DNA matches obtained from database searches."

They all looked at each other. Heather's face was blank. Grant's was confused. Zachary couldn't see his own expression, but he could barely control himself. Fury rose up inside him that Able would lead them along for weeks and then announce that he was unable to do what they had asked him to.

"You can't even search it?" Grant demanded. "I understand that you'd have to get a direct match to prosecute someone, but you can't even use it as an investigative tool?"

"Vermont's current policy is such that we are prevented from doing so."

"You can use a partial license plate, why can't you use a partial DNA match?"

"I'm sorry, sir, that's just what the state legislators have determined."

"So you can't give us anything," Zachary said flatly.

Able looked at him. There was a gleam in his eye. Zachary tried to understand what Able looked so smug about. That he was telling Zachary what he had told him weeks before; there was nowhere to go with the case and he shouldn't bother investigating it? Was Able happy that he hadn't been able to get anywhere? Had it just been a ruse to get them off his back?

"Why didn't you tell us before that you wouldn't be able to do a partial match? You knew we weren't looking for the baby in CODIS."

"With all of the advances in technology, it can be difficult to keep track of what the policies are and what's allowed or not allowed," Able said slowly. "Sometimes, for instance, a policeman might put a DNA profile into the system before he's told that he isn't allowed to use a partial match. Most states allow a partial match, so CODIS is set up to allow it."

Zachary raised his eyebrows. He looked down at the paper in front of Able.

"So you ran the DNA and *then* were told it wasn't allowed?"

Able nodded.

"Was there a hit?"

Able shook his head. "He was not there. No partial matches."

Zachary smacked his palm down on the table, making everyone jump. "There's nothing? You called us in just to tell us that there was nothing?"

"*Nothing* is still a result," Able pointed out. "It means this guy has not been convicted of any other felony. Not since all felons have been required to give a DNA sample, anyway."

"That doesn't help us at all!"

"I can't give you what I don't have," Able said reasonably.

Zachary's blood was boiling. He had put all of his hopes on this one piece of evidence. He had been sure that the baby's father would be in CODIS.

Heather put her hand on Zachary's arm. "It's okay, Zachary. We knew it was a long shot."

Zachary shook her off, irritated. In his brain, the wheels spun, unable to find purchase. After all of the research he had done, there had to be something more they could do.

"What about public DNA profile repositories like GENEmatch?"

"Did you not understand what I told you? Vermont cops are prohibited from using partial matches. In CODIS or any other database. The only thing we could use in GENEmatch is a direct match to the donor, but we don't have the perp's DNA."

Zachary was stymied. He looked at Heather. He did not want to let her down. There had to be a way for him to pursue it further and get more information. According to what he had read, there was a twenty-five percent chance that submitting the DNA to GENEmatch would link the DNA profile to relatives. Those relatives could help them triangulate a single branch of the family tree, isolating two or three suspects.

"Since you can't use the pacifier, can we get it back so we can test it?"

"It's already booked as evidence. It won't be released."

"Can your lab give us the raw genome data, or transfer it to another lab?"

"No."

Zachary stared at Able. The man had acted like he was being helpful, but he had just destroyed what chance they had of matching the DNA in GENEmatch. He should have told them to start with that he couldn't use a partial DNA match. Then they could have tested it privately and used the results.

"Zach... we still have the mittens," Heather pointed out.

But were the mittens going to have enough DNA on them to test? Skin cells on the inside, but how much? Maybe the baby had sucked on his hands while he had the mittens on, but as far as Zachary could remember, babies didn't find their own hands and feet to suck on until they were older.

"The reason they put them on is because he was scratching his face," Heather said, as if she could see the inner workings of Zachary's brain.

Maybe he got blood and skin under his sharp little nails. Maybe that tissue was transferred to the inside of the mittens. Maybe he'd drooled on them or spit up. There were a number of different ways the baby could have contributed DNA to the mittens. And hopefully, no one else had. It wasn't as good a source as the pacifier, but it would have to do.

"If you have another source, that's your best bet," Able confirmed. "There's only so much we can do."

Zachary shot him a look, but didn't say any of the things he was thinking.

128

CHAPTER TWENTY-SEVEN

Z ACHARY WAS STILL ANGRY and was exhausted by his anger by the time he got home. He had talked with Heather and Grant as calmly as he was able after leaving the police conference room, telling them that he would send Heather the information for the private DNA lab he had come across during his research, and she could send the mittens there. He would contact them ahead of time to explain the situation, and they would give him the raw genome data to upload to GENEmatch once they had done the gathering, preparation, and sequencing.

He drove home too fast, zipping past commuters on the highway. When he returned to his apartment, he slammed the door, not caring if everybody on his floor heard it. Luckily, Kenzie wasn't there, so he was free to kick doors and furniture, smack the counter, and handle the dishes for his supper as loudly and recklessly as he liked.

He felt a little calmer after having something to eat. Mr. Peterson had tried to reach him during the day, when Zachary hadn't been in any mood to talk, so once he'd had a bit of time to unwind and to regain his composure, he called back.

"Zach, how are you doing?" Mr. Peterson greeted cheerfully.

Zachary let out a long breath, trying to stay calm and centered. He didn't need to dump on Mr. Peterson. He was having a hard time even understanding where all of the anger was coming from, but it certainly wasn't Lorne's fault. He forced a smile, knowing that Mr. Peterson would be able to hear it in his voice.

"It's been a frustrating day. But I'm okay."

"Oh, what's going on?"

"Heather's case. We ran into a brick wall with the police. Which he could have told us about three weeks ago, but didn't bother to do."

"I can see how that would be annoying. I know how pleased you were that they were going to run the DNA and maybe be able to identify Heather's attacker."

"Yeah. Would have been helpful if they had told me that they wouldn't actually do that. Apparently even though it's allowed all over the country, Vermont won't allow the police to do partial matches."

"Ouch. Why didn't he tell you that, then?"

"I guess he decided to go ahead and run it anyway and get forgiveness later. But... there was no match in the database."

"So it doesn't really matter that it's against their policy. He wasn't there anyway."

"But that meant he logged the soother and used the DNA and the police won't share the data. So we're stuck trying to test another piece of evidence, and I don't know whether we'll be able to get enough DNA from it to use for our own purposes."

"What would you test it against, if he's not in the police database? Is there some super-secret private investigator database?"

Zachary had to laugh, as angry as he was. "No, there's a public database. People upload their DNA onto it for genealogical research. Anyone can access the shared data. If there's a match there, we can trace the family trees and narrow down what family the perpetrator came from."

"Really?" Lorne whistled. "That's amazing. People share that information publicly? Why would someone who had committed a felony voluntarily post their DNA to a public site?"

"It's not necessarily the criminal who does it. It might be his second cousin, or his aunt, or several different people, which allows you to really narrow down who it is, sometimes to just one or two people. Then you get direct DNA from them, and see if there's a match, and presto... you have something to build a case on."

"Isn't that automatically enough to convict?"

"It depends on the source of the DNA. People can leave DNA wherever they go, and it can be picked up by someone else and transported to a new scene. So I could leave hair or skin cells on a doorknob at the coffee shop, and then the next person could transfer it to... their boyfriend's apartment. The police could pick it up there and put me at the scene, even though I had never been there."

"But in this case, where you're testing the baby's DNA, then you know for sure that whoever the father is, he's the one who assaulted her."

"It's only a partial match, because we don't have his DNA from the rape kit. We only have half of his DNA from a baby that he fathered. They can determine paternity to a certain percentage, but it isn't ever going to be one hundred percent. And they still have to prove the circumstances, that he and Heather didn't have consensual sex at some point. She says the only person she had intercourse with was the rapist, but a jury would have to believe her. The defense would do whatever they could to prove that they might have had consensual sex at some other time."

"Ah. That makes sense, Zachary. I guess I wasn't thinking about it that way. You believe Heather, and so do I, so it didn't occur to me that someone else might not believe her story. We know she was attacked violently."

"But that doesn't mean she'd never had any other contact with anyone else and that the baby was definitely conceived in the attack. The timing is right, but…"

"Yeah. Poor Heather, she must be frustrated too."

"I think she took it better than I did, actually. Maybe it will hit her when she gets home. But at least she's got someone with her. She's not alone."

"Good. I worry about you being alone. At least Kenzie is there more often now."

"I'm fine." The words came too loudly, and he was worried that Mr. Peterson would think he was angry at him. "Sorry. I'm just… frustrated and irritable."

"Understandable. You had quite a disappointment over the case. Have you eaten?"

"Uh…" Zachary had to stop and think about it. "I'm not sure." He looked around him and saw the used dishes. "Yes. I ate." Provided the plates weren't from the previous day. He usually remembered to wash them.

"Is that Zachary?" He heard Pat's voice in the background. "Say 'hi' for me."

"Tell him 'hi' back," Zachary responded.

"He heard you. He says 'hi,'" Mr. Peterson passed the message along.

Pat said something else, his voice lower, and then he was apparently gone. Mr. Peterson didn't return to the conversation immediately.

"How is he doing?" Zachary asked.

"He's really having trouble with Jose's murder. And even more than that, with you getting… injured."

"I'm fine. Tell him everything is okay. I'm keeping busy with work, all healed. Nothing to keep worrying about."

"He blames himself for you getting hurt. You never would have gotten involved if it hadn't been for him."

"It's my own fault for not thinking about the consequences. Being too impulsive. I was supposed to wait until I met up with Dougan. I didn't do that and I walked right into Teddy's operation. I should have realized it was too dangerous."

"The two of you," Mr. Peterson sighed. "It wasn't Pat's fault and it wasn't yours. It was Teddy's. He's the one who hurt you. He's the one who killed Jose. He's the one who chose to break the law and to hurt people. Neither of you wanted anyone to get hurt. It was *Teddy's* fault."

Zachary shrugged to himself. He knew what had happened. He knew that if he'd made other choices, he wouldn't have gotten himself hurt. He might not have 'asked for it,' but he certainly could have been smarter.

"Pat knows that it was more than just physical injuries," Mr. Peterson said slowly. "He knows that even though the physical injuries have healed, you're still suffering from the emotional fallout. And that your relationship with Kenzie…"

The knot in Zachary's stomach tightened. His chest hurt. "What?"

"We've all noticed how it's affected you."

Zachary thought about it, the seconds passing.

"Zachary?" Mr. Peterson prompted. "You there? Are you okay?"

"Kenzie."

"What about Kenzie?"

"You *all* know that Kenzie and I are having personal problems."

Mr. Peterson didn't reply.

"How would you know that? Because I didn't tell you we were having any issues."

"I've talked to Kenzie," Mr. Peterson admitted after an awkward pause.

"You've been talking to my girlfriend behind my back."

"Don't think of it that way. That's not how it was. Kenzie is worried about you. We're worried about you. We talk to each other…"

"Did she call you?"

Lorne didn't answer, obviously weighing his response. He didn't want Zachary to think that he'd been invading his privacy. But he also didn't want to get Kenzie in trouble.

"Did Kenzie call you?" Zachary repeated.

"Yes."

"Kenzie called you to discuss our private relationship."

"It wasn't like that. She called because I know your history. As much of it as anyone. She called for advice."

"How to deal with our relationship."

"Yes… but that's not a bad thing, Zachary. She didn't dump you. She didn't tell you that you had to change to suit her. She called to ask about the best way to… stay with you."

"It's not bad for my girlfriend to call you to discuss what's wrong with our sex life?" He could barely keep his voice under control.

"I wish I could explain… that's not how it was."

"We have a good relationship," Zachary said hotly. "I've done everything she wanted. I don't ignore her or push her away. I started going back to therapy. We're working through the stuff between us. Why would she have to call you?"

"I guess… she needed someone to bounce ideas off of. How to handle the problems you were having. She wanted to know if I knew about… previous problems. What would you want her to do? Call Bridget?"

Bridget.

Darkness bloomed in Zachary's brain. He felt himself falling down a deep dark hole. A black hole.

"Zachary?" Mr. Peterson prompted, trying to bring him back.

"This is about Bridget?"

"No. It's not about Bridget. She wasn't calling about Bridget. I was just saying, who else would she go to? Who else knows anything about you and your previous relationships?"

"Bridget..."

"I told you, it's not about Bridget."

Zachary swallowed. He didn't know what to say or do. He was used to being able to talk to Mr. Peterson without any problems. Lorne was next to perfect in his eyes, always supportive and compassionate. He let Zachary have his privacy and had never gone behind his back, as far as Zachary knew, with either Bridget or Kenzie. And other than Bridget and Kenzie... there hadn't been anyone else in Zachary's life. No one serious. No one that he had introduced to Mr. Peterson and Pat.

"What did you tell Kenzie?"

"I... I just said she should be patient, give you time to work it out. Bring it up with you directly."

"But she wanted to know about my past."

"To know how much of this was new, and how much... might have already existed before Teddy."

"And what did you tell her?"

There was an uncomfortable pause. It was the point at which Mr. Peterson was going to have to admit that he had given Kenzie personal, private information about Zachary without his permission.

"Zach... it's not something that you and I have ever talked about..."

"Yeah. So...?"

"I told her that... you had probably been abused in foster care. That I didn't know any details, but with the number of different homes and institutions you had been in, it was probable. That there were red flags."

Zachary swallowed. What else could Mr. Peterson have said? He hadn't been there. He couldn't give Kenzie any details. He was just confirming the suspicions that Kenzie already had.

"And Bridget never came up?"

"She asked about Bridget, sure. Whether... either of you had ever mentioned anything about your relationship."

"Our sex life."

"Yes."

"And...?"

"You never said anything to me. That's not the kind of relationship that we have. And Bridget..."

Zachary could just see Bridget ranting to Lorne about Zachary's failings. She had no filter when it came to complaining about Zachary's inadequacies in other areas of his life. Why not the bedroom as well? Zachary covered his eyes with his hand, as if that could block out whatever Mr. Peterson was about to say.

"And Bridget?" he repeated.

"Zach… you know I would never say anything negative to you about Bridget. I know how much you loved her and how hard it has been to let her go. But… your relationship with her was toxic. Things might have seemed idyllic back in the beginning, but I was never comfortable with her. You weren't yourself with her. And she treated you like a project, something she was going to fix. It was never a partnership."

"What did she say to you?"

Mr. Peterson's voice was strong. "I never let Bridget run you down in front of me. Not with you there and not when you were out of the room. Whatever she had to say about your private life, she didn't say it to me. And that's what I told Kenzie. I don't know whether you had intimacy issues with Bridget and I preferred not to hear about them from Kenzie either."

Zachary chuckled. He could see Mr. Peterson telling her that and could see Kenzie's frustration at being told that it wasn't appropriate. Zachary had never wanted to know any details of Mr. Peterson's and Pat's intimate life, and Mr. Peterson had never asked for any details about Zachary's.

Lorne sighed. "I'm sorry. Maybe I should have said something to you at the time… but it was just a brief discussion, pretty much me telling her that her guess was as good as mine and if she wanted to know, she should ask you."

"Yeah."

"And you two *have* been talking, haven't you…?"

"Yeah. Sorry if I overreacted. I just… this stuff is…"

"Personal."

"And really hard. I don't understand my own reactions. I don't *want* to react the way I do, but I can't help it."

"How could your experience with Teddy *not* affect you? Would you expect Heather's assault not to color her future experiences? It's not a matter of choice."

"But before… I could shut it out before. I thought that was all in the past."

"It's stirred up some old memories?"

"Yeah."

"You said you're going back to therapy."

"I thought… it was time. If I want to be able to get over these problems with Kenzie… ignoring it wasn't making it go away."

"You guys will work it out. Give it time."

CHAPTER TWENTY-EIGHT

Z ACHARY KEPT BUSY OVER the next few weeks as they waited for the results of the second DNA test. The lab assured Zachary that they had retrieved enough DNA from the tiny mittens to run a profile, and after that it was just a matter of waiting while it worked its way through the system.

Zachary didn't tell Kenzie that he knew about her going to Mr. Peterson behind his back. He knew she wouldn't see it that way; she thought she was totally justified in digging into his past life to gain some insight into dealing with Zachary's anxiety and dissociative episodes. But he found excuses not to be with her and to put her off most of the time when she wanted to get together. He spent almost a full week on night surveillance, which eliminated any time they could get together that week other than lunch hours, which they took close to the morgue rather than at the apartment.

Then he needed a week to organize and write the reports and to train Heather on some of the basics of investigative work. Since she was available during the day, he relegated his report writing to the evening, and the rest of the time he slept.

He was starting to run out of excuses not to see Kenzie, but he was also expecting the DNA results back from the lab any day. He would upload the results to GENEmatch, and it would spit out the names they needed, and he already had the name of a genealogist on hand who would help them make sense of the relationships and home in on the suspects.

Ella Day, the professional genealogist, was a small woman with thick blond, curly hair. She had a bright red lipstick smile and greeted Heather and Zachary warmly. He had the sort of feeling meeting her that he might have had in meeting with a medium or fortune teller. What she could do with DNA and genealogical information would have seemed like magic just ten years before. If Zachary hadn't thoroughly checked out her background and references, he would have taken her for a scammer for sure.

She welcomed them and had them sit down in her comfy living room. She offered coffee and tea or cold beverages. Grant had not been able to make it due to a work commitment, so it was just Zachary and Heather for the meeting.

Zachary was all edges, worried about whether they were going to get any information or whether it would just be another report of 'he was not there.' They needed to find the guy for Heather's sake. Zachary knew how important it was in his own case to know who it was who had hurt him, to be able to put a face and a personality to dark shadow who had spoken to him and tortured him that night. When he allowed himself to think of what had happened, he wanted to know that it wasn't some faceless bogeyman, but a real person. A person who was behind bars and would not hurt him or anyone else again.

Ella set down the drinks on the coffee table, smiling sweetly at Heather and Zachary. She still seemed to be emitting some sort of vague, other-worldly vibe, and Zachary didn't know why. What she did was science-based. It was genetics, not ethereal vibrations or listening to ghostly voices. She was not an artist, but a kind of a scientist.

"Tell me about your story," Ella told Heather, as she sat down and smoothed her skirt. Maybe it was the flowered skirt that was giving Zachary such a weird vibe. She should have been wearing neatly-pressed slacks or faded bluejeans, depending on whether she liked to present a professional appearance or a geeky one. The flowery skirt didn't fit either image.

"What do you want to know?" Heather asked, guarded.

"This is your baby, right? You're trying to track him down?"

"Well… no, not exactly. We're trying to track down his biological father."

"You lost track of each other, want to reunite? Or does your son want to meet him?"

"We want to put him in prison," Zachary said, wanting to put a quick end to Ella's fairy-tale notions. "This was no love affair. It was a brutal assault. We want to track the guy down, lock him up, and throw away the key."

"Oh." Ella nodded. "I'm sorry. I see."

"You can help, right?" Heather asked.

"You've already uploaded it to GENEmatch and got some hits?"

Zachary pulled out the USB key and held it up.

"Great. Why don't I get that loaded while the two of you relax for a bit? I'll see what pops up."

"Will you be able to do it today? Identify the biological father?" Zachary asked.

"There's no guarantee. I'll need to work the family trees and see if I can identify who the potential father is. It can take a few hours to a few weeks, but sometimes it is only a few minutes' worth of work. You just don't know ahead of time. But I'll take a preliminary look at the results, and then I'll have a better idea of the timeline for you."

Zachary and Heather nodded together. Ella retreated to her computer on the other side of the room and sat down. Zachary watched her out of the corner of his eye for the first few minutes, saw her put the USB key in and start tapping away, waiting, mousing here and there, clicking, mousing some more.

He couldn't really tell what she was up to, and in a few minutes returned his attention to Heather, who was doing the same thing, looking away from Heather and back at Zachary. They both gave a little laugh.

"Leave her to it, I guess," Heather said.

"Yeah. Hard to do. I keep expecting her to jump up and shout 'eureka!'"

"At least we know it was good DNA and that there were matches."

"The lab said they got a good DNA profile."

"I was terrified of cross-contamination. That it would end up being the DNA from someone's cat."

"If it had been cat DNA, I think they would have told us before they sequenced it."

"I know." Heather bounced her legs up and down, sneaking another look at Ella. "I just feel like it is all going to go wrong. If I get my hopes up, I'm just going to end up being disappointed."

"We can't predict the results. All we can do is pursue every lead."

"Well, you've done that. You're really good at this."

"I want to help you."

Heather nodded. Her cup rattled on the saucer when she picked it up. Zachary wished that Ella had just served their drinks in regular mugs. He felt like he was going to smash something. Heather steadied her cup using both hands and took a little sip. She made a face and Zachary thought she probably wasn't usually a tea drinker. It wasn't his preference either, but he often had it with clients who were nervous, because it helped them to calm down, when coffee just make them more jittery. That was why he had suggested it to Heather when Ella had offered. Heather set her cup down again with a clink.

"How is Grant?" Zachary asked. "Your kids? What have you been up to lately?"

She rolled her eyes, recognizing that he was forcing small-talk, but she answered anyway, needing the distraction.

"Things have been really good with Grant. It's like… talking about this has opened things up for us. It's like we're newlyweds again, just learning about each other and exploring new sides of each other that we'd never seen before."

"You too? I mean… are there things that Grant has told you about him that you didn't know before?"

"Yes… because he didn't share. He knew that I was holding back on my history, and that I didn't want to talk about anything to do with sex, so we just never did. We had a relationship… but it was just an outward, physical thing, without much passion or imagination."

"Going through the motions," Zachary said, remembering Kenzie's words.

"Yeah. Like that. Going through the motions. I had two kids, so obviously we had a physical dimension to our marriage. But it was never emotionally fulfilling. Just… an appetite to be satisfied."

"And that changed when you told him about what had happened to you?" Zachary tried to wrap his mind around that. He would have expected the opposite. That Grant would push back, not wanting to do anything that might make Heather feel bad. Or he would not want to have anything to do with someone who had been spoiled before they ever met. He hadn't expected that it would have helped them to grow closer physically. Emotionally, maybe, but he had expected it to put a wedge between them as far as physical intimacy went.

Heather made some answer, but Zachary didn't hear what it was. Ella's typing suddenly got louder and sharper, like the final percussions in an anthem. They both looked over at her, looking for a change in her expression.

"*Yes*," Ella said. "We can narrow it down to one family tree."

Heather sat straight up in her seat. "Who?" she asked. "What is the family name?"

Despite the fact that her attacker had been masked, it could still have been someone that Heather knew. Someone who was afraid that she would recognize him. It was thirty years later, but she might still remember the name and be able to match it to a face or role in the neighborhood.

"Reid-Clark," Ella said, staring intently at her screen, clicking with her mouse and tapping in various searches or commands. "Looks like a union between Reid-Clark and Astor…"

It took Zachary a few seconds to compute this. He looked at Heather. Heather was looking at Ella, her face blank and expressionless.

"Heather…? The family you were living with was the Astors. Was there someone who was related to them?" Zachary asked.

"No," she said flatly.

"Your foster mother was in the delivery room with you. Was she the one who put the mittens on the baby? Is it possible that she got her DNA in the mittens when she put them on?"

Heather shook her head.

Ella looked up from her computer at Zachary with an irritated expression. "Don't confuse things," she said sharply. "This is male DNA, not female. And Mrs. Astor would not actually be an Astor if that was her married name. It has to be her husband or someone from his line."

"Heather…?"

Heather was blank. Silent. Her eyes didn't move. Her knees no longer bounced up and down with nervous anticipation.

"Heather, was Mr. Astor at the hospital? Did he handle the mittens?"

"No."

Zachary looked back at Ella, trying to connect with her to get more information and her read on the situation. She was staring at her computer screen and paid him no attention.

"Feathers," Zachary tried her nickname to pull Heather out of the trance. He knew what it was like to get so wrapped up in his brain and his feelings that he couldn't escape the thoughts. "We're here together, Feathers. It's Zachary. We're having tea with Ella. Do you smell the tea?"

There was a flicker of life in her face. In a moment, she looked down at the cup of tea in front of her. She picked it up, took a sip, and again gave a grimace at the taste.

"Do you want some sugar or cream in that?" Zachary looked at the tray Ella had placed on the table. "Some honey? Lemon?"

Despite the fact that she didn't respond, he reached over and squeezed one of the lemon wedges over his own tea, squeezing the rind hard to spray the pungent oils into the air. "Do you want some lemon in yours?"

Heather shook her head. She reached out and touched the outside of the rind as he put it down. She licked the oil off of her finger and wrinkled her nose at the bitterness.

"Heather." He put his hand on her arm. "What do you remember? You told Able that the Astors didn't molest you."

"No, they didn't."

"The story about you being attacked in the woods... was that what they told you happened? Did you remember that, or did they plant it?"

"You think I don't know what happened to me?"

"I think memories can be manipulated. If you're told something enough times and in enough detail, then that's what you remember. Especially if you were in a vulnerable state. You were traumatized. If you were given drugs or alcohol and given their version of what happened, that's what you would remember."

"No. It's not a fake memory. They didn't tell me what happened, I told them."

Zachary thought about the police file, about the things that Heather had said in her statement, the mother being the one to take her to the police, the pictures of what had been done to her. He remembered the scrapes on her back from the rough ground, the leaves and grass tangled in her hair. That hadn't been staged.

"The man who attacked you wore a mask. Could it have been your foster father or one of the sons?"

Heather stood up abruptly. "I have to go."

"You want me to take you home?" Zachary had picked her up from her house. He'd been worried that she would be too emotionally overwrought after the visit to the genealogist, and he was not happy to have been right. He hadn't been expecting the revelation.

"I want to go home," Heather echoed.

There were still no tears, no raised voice. Ella was watching them, a little frown line appearing above the bridge of her nose.

"I'll be in touch," Zachary told her. "I'm sorry this is so abrupt. I'll call you."

She nodded and didn't try to stop them from going. Zachary wondered if her clients always got so emotional. Maybe that was the reason for the soothing atmosphere and the tea. It wasn't a show, she knew it would be an emotionally taxing visit, even if Heather had just been there to try to track down her child.

Zachary took Heather by the arm, leading her out to the car like she was a frail old woman. She walked like a sleepwalker, not looking at him, not looking to the right or to the left. Zachary unlocked the car, opened her door for her, and warned her not to bump her head as he guided her into the seat. He shut her door and returned to the driver's side. She automatically pulled her seatbelt across, and Zachary made sure that it clicked into place.

"Do you want something on the radio? Do you want to talk?"

She didn't answer.

Zachary pondered as he drove her home. It was a shame that Grant hadn't been able to go to the meeting with her. He didn't like to take her back to an empty house with whatever emotions she was going through, finding out that her attacker that day had not been a stranger, but one of the men living under her own roof.

Heather started to rock forward and back. There were still no tears. Zachary tried to keep up a running description to her of the things he was seeing, hearing, and smelling around them, hoping to keep her anchored in the physical world, not stuck in flashbacks of the assault.

How could someone she had lived with not only rape her, but also beat her up so badly? Someone who was supposed to be caring for her and being a loving and kind father or brother? He had lain in wait for her, obviously knowing that she broke the school rule and walked through the park every day. He had worn a mask so she wouldn't be able to identify him, had brutally assaulted her, and then he had lived with her afterward, watching her growing large with his child.

She had to feel devastated. Betrayed. The police had told her that it was her own fault, and now she knew it had been her own foster father or brother.

"Can we call Grant? I'll stay with you until he can come home."

"He'll be home soon. Maybe even before we get back."

Her voice was so calm and measured that someone who didn't know her or the effect that shock could have would have thought that she was unconcerned and feeling no distress over the revelation of her attacker's identity. Zachary understood that the opposite was true. She was so overwhelmed by the news that it had pushed her over the edge. Past being able to feel it or express it.

"Do you want to call your therapist? Or a hotline? Do you have tranquilizers?"

"I'll talk to Grant. It will be okay."

Zachary kept talking to her, kept trying to keep her engaged. When he parked at the curb in front of her house, Zachary pulled his key out of the ignition and released his seatbelt to walk her into the house. She reached for her door handle.

"It's fine, Zachary." She indicated the blue car in the driveway. "Grant is home."

"I'll just walk you in, make sure he knows what happened."

"No," she insisted. "Let me speak for myself."

Back when it had happened, she hadn't been allowed to speak for herself. She'd done what her foster mother and social worker had told her to and had not been allowed to make her own decisions. Zachary had to allow her the chance to have her own voice.

"You're sure you'll be okay?"

"I'll be fine."

"Heather." He stopped her one last time before she could walk away.

"What?"

"Do you know which one it was?"

She stared at him for a long moment, her expression still completely blank and unreadable.

"Thank you for your help today, Zach. And for all the rest. I don't know how I could have done it without you."

CHAPTER TWENTY-NINE

H E DIDN'T FEEL GOOD about leaving Heather alone after receiving such shattering news. But he had to keep reminding himself that she wasn't alone. Her husband was there. He had been fully supportive of her since she had told him about what had happened to her as a child, and he would be there for her now, giving her whatever comfort she needed.

But he didn't get all the way home before finally breaking down and calling her to make sure she was okay. There was no answer. She was probably working it through with Grant, hugging, crying, letting out all of the emotion she had been stuffing down for thirty years. It wasn't a good time to talk to Zachary. She needed to be with her husband, not her brother.

He called again when he got back to his apartment. Again, no answer. Zachary was getting uneasy. She must know how worried he would be. Couldn't she at least answer to say that she was okay? She must be finished crying. He hung up and tried again immediately. He anxiously checked for text messages, emails, or messages in social networking platforms. She hadn't sent him anything. There was nothing to reassure him.

What if it hadn't been Grant's car in the driveway? What if she'd lied to him about someone else being home and had planned to harm herself once he was out of the way? She could already have bled out, or her respiration could be getting too slow after taking pills. Or she could have chosen another way to exit the life that she couldn't bear anymore.

He concentrated, trying to remember his previous visit to her house. Had the car been in the driveway? What had she driven when she met him at the police station? The dark blue car? Uneasy, he called her again.

When there was no answer, he changed tactics. Firing up his browser, he started searching for Grant Garrity. Luckily, the man had an electronic trail a mile wide and it only took Zachary a few minutes to find his phone number.

"Hello?" Grant's voice rang in Zachary's ear, too cheerful to have been comforting his wife for the last hour. Zachary's stomach knotted.

"Grant, this is Zachary Goldman."

"Oh, hi, Zach. Is Heather with you, then?"

"No. I dropped her off at home. She said you were there already."

"I just got here," Grant said, confirming what Zachary had feared. "She's not home."

Zachary swore under his breath. He didn't want to panic Grant, but he was starting to panic himself.

"She said that you were home. She's not answering her phone and I'm worried about her. If she lied to me about you being home... you're sure she's not there? In the bedroom or bathroom? I'm worried... she might have done something."

All cheer had left Grant's voice. Zachary could picture him, his face ashen. "No... I just called out. She didn't answer. I didn't think..."

Zachary could hear him pounding up the stairs. He could hear doors opening and closing. After a few minutes, he was back. "I don't know where she is, but she's definitely not home. Her car is gone. What happened? Why would she...?"

"You know that we were meeting with the genealogist today to see if we could get a hit in the GENEmatch database."

There was a moment of silence from Grant. "No. She didn't tell me that was today."

"She said you were busy at work and couldn't come."

"I had work, but I could have gotten off to come with her. Why would she say that?"

Zachary's brain was spinning. Had Heather known, consciously or unconsciously, what she was going to find? Had part of her brain known all that time who it was that had assaulted her in the park? She might have recognized him by something other than his face. His aftershave. The way he moved. A ring on his finger, belt buckle, shoes. Heather might have been subconsciously repressing it all along.

"I don't know why she wouldn't have told you. Maybe she was confused and thought you had something else going on today. Did she leave you a note? Send you a message or leave a voicemail?"

"No... I don't think so. I don't see anything. She's usually here when I get home from work."

"Does she know how to reach her old foster family? The Astors?"

"No." This answer, after all of his uncertain and hesitant replies, was immediate and strong. "She didn't keep in contact with them. I always thought it was a little strange that she wouldn't have anything to do with them, after living with them for a couple of years. But after hearing what she went through when she was there... well, I can understand it a bit better. I'm sure they were only trying to help her and do the right thing when they forced her to give the baby up, but I think she felt like... it was adding insult to injury."

"You don't have any idea where they are now?"

"Why...? I don't know where they are. I don't know if she ever heard anything, but it wasn't like they moved in the same circles."

"Okay. I'll see what I can find."

"I'll have her give you a call back when she gets home," Grant said, acting as if Zachary were just making a social call.

"Grant." Zachary stopped him from hanging up.

"Yes?"

"Do either of you own a gun?"

"Yes, of course. Heather was always afraid of getting mugged when she was out with the kids or by herself. She's carried one for years. I never really knew why until now, but I felt better knowing she could protect herself if she needed to. You think she's going to need it? What's going on?"

"Grant... the man who raped and beat Heather was one of the Astors."

Grant swallowed his curse, making it impossible for Zachary to tell for sure what he had said. "And you think... she's gone after them?"

"That's why I asked if she knew where they lived."

"But she doesn't. I'm sure of it."

"She might have had some idea... and I've been teaching her how to skip trace. Do you have any sense of which one of them it would be? Did she ever say anything that would have put one of them higher on your list than another?"

"She never talked about them. About any of them."

"Even when she was telling you about what happened to her? It might have been very brief, even just a sense that she was afraid of men of a certain age. Would she react more to a forty-year-old or a teen?"

"I don't know... if I had to pick one, I would say a forty-year-old. But she never mentioned them. I don't even know their names."

Zachary flipped through the file on his desk. He had printed out all of the documents he had taken pictures of, the ones that had originally resided in the police file. "Hang on a second. Their names. That could be an important piece of information."

Grant waited. Zachary skimmed the pages, looking for the original reports that had been made, which listed household members. "Okay. Kevin, Mark, and Robert."

"Uh... Robert... I suggested it as a name for our son. My grandfather was named Robert. But she wasn't having it. She said there was no way our son was going to be named Robert."

"No objection to Mark or Kevin?"

"I don't remember either of them ever coming up. We have a family friend named Mark... I have a nephew named Kevin... she's never said anything about the names bothering her or not wanting to be around them. Just Robert. That she'd never allow her son to be named Robert."

"Okay, that's a pretty good guess, then." Zachary checked the file. Robert was the father. Heather's foster father, likely her attacker. He couldn't believe it.

"What are you going to do?" Grant asked.

"I'm going to track him down. Find out where he is now. And get over there."

"Can I come? I can help. I know Heather better than anyone."

Except that he hadn't even known her secret. Not for thirty years. "I'll call you when I know something," he promised. "I don't know where he is yet and I don't want to put you in any danger."

"Call me as soon as you know."

Zachary said a quick goodbye and hung up. He sat staring at the papers in the file for a long minute, then he navigated to Able's number on his phone and turned to his browser to start typing in searches as he waited for it to ring through. It continued to ring. He waited for voicemail to answer, trying to compose a script in his head. Where was Able? Was he away from his phone or on another call? Or had he decided he'd had enough of Zachary and didn't want anything else to do with him? Should he try getting through the police switchboard, explaining that it was urgent? Or just hang up and call 9-1-1? The trouble was, he didn't yet have any information to give to 9-1-1 and they would probably just write him off as a kook.

"Able."

Zachary looked away from his computer. He waited for the rest of Able's recorded voicemail greeting, but it didn't come. He had answered in person.

"Detective Able. It's Zachary Goldman. We've got a problem."

"We? You and Heather?"

"No. You and me. Heather and I met with a genealogist today to see whether we could match the baby's partial DNA to a father using GENEmatch. Or to a family tree where we could identify suspects."

"Okay."

"It turns out it wasn't a stranger. It was one of the Astors. My money is on the father."

He swore. "You couldn't tell which?"

"Not until we get direct DNA and paternity testing for each of them. Heather... she didn't exactly freak out. More like... shut down. She said she wanted to go home, so I drove her home. She said her husband was there and she wouldn't be alone. But she lied. He wasn't home. She took the car and left."

"You think she's going to hurt herself?"

"I think she might... but I think she might also go after him. Or all of them."

"Has she kept in touch?"

"No. Her husband doesn't think that she knew where they were anymore."

"Then we've got some time to track them down and head her off. You don't know where she's gone?"

"Well, that's the thing." Zachary tapped another search into his browser, quickly opening tabs and scanning through the information he found as he talked on the phone with Able. "In the past few weeks, while we've been waiting for the DNA results, I've been helping Heather out. She wanted to change the way she was living. Do volunteer work or develop some marketable skill. So I've been helping her."

"With what?" Able's voice was gruff, and Zachary figured he'd already figured it out.

"With basic detecting. Skip tracing. Finding missing people."

Able swore again. "How much of a head start does she have?"

"A couple of hours. But she is a beginner, it might have taken her a while to find him with only internet search capabilities. She's not hooked into all of the databases that I am, or that you have access to. Can you check DMV for current address?"

He heard Able start to tap computer keys on his end. "What's the name?"

"Robert Astor. Age seventy-two. Do you need his social?"

"You got DOB?"

Zachary gave it to him. Able typed the information in. "Got it. Thanks for the heads-up. I'll get someone sent right over on a welfare check. But I don't think Mrs. Garrity presents much of a threat."

Zachary was about to ask who Mrs. Garrity was, before he remembered that was Heather. Even though they hadn't seen each other for such a long time, it seemed incongruous that she should have a different last name from his. But they could all have different last names. Any of the children could have married or been adopted or just taken on the name of a foster family or started life with a new identity when they had aged out of foster care.

"Heather carries a gun."

"She what?"

"I asked her husband. She's a former victim. She wanted to be able to protect herself from an attack."

"Great. Okay. I'll give them a heads-up that this might be more than just a welfare check, then. I don't want cops getting killed."

"Give me the address. I'll head over there too. I might be able to talk her down."

"You think I'm going to give you that information? I don't want you interfering. I'll call you back when everything has been sorted. That's the most I can do."

Zachary looked at the address on the screen in front of him. He read it aloud to Able. "Is that it? Is that the address on his operator's license?"

Able's muttered curse gave him the answer. "Stay out of this, Mr. Goldman."

"I don't want her getting shot by some jumpy policeman, either. She's my sister. She's more of a danger to herself right now than to anybody else. I'm going."

"Give the police department some credit. We can manage this."

146

"I'm a ways out. If it's handled by the time I get there, then there won't be anything for me to do when I arrive. If it's not, you might very well be looking for someone who can talk to her."

Zachary hung up before Able could make any further objection. He jammed the phone into his pocket, sent the information on his screen to himself, and grabbed his keys. He was back in his car in no time, headed back to the highway. He ignored the calls coming into his phone from a blocked ID. That would be Able, and he didn't want to talk to Able. After Able gave up and stopped dialing him every two minutes, Zachary called Grant back.

"I've got an address for Robert Astor. The police are sending someone over there. I'm on my way. But I'm going to be a while, even speeding on the highway."

"Where is he?"

Zachary tapped his phone to bring the address back up again, and read it out to Grant.

"Don't go in if the police aren't there yet. Wait for them. Tell them that you can talk to her, there's no need to go in guns blazing. I'll be there as soon as I can. We need to give her some time to cool off. We don't know what kind of shape she's going to be in."

"Heather wouldn't hurt anyone. She's never hurt a fly."

"He hurt her. And if he triggers her, there's no telling what she'll do with a gun in her hands to protect herself this time."

CHAPTER THIRTY

I T WAS A GOOD thing that Kenzie wasn't in the car with Zachary, because he was going much faster than she would have tolerated on the highway. Having driven with her before in an emergency, he knew she would have been freaking out.

But he was a good driver, and his ADHD meant that he could hyperfocus and react quickly if something unexpected happened. That wouldn't necessarily help him if a cop happened to see him, but he hoped that the traffic gods would be on his side and there wouldn't be any police on his way there.

It was possible he would beat Grant there, but he didn't expect to, not unless Grant was a real old-lady driver. If he stepped on the gas and ran a few lights or stop signs, he'd get there ahead of Zachary. The police would be there too. Zachary hoped that Able had activated whatever tactical team or hostage negotiator that he had to, and that they knew enough to approach the house quietly and not just rush in. He wanted Heather to see her way out of there. He didn't want her to be a headline on the next day's news, another statistic in police-involved shootings for the year. He prayed that they set up a perimeter and took it slow.

And that Heather hadn't already killed the sicko.

He had let his mind wander as he thought through the possibilities, and he almost missed his exit, which would have been bad because there weren't a lot of places to get turned around and get going in the right direction again. He'd miss the whole town or have to wind his way through tiny streets at a crawl, watching for children and elderly pedestrians.

When he pulled onto the block, he knew he had the right place. Lots of police cars. A nice wide perimeter around the house in question. It probably looked almost normal from the inside of the house. But past the house's viewlines, activity buzzed and everybody was working on their particular jobs, keeping the public back where it was safe and letting the experts work out what they were going to do.

Zachary left his car behind the barricades and walked in. He was looking around for whoever was in charge, not sure whether Able would be there, and if he was, what kind of authority he would have over the operation. Zachary didn't try to breach the barrier, but walked up to one of the cops keeping the public at bay.

"That's my sister in there. I'm the one who called it in."

"That's nice, sir, but there's nothing you can do at this point. Just stay back out of the way and let the police do their jobs."

"Is Detective Able here? Who is in charge?"

"Not Able."

"Is there a hostage negotiator? What's the plan here?"

The cop looked irritated. "Buddy. You got no special standing here. You're going to have to wait and see what happens, just like everybody else."

Zachary looked over the faces of the police inside the taped-off area. "Is her husband here yet? Grant?"

The cop's eyes went to the side, and Zachary identified a small knot of people that must have included Grant Garrity. He walked along the outside of the perimeter toward them, pulling out his phone and dialing Grant's number. Grant jumped when the phone rang, and pulled it hurriedly out.

"Yeah? Zachary?"

"I'm behind you. Can you talk to whoever is in charge about letting me inside?"

Grant turned and looked, then waved at Zachary. He spoke to one of the cops, turning and pointing Zachary out. A couple of times. Until the cop finally nodded and spoke into his radio, and in a moment, there was a hulking big uniform in front of Zachary, looking him over like he was some kind of bug.

"You're Zachary Goldman?"

"Yeah. Are they going to let me talk to her?"

"Talk to her?" the big ape repeated. "I doubt that!" He laughed.

But he led Zachary into the perimeter, and he was allowed to go over to Grant to talk to him.

"Have they verified that Heather is inside?" Zachary asked. "That we guessed right?"

Grant nodded slowly. He seemed distracted, like he wasn't sure what to think of his wife being inside, the subject instead of the victim. He'd probably never even thought about her that way before.

"They put listening devices on the windows. So they can hear what's being said inside. Heather is there."

"Doing what? Talking to him? Threatening him?"

"They won't really tell me anything other than to just be quiet and wait for them to do their thing."

"Who is in charge?"

Grant scanned the various worker bees, shaking his head a little as if he were lost. He pointed to a long truck on the other side of the perimeter, some kind of mobile command center. "I don't know his name, but he's in there. Or they are. I don't know if it's one guy or if there are different departments or what."

Zachary moved toward the truck. He was stopped by one of the apes. Either the same one as had escorted him through the barrier, or another very similar. Zachary hadn't been paying any attention to their faces.

"You can't go in there."

"I'm Heather's brother. I need to talk to her. They're the only guys who are going to have any say in whether I can talk to her or not."

"You can't talk to them."

"Just let me go talk to them. They'll want to deal with someone with a clear head. Someone who knows Heather."

The big cop didn't like it, but he shook his head and escorted Zachary over to the bus. He knocked on the door with loud bangs, and eventually, someone pushed the door open. "What is it?"

"This is apparently the perp's brother?" the cop said it as a question, and shrugged. "He said you might want to talk to him? I don't know."

The other cop looked at Zachary for a minute, then motioned him up the three stairs into the bus.

"Come on, come on," he urged.

Inside the bus, Zachary took a look around. Lots of electronics and people wearing headphones. Talking to each other, talking to someone off the scene, coordinating whatever plan they were setting up.

"I thought the husband was here," commented the man who had let him in. "I'm Jones."

"Jones. Uh. I'm Zachary Goldman. I'm Heather's brother. I was with her earlier today when she... got some disturbing news about Robert Astor. If I could talk to her, I think I could help."

"Her husband is out there. What makes you think you're in a better position to talk to her than he is?"

"Because... she initially came to me about it. She talked to me about it before she talked to him. Because... we've both had some similar experiences. Some experiences that help me to understand what it is she's going through in there."

"She's not going through anything. She's the one putting someone else through pain and distress. She may have been the victim before, but she's not now."

"She still is. At least in her mind. So let me talk to her. What's it going to hurt?"

"Having the wrong person talk to her, or the right person say the wrong thing, and she could go nuclear. No one wants that. We're just going to take this slowly, one step at a time."

"Exactly." Zachary nodded. "That's exactly right. Nice and slowly. Has she talked to anyone? Does she know you're here?"

"Oh, she's knows we're here. We've had some contact."

"What did she say?"

"She doesn't have any demands. She just wants to kill the guy. But she hasn't done it yet, and that's a good sign."

"How long has she been in there?"

Jones looked at his watch. He had dark hair and bright, intelligent eyes. Every movement looked like it was choreographed. "Thirty-five minutes."

Zachary had been right, it had taken her a good amount of time to track down his address and get there. They had caught up to her quickly. And maybe that meant she wasn't too invested yet in killing him or being killed herself.

"How long have the police been here?"

"Twenty, give or take. The phone contact was… ten minutes ago, maybe. She's doing well; she didn't drop him as soon as she arrived, and she didn't do it when we got there. So far, she's kept her cool."

Zachary shook his head. Cool, Heather was not. She might come across that way, but she was traumatized and Zachary knew that she wasn't feeling calm and collected at all. She felt like the whole world was coming down around her and she didn't know what to do.

"I want to talk to her. I have my cell phone, does she have hers? If I call her, she'll pick up."

"No unauthorized contact. That's just playing with fire."

"I can talk to her. I know I can."

"You're not a trained negotiator. And you may think you know your sister, but in a case like this, you have no idea what's going on in her head."

"She came to me to help her to find out who hurt her. I need to finish it. I understand what's going on in her head. He hurt her and she wants to hurt him. He ruined her life and she wants to ruin his too. It's not enough to just shoot him. She needs him to be just as afraid of her as she was of him. Physically, it doesn't really matter how badly he's hurt. She wants him to hurt on the inside. To be as broken and terrified as she was."

Jones looked at Zachary in silence, chewing on his gum, considering. Finally, he nodded. "Give me your phone."

Zachary handed it over uncertainly, expecting Jones to dial Heather's number on it. But Jones slid it away in his own pocket. He motioned to one of the techs. "Get Mr. Goldman a headset."

In short order, one was placed over Zachary's head. He looked at Jones. "What do I do with this?" There was no keypad, no way he could see to dial out.

Jones smiled. "Just keep it on. We'll do all the work. Understand that we can cut you off at any time. We can also whisper prompts in your ear. Our job here is to deescalate. Get her calmed down and hopefully she will come out of there of her own free will, without any guns and without any harm done to Mr. Astor."

"Right."

Though Zachary himself would have liked to have been left alone with Mr. Astor for a few minutes. He was not a violent person, and had never been the instigator of a fight in his life. But he would have liked to hurt Mr. Astor. Just like he would have liked to hurt Teddy.

CHAPTER THIRTY-ONE

THERE WAS A RINGING on his headset, and everybody in the bus was suddenly silent, listening in. Zachary rubbed his clammy hands down his pants. He waited to see whether Heather would pick up. Maybe she was too far gone. But they were monitoring her through the windows. They would know if she had already killed Mr. Astor.

"What?" Heather demanded.

Zachary took another breath. He forced a smile, which he hoped would make his voice sound cheerful and unstrained. "Hi, Feathers."

"Zachary?"

"I guess I should have walked you in."

She grunted. "You weren't going to get in my way."

"How are you doing in there?"

"Things aren't going quite the way I expected," she growled.

"It's a little harder than they make it look on TV, isn't it?"

There was a lengthy silence. Zachary wondered if he had said the wrong thing. But she wasn't shooting Mr. Astor to bits, so he supposed it could have been worse.

"I thought... I could come here and talk to him and he'd admit what he did. I'd tell him that I had proof he was the baby's father and he'd admit what he did."

"But he's not budging?"

"He's... weird."

"What does that mean? Weird how?"

"He's smaller than I remember. He was all... authoritative when I was a kid. He was... like God."

"And now, he's just a regular man. A regular man who isn't as big and scary as you remember him."

"Yeah."

"What did he say about the assault?"

"He said... he couldn't believe I thought he had anything to do with it. That there must be a mistake. Someone screwed up the DNA samples."

Zachary's first reaction had been that the mittens had been cross-contaminated and that it wasn't the baby's DNA that they had ended up testing. But Heather swore that Mr. Astor had never touched the mittens. So how could his DNA end up being on them? Or the DNA of one of the boys?

Zachary had told Mr. Peterson about DNA transfer. Heather could unwittingly have transferred the DNA. She would have touched other things that had the Astors' DNA on them at home. Then she could have transferred it to the mittens herself. Maybe it wasn't the baby's DNA at all. Maybe it was one of the other boys'.

"Do you think that's true?" he asked Heather. "What do you remember about your attacker? You lived with Mr. Astor every day. He couldn't fool you just by wearing a mask."

Zachary jumped when he heard Jones's voice in his ear. "We're trying to settle her down, Mr. Goldman. Not make her more angry toward the victim. If she has doubts about him being her attacker, that's a good thing."

He looked over to Jones, then away again, trying to stay focused on Heather. He couldn't talk to her if he was being interrupted by someone else's thoughts. But he remembered Jones's warning that they could shut down the call any time they wanted to.

"I know it was him," Heather confirmed. "As soon as that lady said it was from one of the Astors, I knew."

"Because of the way he behaved toward you? Had he... been inappropriate before?"

"No." Her tone was confused. "He was always really strict. He wasn't creepy. He didn't sit on my bed or touch me when he talked or anything like that. He never tried to be the only one in the house with me, and when he was... nothing ever happened."

"So he never gave you any sign that he had designs on you?"

Heather sighed. "He ignored me most of the time. It was Mrs. Astor who was the parent. He would go off to his office and just work on stuff there. I never even knew what it was he did. He just wasn't even there most of the time."

Zachary shook his head. He touched the earphone over his ear uncomfortably. He didn't like over-the-ear models. He liked the ones that fit inside his ear. That was what he used for his phone. They were distracting him from the conversation.

"So he kept to himself. Whatever he was thinking, he just kept it inside. You didn't have any way of knowing what he was up to. You couldn't have known."

"Yeah. No warning," Heather agreed.

Would it have been better if she had known his inner thoughts? Or would that just have drawn the torture out?

"He knew that was the way you came home from school?"

"It's the only way I ever came home. He knew. I had fights with Mrs. Astor about it all the time. She'd get calls or notes from the school. Then she'd get after me, tell me I had to obey the rules and go around the park like everyone else. Because that was the rule. But... I didn't like going around. I didn't want to be out on the road, with all of the traffic. Why should we have to avoid the park? It was a public park, it was meant to be enjoyed. I like being in nature. At least, back then I did."

He wondered how she enjoyed nature now. Did she still go out for walks in the park? Or did she stay at home, where she felt more safe?

"Could I come in, Heather?"

Jones spoke in Zachary's ear again. "You are not allowed to go in there. No one is allowed to go in."

He put his hand around his mike to muffle it, not sure if he had a mute button somewhere. "If she wants me to go in, I can go in and help to calm her down. I can keep her from shooting Mr. freaking Astor. As much as he deserves it."

"It's against policy. We can't send more potential victims in there. Especially civilians."

Zachary grunted. He looked for a way around the rule. There was always a way around. He was an inveterate rule-breaker. "What if I go sit on the doorstep. Can I do that?"

"No."

"She could come out to talk to me. I wouldn't have to go in. You want her out of there, don't you?"

"You would still be putting yourself in the line of fire."

Zachary shook his head. He took his hand off of the mike to talk to Heather. "Never mind. They won't let me come in there."

"That's probably a good thing."

"Do you think it's time to come out?" he suggested.

"I need to do this."

"I don't think you can. Can you?"

"I can. I just need to get my courage up. It would help if he wasn't such a weaselly little snot. That isn't what he was like when I was little. He was the dad. I was so used to... you know what our dad was like. You didn't disobey him, or he was likely to take your head off. We all knew that. When I went to the Astors, I just thought... he was the dad. He had to be obeyed like that. He was the authority."

"Yeah. It's always different when you're at another home, the rules change, the roles change, it takes forever to figure out the way things work. And for me, by the time I figured things out, I was always on my way somewhere else. You know?"

"You changed families way more than I did. I just had the Astors."

There was a voice in the background that Zachary couldn't make out. Then Heather's voice shouting directly into his ear. "You shut up!"

Zachary waited for the ringing in his ears to stop. He glanced around the command center at the others listening in on the call and saw that a number of them had pulled the earpieces away from their ears momentarily.

"Hey, Heather. What's going on there?"

"I don't want him to speak!"

"Okay. Gotcha. Is he... physically okay?"

"Have I hurt him?"

"Have you?"

"Why do you care? You know about people like him. You know what he did to you."

Zachary noticed her pronoun confusion and tried to let it float over him. Mr. Astor hadn't done anything to Zachary. It had been Archuro who had hurt him. But Archuro wasn't in there. Zachary wasn't with him. He breathed through his brain's attempts to sweep him back in time.

"I'm just wondering," he said casually. "The cops are wondering. Whether he's tied up, or injured, or you've got your gun pointed at him. You know. They want the whole picture."

"He banged up his face a bit. I told him to take his clothes off to humiliate him, but I can't stand looking at his body, so the joke's on me. He's sitting here in his tighty-whities looking like some dead fish the dog drug in. But he *won't shut up!*" She shouted the last few words again.

Jones was looking anxious, but Zachary shook his head at him. It was good for Heather to be getting her frustration out by yelling. She had said a couple of times that she was trying to work herself up to killing Astor, but Zachary thought that if he kept bleeding off her anger safely, he could bring her down.

"What's he saying?" Zachary asked.

"I don't know. He's saying that he'd never hurt anyone. But he did! You know what he did to me."

"I know. He should have to pay for that. He should have to go to prison."

Zachary motioned to Jones for his phone, but it took a few mimed requests before Jones got it out and handed it to him, frowning. Zachary thumbed through the photos, turning to one that just showed teenage Heather's face, battered and bruised, which he turned around and showed to Jones.

Jones's lips tightened as he looked at the young teen's injuries. He shook his head slowly. "I hate it when we have to protect scum like that," he said in Zachary's ear, "but it's part of the job."

Zachary nodded his agreement. "You want him to go to prison, don't you, Feathers?"

"Yes." Her voice sounded teary and sullen.

"If you want him to go to prison, then you need to let the police arrest him. You need to let them in there."

"But he has to say what he did! They won't arrest him if he doesn't admit it."

"He'll admit it. He's just scared right now. Once he gets out of there and gets a lawyer, he's going to be trying to get a plea. That's what his lawyer will tell him to do. They'll know that we have him dead to rights and they'll tell him to plead it out."

"I don't want him to plead!"

There was a loud crash. Zachary pulled his earpieces away from his ears, looking anxiously at the other people in the command center. No one seemed to be panicking or ramping up a response to the next level, so the loud noise had been something other than a gunshot.

"What was that?" Zachary asked.

"His chair fell over," she said more calmly.

There were a couple of muffled laughs inside the bus.

"He peed himself," Heather said, disgust in her voice. "How could I have been so scared of this little rat? I spent every day of my life worrying that the man who raped me was going to come back and do it again. I was afraid to go out of the house, to take my kids to the playground. I thought he was a big, scary monster."

"But he's just a man. And not even as big as you remember him being."

"He barely even had to raise his voice and I'd start shaking. I never let anyone see it, I always put on a front, but you know what it was like. They were all bigger than we were. The grown-ups who controlled our lives."

Zachary could taste the fear when she talked about it. He remembered how his heart would freeze as soon as one of his parents raised their voices. He put on a brave face for the younger kids, telling them how everything would be okay and that he would take care of them, but he still felt it.

He still knew that bowel-loosening terror that one of his parents was going to kill the other, or that they would turn on one of the children. All of the kids had been in the hospital at one time or another after suffering an 'accident' at home. Falling off a ladder, jumping a bike off a ramp, climbing up a dresser or bookshelf and pulling it over onto himself; he and the others could all be very inventive explaining their injuries to the authorities.

They had taken that fear with them to all of the families they went to. They still carried it with them.

"I know," he whispered, unable to raise his voice as the memories flooded his brain. As if one of his parents might hear him and fly into a rage. "I know, Feathers. But it's okay now. He's not going to hurt you anymore. None of them are."

The specters of their parents would never be gone. They would continue to taint every relationship he had. Even Mr. Peterson, who had always remained calm and had never raised his voice to Zachary, could still set Zachary off by touching him when he didn't expect it.

Heather's foster father had done more than accidentally triggering her. He had betrayed her trust and taken something precious from her.

Zachary realized that Heather was crying. He tried to swallow the lump in his own throat and to comfort her.

"Grant is out here. He doesn't want anything to happen to you. And I just met you again. I want to get to know you and the strong, loving woman you became. Don't give that scumbag another thought. He's not worth all of the time and agony you've wasted on him. He's in the past now. You have so much to look forward to."

She tried to answer, but her words were scrambled and he could only hear her crying.

"Put the gun down. You don't need it anymore. You're free of that fear now. Come on out. You have so much more to look forward to now."

Zachary was aware that the others in the bus were watching him, everyone so silent they would hear a pin drop, waiting for Heather's response.

"She's on the move," someone said in Zachary's headset. He didn't know if they could see her through the window or were watching her heat signature through the side of the house. He waited, holding his breath. "Subject is moving away from the hostage."

He hated that they referred to Mr. Astor as the hostage. He was the one who had held Heather hostage for three decades. But they didn't care about the history. Only about whether she was going to shoot him or not.

There was a dial tone in his headset for a brief moment before it was cut out by whoever was managing the audio.

"Subject has terminated the call."

Zachary headed for the door of the command center.

"Stay here, Mr. Goldman."

"I need to go out and meet her."

"Stay inside where it's safe. They will need to secure the sub—your sister— before you can see her."

"I can at least be out there so she can see me, see that I'm there for her."

"She already knows that, you've just been on the phone with her."

Ignoring him, Zachary stepped more quickly and got out of the bus without any of the cops grabbing him. Outside the command center, it was another story. He immediately ran into a wall of cops, most of whom were watching the house, listening to their earbuds, radios, and headsets. But a few of them were alert enough of their surroundings to immediately identify Zachary as a civilian who shouldn't have the run of the secured area, and a couple of them grabbed him to prevent him from going any farther.

"Sir!"

Zachary could at least see the door of the house from his position, so he didn't fight their hands, but stood still, watching. On cue, the door swung open.

Heather stood framed by the door, her hands held up, empty. No attempt at suicide by cop; she was surrendering. Zachary breathed a sigh of relief.

She was swarmed by a black-suited tactical squad. They took her to the ground, but they didn't throw her down. They weren't yelling or hitting her, but had to frisk her to make sure she didn't still have the gun or any other weapons. Zachary tried not to react to the sight of her being frisked and handcuffed. Just because she was being taken into custody, that didn't mean they were going to charge her with kidnapping or assault.

There were extenuating circumstances. Once the authorities understood what had happened, they would go easy on her. She could plead down to minor charges, maybe not have to serve any time. Some community service, a suspended sentence, probation…

"Now let me go see her," he told the cops holding on to him, once Heather was in handcuffs and on her feet again. They looked around for someone to give them directions. Jones was standing behind them, in the doorway of the bus. He nodded.

"Go ahead. But escort him over, I don't want chaos."

Zachary allowed the two big cops to walk him toward the house. Heather was back on her feet and a group of them were moving her toward a vehicle. Zachary hastened his step.

"Heather. Wait. Please let me see her."

They were talking in loud, clipped voices, but Zachary managed to make himself heard. They turned to him.

"Just let me see her. Let me talk for a minute."

Heather turned to him. Her eyes were sunken and her face streaked with tears. That morning, she had looked so fresh and bright and neatly-pressed, but the day had taken its toll on her.

"Heather. It's okay. He's going to be arrested and you're going to be alright. It's okay."

"I wanted to hear him say it. I wanted him to admit what he'd done."

"He still will. And he'll say it without a gun to his head."

He wanted to give her a hug, but didn't figure the cops were going to let him get that close to her. He sniffled back tears of his own. "You need to let her see her husband too. Let him know where you're taking her so he can pick her up."

The head of the tactical team looked at him. "She's not going to be going home."

"You just watch. When the media and the judge see the pictures of how she looked after he raped and beat her, she'll be going home."

They turned her away from him and continued getting her into a car for transport.

CHAPTER THIRTY-TWO

ACHARY WAS EXHAUSTED. JONES caught up with him after Heather was given a chance to speak to Grant and then transported from the scene. Zachary was watching the house, waiting for the men who had gone in to escort Robert Astor out. He wanted a good look at the man who had hurt his sister.

"You're a private eye?" Jones asked. He'd obviously talked to someone. Zachary's face and name had been in the media a lot over the past months and somebody had recognized him.

Zachary nodded. "Yeah. Zachary Goldman. Goldman Investigations."

"What do you have by way of proof that Astor was the one who assaulted your sister?"

"Besides her word?"

Jones shifted uncomfortably. He nodded. "Besides her word."

"We have the DNA profile of the baby she conceived as a result. It leads back to the Astors. You do a paternity test, and it will verify that he is the father. She was fourteen."

"We'll need a sample to test for ourselves."

"It's already in the hands of the PD. Talk to Detective Able. He should be around here somewhere, he's the one who called this in."

Jones gazed around, then nodded. He put his hands in his pockets, trying, Zachary thought, to look casual and relaxed. "You did a good job talking her down. A little irregular, but it worked."

"Yeah. I'm glad she didn't kill him. I was afraid she might before we got here…"

"He's a lucky man."

"Are you going to arrest him?"

"We're going to… invite him in for questioning. And if he doesn't give a DNA swab voluntarily, we'll get a warrant."

Zachary looked toward the door again. "I don't think you'll need a warrant."

"You think he'll give it voluntarily?"

"I think Heather already saw to that. Is he in there changing out of wet underpants?"

Jones's nose wrinkled in distaste.

"Bag them up and test them," Zachary advised. "Then you can confront him with the evidence."

Eventually, Zachary saw the door open, and several uniformed policemen escorted Robert Astor down the sidewalk to a waiting car. He wasn't handcuffed like Heather had been, but Zachary knew that he was going to have to face some pretty tough questioning anyway. There wouldn't be any way for the police to look the other direction and say that she was just some crackpot making wild accusations. After causing such a big circus, they were going to have to show either that she was right or that she was wrong. There would be no waffling about it. She wasn't going to be relegated to a quiet corner somewhere.

Astor was not a big man, as Heather had observed. Taller and heavier than Zachary, but that wasn't saying much. Zachary had always been the smallest in his school classes. Astor was in his early seventies, so he no longer looked like the man that Heather had respected and feared as a father figure. He was slightly stooped, had brown spots on his skin, and had hair that was more gray than its original dark brown. He didn't have a lot of wrinkles, so his face probably still looked pretty similar to what it had when he had been Heather's foster father. For the moment, he looked beaten-down and frightened. Zachary didn't know if that would last, or if he would be yelling about his rights and insisting that they release him once he'd had a chance to recover from the encounter with Heather. At least things had ended pretty quickly. He hadn't been locked in the house with Heather for hours on end. Some standoffs went on for hours or days.

After he was directed into the car and was sitting in the back seat, a woman was escorted over to see him. His wife, Zachary assumed. Her hair was a somewhat unnatural shade of red, gray at the roots, and she had a sad face with more wrinkles than her husband. She looked like she had lived a hard life.

She talked animatedly with the police officers around the car, obviously arguing to have her husband released or to let her talk to someone in authority, or whatever other concessions she could get. She didn't like the idea of them taking Astor in for questioning. She kept shaking her head, looking at her husband waiting in the car, and shaking her head again. Zachary drifted closer, hoping to be able to hear some of what she was saying. He caught Jones watching him, but Jones didn't stop him from getting closer, and neither did any of the other cops or authorities present. He listened carefully, trying to read her lips to catch the portions that he couldn't hear.

"I don't understand why you think he's done anything," she said. "How is it that the victim of violence gets blamed for what happened? You can't take him in to the station. If you want to talk to him, you can talk to him here. And you can wait until he's feeling better. This... this doesn't make any sense. This isn't how you treat a victim."

"The subject in this case made a lot of allegations. We'd like to get everything cleared up."

"What allegations? I don't know this person. Heather Garrity? Is she just some random person? She's crazy. She just picked this house out because it reminded her of something from her past. There's no way she knew what she was talking about."

Zachary frowned. For someone who didn't even know what accusations had been made against her husband, she had made an awful lot of defensive statements.

The cop who was trying to handle Mrs. Astor looked around and saw Jones watching. "Boss, you want to talk to this lady? Explain to her what's going on...?"

"I thought you were doing a fine job all by yourself, Walton."

"Boss..." Walton made a gesture toward her, frustrated, not wanting to deal with the disgruntled woman. He just wanted to get Astor in to the police station. Hopefully, he wasn't the one who had been tasked in questioning him, and someone who had a little more training would be trying to get a confession out of Astor. Maybe Jones himself. Maybe a woman detective who knew how to handle scumbags like Astor.

"You're Mrs. Astor?" Jones asked gently, looking at her.

"Yes. And I don't see why my husband is being detained when he was the victim here! It's ridiculous. Why should people who have been targeted be victimized all over again by the police like this?"

Why indeed? She had seen it happen to Heather. Was she remembering that, or was she only concerned about her husband?

"Your husband has been asked to come in to answer some questions about Mrs. Garrity and his history with her. I'm sure he can fill you in on it later."

"My husband? How would my husband know anything about her?"

In the car, Mr. Astor put his face in his hands. As if that could shut out his wife's argument and her voice.

"Robert? You tell him. You tell him that you don't know what they're talking about. Who is this person? She's not anyone that we know."

"Margaret..."

"What? You don't know her, so you can't answer any questions about her. This is ridiculous. They shouldn't be allowed to just interrogate anybody they want. There is a limit. And you don't have to agree to talk. You can refuse and they can't do anything about it."

"Margaret!" he said in exasperation.

She looked at him. "What?"

"It was Heather, Margaret. Not some stranger. Heather, our foster daughter."

"Heather," she repeated, her face suddenly going slack. "What would she be doing here? She hasn't lived here for years and years. And she never lived in this house. What did she want? Robert, you told her to leave, didn't you? Someone can't just go into your house and start threatening!"

"Margaret, please… shut up."

She stared at him, unable to believe he would talk to her that way. Zachary took another step forward, watching with interest. Heather had said that she was afraid of Astor, that he was authoritarian, but Zachary wasn't seeing a man who asserted his own position and bullied his wife. Zachary watched them both for the minutest tells.

Margaret Astor regained her composure, and deferred to her husband rather than making further accusations.

"What is this, then?" she asked. "I don't understand."

"She's accused your husband of aggravated sexual assault," Jones told her.

"Him?" Margaret's voice was scathing, and Zachary expected her to run down her husband's manhood right there. "He's an old man. Why would he chase after some girl from the past? Heather Goldman was never any great beauty as a girl. She was knock-kneed and pimply and I don't imagine she turned out to be much of anything. We did everything we could for that girl, officer, but she was sullen and ungrateful and it didn't matter what we did for her, she never appreciated it. In the end, she left us and ended up in a group home for girls like her."

Zachary clenched his fists. He would have liked to have clocked her one for running down his sister after all that she had gone through at their hands. They thought that they had done everything for her? All they had done was to damage and traumatize her further.

"Not recently," Jones said, once he could get a word in edgewise. "She says that your husband assaulted her when she was fourteen. When she was living with you."

Mrs. Astor's mouth snapped shut like a trap. She looked at her husband but didn't say anything to him. She didn't immediately jump to his defense, which Zachary found interesting. She was not afraid to speak her mind, but one thing that she hadn't said yet was that Robert Astor had been a saint and that he had never done anything to hurt anyone. She didn't immediately protest that he hadn't raped Heather. That he couldn't have.

"Trust that little minx to come up with something like that," she snapped, and shook her head. "I don't know what happened in the woods that day, Mr. Jones, but my husband was at work, not at home or in the park. He could not have done that to her." Her mouth closed, and her lips formed a long, thin, straight line. She glared at Jones, but she couldn't keep quiet about the injustice being perpetrated on her husband.

"The police investigated it at the time. If there had been any reason to suspect my husband, they would have arrested him at the time. She's just making things up, and why she's doing it now, thirty years later, I don't know. The woman's off her rocker. That's obvious from what happened here today, isn't it?"

"She was highly agitated," Jones agreed.

"Probably off her meds. Those kids were damaged. All of the children in that family. I used to hear about their exploits sometimes from the social worker or the other foster parents. They were uncontrollable. Lighting fires, starting fights, running away. Our little Heather was quiet by comparison. But that didn't mean she didn't get in any trouble. Never thought she had to follow anyone else's rules, that one. Did she think that they were told to stay out of the park because the school had nothing better to do than to think up unnecessary rules? But no, little Miss Delinquent had to do it anyway. And you look at what happened to her when she did."

Zachary swallowed. So there *had* been a history around the park. Maybe Robert Astor saw it as his own personal playground. And it hadn't mattered to him that one of the girls was his own foster daughter. He wasn't afraid of it being too close to home. After all, he wore a mask. No one could identify him.

"We went to the police at the time," Margaret insisted again. "Heather didn't want to go to the police. She didn't want to report it. But I did the right thing. I took her in. They questioned her and they gathered all of the evidence they could. None of it ever pointed at my husband. He was never a suspect in her case."

Jones took all of this in with equanimity. He nodded understandingly, making Mrs. Astor feel like he was on her side. "I understand there was a *baby*," he said, as if this were a shocking secret, something that pointed at Heather's delinquency.

"Yes, there was," Mrs. Astor said with relish. She appeared to be perfectly happy to dish up the details on every detail of Heather's ordeal. "She was terribly sick with morning sickness. I had hoped to leave her in school until later on in the pregnancy, but she was so sick all of the time that we had to pull her out. Said that she had mono and would be back the next year." Mrs. Astor leaned toward Jones to confide in him. "There was no talk of abortion and no talk of her keeping the baby. It wasn't like that then. She only had one choice, and that was to have the baby and put it up for adoption." She straightened up and shrugged her bony shoulders. "I hoped that she'd miscarry and not have to carry it all the way to term, but in spite of the morning sickness, she was healthy enough. When the baby came, we wrapped everything up lickety-split and had that baby to his adoptive parents within a couple of days. That's the way it should be done. Not all of this nonsense they have now."

"We have a sample of the baby's DNA. We will be able to identify your husband as the baby's father or rule him out. That should settle the question of whether he was the one who assaulted her once and for all."

Mrs. Astor went still again. She looked at Jones, and looked at her husband. Zachary wondered whether she had known or suspected back then. Surely she wouldn't have insisted on Heather going to the police station and having a rape kit done if Mrs. Astor had any suspicion that her husband had been Heather's rapist.

But she didn't say anything further and neither did Robert Astor.

CHAPTER THIRTY-THREE

ZACHARY EVENTUALLY SAT IN his car, eyes closed, going over the events of the day. He was beyond tired. Exhaustion had come and gone several hours before. Everyone was at the police station, but he hadn't been invited. In fact, Jones had made a particular point of non-inviting him, telling him to go home and not to show up at the police station.

"You leave it to us now. You've done your part. It's our turn to tie it all together and see if we can build a case that will stick."

"You'll take care of my sister? Don't let her talk to that woman or to him. Make sure that she's comfortable, and that she sees a judge as soon as she can...?"

"The wheels of justice move slowly, as I'm sure you know. They won't be too quick to release an armed gunman. But I think things will play out, if you're patient. She'll be able to see her husband at the police station for a few minutes. Probably best if you aren't working the case."

"Okay. But if she needs anything... call me."

As Zachary sat in the car by himself, reviewing it all in his head, his phone did ring. He worked it out of his pocket and looked at it. Tyrrell. Zachary looked out his window at the floodlights that had been set up around the house. There had been plenty of news reporters there to comment on the hostage-taking and the rumors surrounding what had happened there. Zachary had been sorely tempted to put in a few words of his own, but he hadn't. He needed to let justice take its course, as Jones had suggested. Zachary didn't need to be in the spotlight yet again.

Zachary answered the call. "Hi, T."

"Zachary? Was that Heather on the news? What's going on? What happened?"

"Sorry I didn't call... things have been moving pretty fast."

"It was Heather?"

"It was Heather."

"But who did she go after? You found the rapist? After all this time?"

"Yeah. It was the foster father all along. She went a little crazy when she found out it was him. But she remembered enough to know that it was true."

Tyrrell swore. "Poor Feathers. Is she okay?"

"She's safe. Her husband is with her at the police station. It might be a few days before they release her, but when the media gets wind of the story behind the hostage-taking... they won't let her stay in jail for long."

"I hope not." Tyrrell swore again. "At least she knows who it was, now. I think that was probably the worst part for her, not knowing who it was. At least if she knows, she has a direction to aim her anger. Without that, it's just everything. Never knowing where he might be, if it's the guy standing next to her in line. She could never start the healing process."

"Yeah." Zachary knew which way to aim his anger, but he was far from healing. He hoped it wouldn't be thirty years before he was able to face what had happened to him. He knew who the perpetrator was, and despite what he had told the police who had interviewed him, he remembered everything that had been done to him. But being able to move on... that was still too far in the distance to even see a pinprick of light at the other end of the tunnel.

"Zach."

"Yeah?"

"You okay?"

"Yeah."

"You want company tonight? You want to stay over here?"

"No. Thanks. I need my own space."

"Okay, man. But if you need to talk, just give me a call. Even in the middle of the night. I'm good at middle-of-the-night calls."

He didn't call Tyrrell in the middle of the night. He didn't call Kenzie either, and she didn't call him, though he was sure that, like Tyrrell, she must have seen the coverage on the TV and internet and known what it was all about. She kept her distance, waiting for him to acknowledge that he needed her. That was for the best. There were messages on his phone and in his email from Mr. Peterson, Mario Bowman, and a few other acquaintances as more details became available and they wanted whatever tidbits they could get from him.

He knew he wasn't being fair. They were people who, for the most part, really did care about him and wanted to know how he was more than just gathering juicy gossip they could share online. But he felt like they were vultures circling his dead carcass.

Or watching his dying body for his last breath, when they would swoop in and start the feast.

There was a message from Rhys. Not a voicemail message, of course, which would have been too difficult for him, but one of his gifs, sent over a messenger app, waiting for Zachary to open it.

He mentally prepared himself to interpret Rhys's intention.

Sometimes Rhys was more cryptic than others. Zachary didn't know whether he was intentionally vague or symbolic when he could have been more clear, or if that was just the way that Rhys's brain worked after the traumas he had been through.

The gif was not at all hard to interpret. It was the same one as Rhys had shown him the last time they had visited face-to-face. The drowning man, giving the three-two-one count and waving bye-bye.

Two meanings. Either Rhys was feeling worse and reaching out for help, or he was worried that Zachary would be feeling low and needing extra help. Despite the late hour, Zachary called Rhys's grandma.

"Vera. It's Zachary."

"Oh, Zachary. It's good to hear your voice. I'll go get Rhys."

"No, wait. Is he okay?"

She paused. "Is Rhys okay? Yes… why?"

"He sent me a message. I wasn't sure whether he needed help…"

"Or whether you do?"

Zachary laughed, a little embarrassed. "Well, yes."

"He saw you on TV again. He's always impressed when he sees you on TV. But he always worries, especially if he can't reach you."

"He's very intuitive."

"That he is," Vera agreed. "Now hold on and let me get him. It will only be a minute, you know he doesn't chatter on like some of us."

Zachary waited while she walked to Rhys's room. He heard her knock on the door to announce herself and then open the door.

"It's Zachary, Rhys."

Zachary closed his eyes, envisioning Rhys lying on his bed with his computer or his own phone, and tried to imagine how he would communicate what he wanted to say. Facial expression, body language, simple signs and gestures, and maybe a word or a picture displayed on Rhys's phone.

"Are you at home, Zachary?" Vera asked, after a few minutes of silence.

"Yeah. I'm home."

"Is Kenzie there?"

"No… I'm by myself."

"You should go to the hospital." Vera paused and double-checked with Rhys. "Is that right, Rhys? You think he should go to the hospital?"

Zachary sighed. He had told Rhys that he would check himself in if he was feeling any worse. And in the stillness of his apartment, isolated from the people who cared about him, wondering whether Kenzie was gone for good, what was going to happen to Heather, and stuck in a morass of his own memories, the darkness weighed him down inside and out.

He texted Rhys a selfie or himself in the hospital waiting room as he waited for his name to be called so that Rhys would know that he had followed through. Rhys texted him back a thumbs-up and a sad emoticon. Zachary didn't make any attempt to carry on a further conversation with Rhys. He powered off his phone and sat there waiting. His elbows on his knees and his head in his hands, he stared down at the floor.

He knew he should have sought help sooner. Everyone had known that he was shattered after Archuro. They had all told him that he had checked himself out of the hospital too soon. When he had finally gone back to his therapist, she too had suggested that at the very least, he needed a med review, and that he should seriously consider a couple of weeks at the hospital to get stabilized.

But like Heather, he was stubborn, and he figured he could just tough it out on his own. Checking himself into psychiatric always made him feel like a failure. The kid who couldn't control himself. A lunatic. No different from the homeless schizophrenics he saw wandering downtown in the city, mumbling or even yelling at their hallucinations.

"Mr. Goldman?"

He looked up to see a nurse hovering a few feet away from him, clipboard in hand.

"Would you come with me, please?"

CHAPTER THIRTY-FOUR

TYRRELL VISITED HIM. MR. Peterson visited him. Kenzie did not. Zachary didn't get any calls or messages from her. The staff in the unit didn't mention any inquiries from her. Zachary knew he should call her, but he couldn't bring himself to do it. As long as he didn't talk to her, it wasn't officially over. He could pretend that she was too busy, like he was, and that when life settled down for both of them, they would again be cuddling on the couch to watch an old Phillip Marlowe flick with a big bowl of popcorn resting on both of their laps.

And Heather came. Grant was with her, but he stayed in the background, letting her visit with Zachary.

"Hey, Feathers," Zachary awkwardly gave her a hug around the shoulders. "How are you doing?"

She looked around the unit. "Glad it's you here and not me." She laughed. "I guess that's a pretty tactless thing to say, isn't it? I guess I mean I'm lucky they didn't commit me involuntarily. After what I did... they certainly could have said that I was a danger to others and needed to be evaluated."

Zachary nodded. He wasn't offended by her saying that she didn't want to be there. "So is everything going to work out? Did they... do the DNA test against Astor?"

"It could drive a person crazy how long it takes to get results back, even when they are rushing it. But I know what it's going to say."

She sounded certain of herself. And she was calm about it. She didn't set any alarm bells ringing for Zachary. She sat down with him and held his hand for a minute. Her touch was reassuring, and in his mind's eye he could see the little mother he had known. A blond, scraggle-haired gamine with freckles sprinkled across her nose, taking him in hand to teach him life lessons and to try to keep him from running wild or attracting the attention of their parents. She gave his hand a squeeze, and he suspected that she was thinking of a short, spindly-legged boy with buzzed dark hair and the attention span of a gnat.

"I got a call from Ella."

He frowned. He took a minute to recall who Ella was. Ella Day, the genealogist who had worked on the genetic family tree. She had probably been concerned about Heather and wondered whether she wanted any further details of the baby's heritage. He wondered whether she had been able to pin down the father as Robert Astor from the GENEmatch database, or whether she'd only been able to isolate that branch of the tree.

"What did she have to say?"

"There are different flags that can be set in the GENEmatch database, for privacy and contact information. How much you want to reveal to the public if someone ends up being a close hit."

He nodded. "Uh-huh."

"When she uploaded the DNA profile, it triggered another match that wasn't public information. But I guess the person who uploaded his information got an email notification about it, so that he had the option of seeing what had been posted and making contact."

Zachary looked into Heather's eyes, and saw happiness rather than fear. "Was it...?"

"My son." Her eyes teared up. She looked at the ceiling and dabbed at the corners of her eyes. "The baby that I gave up."

"Did you meet him?"

"Yes. It was..." She closed her eyes, searching for the words. "It was such a comfort." She opened her eyes again. "He has a wonderful family. It wasn't like us, being raised in foster care. He had a stable, loving family and he's very attached to them. It's what I wanted for him."

"And now he knows who his biological mother is too."

She nodded. "He's going to keep in contact."

"That's cool." Zachary smiled. "Awesome."

"Thank you so much for helping me. Not just for solving a cold case that everybody said was impossible, but for helping me to find him too. I was afraid that I would resent him, or see Mr. Astor in him. But he's okay. I can look at him and just see Mikey, my son, and not anyone else. And know that he turned out okay."

Zachary walked out of the hospital to wait for his cab. It felt good to be out in the fresh air. He wasn't one hundred percent okay, but when was the last time he had been?

He'd been through some intensive therapy, another overhaul of his meds, and had been kept under observation for a couple of weeks to ensure that he was sleeping properly and wasn't being overwhelmed by suicidal thoughts. Healing would be an ongoing process, as it always was.

He did a double-take and blinked at the figure at the end of the sidewalk outside of the hospital entrance. The man turned and saw Zachary at the same time.

"Oh." He looked awkward. "Zachary. Hello."

Zachary approached Gordon hesitantly. His brain went spinning wildly with speculations of why Bridget's partner would be at the hospital. Bridget had been ill. She had said that the cancer wasn't back, but maybe she just hadn't known yet. Something had obviously been wrong. Gordon wasn't there for himself.

Gordon nodded to the cigarette in his hand, holding it away from himself as if it belonged to someone else. "Filthy habit. Just when you think you have it licked, some stressor kicks in and you're out on the sidewalk smoking again, everybody coughing and glaring at you as they walk by."

"Is everything okay?"

"Yes, she's fine," Gordon said immediately. "Just getting dehydrated. Can't keep anything down and we needed to get some fluids into her."

Zachary swallowed. Bridget must be on chemo again. Why had she lied to him? She'd said right to his face that the cancer wasn't back. He knew that a second appearance of the cancer so soon did not bode well for her chances of survival. Every time it came back, her odds went down significantly.

"Why didn't you tell me?"

Gordon didn't owe him any explanation. There was no rule that said Bridget had to report a recurrence of her cancer to her ex, or that Gordon should. Zachary was supposed to be living his own life, not always getting wrapped up in hers.

Gordon looked at him blankly. "Bridget said she had seen you. She didn't tell you?"

"I asked her, she said the cancer wasn't back."

"Oh, no." Gordon agreed. He touched Zachary's forearm briefly. "Heavens, not that." He searched Zachary's eyes. "She's pregnant."

CHAPTER THIRTY-FIVE

ACHARY WAS STILL REELING when he got back home. He busied himself with housekeeping details, putting on the coffee machine and taking out the garbage that he had neglected to dispose of before going to the hospital and which smelled to high heaven. He filled the sink to soak the dishes with petrified food cemented to them.

He didn't realize that he'd left the door open when he took the garbage out until he looked up and saw Kenzie standing there.

"Oh. I didn't hear you come in."

"Yeah, you seem a little distracted."

Zachary didn't know what to say to her.

"Lorne said that you were getting out today," Kenzie explained. She stepped into the kitchen and wrinkled her nose at the smell of the garbage that still lingered there. "I figured it would be a good time to stop by and get my things."

"Kenzie, I…"

"I pride myself on being able to take a hint, Zachary. You've been avoiding me. Pushing me away. I get it."

"I just…" He didn't know what to say to her. He didn't know what he wanted. He had hoped that once he was ready, she would come back, and they would be able to resume where they had left off. But he had screwed up by not talking to her about it. He had instead been a coward and avoided talking to her. What was she supposed to think?

He didn't want her to take her things. He didn't want her to be angry and disappointed in him. He'd never thought that she would just give up on him.

She faced him, her face pink. "Lorne told me that you were upset about me talking to him about our relationship."

"Well… yeah, sort of…"

"No 'sort of' about it. Be honest with me, Zachary. You can at least do that."

He looked down at his hands, anxious and embarrassed. He hadn't wanted to make a big deal of it. But it *had* bothered him. He forgave her for it; he knew that she was only trying to sort things out and figure out how to have a relationship with him, or if she even could.

"I was upset," he admitted.

"I shouldn't have talked to him. Not without your permission. I should have talked more to you about it, or asked if we could see your therapist together to discuss it. I just thought that Lorne might have some insight. He's known you longer than anyone else, saw you as a kid, and single, and with Bridget, so I just thought… he could help me to understand what you were going through and weren't ready to talk about. I knew that whatever happened with Archuro had triggered some really bad stuff. But I didn't know if it was all Teddy, or if it went deeper than that."

"I guess… it's deeper," he admitted. Too little, too late.

"I guess so," Kenzie agreed.

She headed toward the bedroom to gather up her belongings. Zachary followed her. He watched as she went through the drawers and closet and the little bathroom to search out anything that was hers.

"Kenzie, can we still—"

"Oh, don't give me the 'can we still be friends' speech. Show me a little respect."

He stood there, tapping his fingers to the sides of his legs, unable to be still.

"You should know that I talked to Bridget too," Kenzie said, without turning around to face him.

"What?"

"I know. It was stupid. I was desperate. You were so… it was obvious how badly you were hurting. And then when we started to get more intimate and it was obvious that you were just… totally checking out, I wanted to know if it had always been that way. And there was only one person I could think to ask."

Zachary remembered how Bridget had called him out of the blue, saying that she wanted to check on him. Had that been after she had talked to Kenzie? Kenzie had acted so indignant that Bridget had called. Was that to cover up the fact that she had spoken to Bridget herself? How could she expect Zachary to go on with his life and forget about Bridget, when she herself had involved Bridget again? How was Zachary supposed to move on?

"She's pregnant," he told Kenzie.

Kenzie had just picked up a bottle of pills and it fell to the floor of the bathroom with a loud clatter. She turned and looked at him.

"What?"

At least Bridget hadn't told Kenzie and refused to tell Zachary.

"I just ran into Gordon at the hospital. She's been admitted because she's dehydrated. Throwing up too much."

"And he told you she's pregnant? Not that she's sick, but she's *pregnant?* He said that?"

He was glad she found it just as shocking as Zachary did. He had told Kenzie their history. How Bridget had said that she never wanted children. The pregnancy scare that turned out to be cancer. Zachary remembered how the doctor had suggested Bridget have the eggs in her cancer-free ovary frozen before they started treatment, to bank them for later. Bridget hadn't even wanted to. She'd said she wasn't ever going to use them.

Apparently, she had changed her mind after meeting Gordon.

He nodded in answer to Kenzie's question. "He thought she had told me. But she hadn't. I was so worried that the cancer was back."

She looked at Zachary for a minute, shaking her head in disbelief. He wished that she would walk up to him and give him a hug and tell him that it was all going to be okay. Zachary would be just fine without Bridget. Bridget could have babies with Gordon, and Zachary would be just fine.

But she didn't.

She bent over and picked up the dropped pill bottle and readjusted her grip on the items she had collected.

"I should have brought a suitcase. I didn't realize how much stuff I had left here. Do you have a bag I could use?"

He went back to the kitchen for a couple of the plastic shopping bags under the sink that he never got around to recycling. He handed one to Kenzie and helped to fill the other, his eyes burning and a lump in his throat.

"I'm sorry about Bridget," Kenzie said. "I know that must be very difficult for you." She took both bags and let out a deep sigh. "Good luck. I hope you can be happy."

Zachary nodded, not trusting his voice.

She walked out of his apartment without another word.

**Did you enjoy this book? Reviews and recommendations
are vital to making a book successful.
Please leave a review at your favorite book store or review site
and share it with your friends.**

Don't miss the following bonus material:
Sign up for mailing list to get a free ebook
Read a sneak preview chapter
Learn more about the author

Sign up for my mailing list at pdworkman.com and get Gluten-Free Murder for free!

JOIN MY MAILING LIST AND

Download a sweet
mystery for free

PREVIEW OF HER WORK WAS EVERYTHING

Z ACHARY had heard about the death of Lauren Barclay in the news before he was contacted by Barbara Lee. It seemed like such a tragic waste. A promising young investment banker, she had been tragically killed in a slip-and-fall accident in her home. It wasn't particularly newsworthy, except for the fact that she had been an attractive, brilliant young woman, and that played well in the press on a slow news day. There were a lot of quotes from family and friends about how awful it was and what a wonderful person she had been. There would be a lot of mourners at her funeral.

But he hadn't really given it anything more than a passing thought. He had that little twinge of regret that he got when he read about a tragic death, but since he hadn't known her and there didn't seem to be anything unusual about her death, he had just given himself a second to feel bad for her and her family, and then moved on with his day.

Barbara Lee had told him that she wanted to meet about the death of a friend, but it wasn't until they sat down together for coffee that Zachary found out the friend was Lauren Barclay.

"I just can't believe it." Barbara sniffled and wiped at the corner of her eye. "She was so brilliant, so full of life, I can't believe she's gone. It just isn't fair. She was so young!"

Zachary nodded. "I read a little bit about it... there wasn't any hint in the news that there was foul play, though. They said it was an accident. She slipped in the tub?"

"I can't believe that. You don't think that's really what happened, do you?"

He looked into her bloodshot eyes. She was probably an attractive woman when she wasn't a complete mess. Her eyes were red, her face was blotchy, it looked like her hair had been put up into a partial bun at some point, but she had wisps of hair going in every direction, and she might have slept on it once or twice since she had put it up. She smelled of sweat.

"I don't know anything about it, so I wouldn't venture a guess," he said. "Why don't you tell me what you know about it? Why don't you think she slipped?"

Barbara rummaged in her handbag for a tissue and wiped her red nose. "I didn't even know she was home. She worked all hours, she was always at the office. I hadn't seen her for days. Then I got home... it was the middle of the day, and I could tell that she'd been there. I called out to her, but she didn't answer. I figured she probably came home to change and then had left again. Or maybe she'd fallen into bed and was catching a few winks before she had to go back. But she wasn't usually home during the day, so I didn't expect... to find her..."

Zachary thought he should touch her arm or make some other comforting gesture, but he wouldn't want it to be taken the wrong way. She might not think he was professional and would decide not to hire him.

"I'm so sorry... you were the one who found her?"

Barbara nodded, giving another sob. A bubble of snot blew out her nose and she wiped it away. If she had been the one to find her friend's body, it was no wonder she was such a mess. He couldn't imagine what that would have been like for her.

"Take your time," he told her. "You don't need to rush into this."

"I just want... to get it all out. Everybody wants to know, but nobody wants to hear about it. They all think that they want to hear the details, but... it isn't like watching a murder mystery on TV. It's something that... it's so unreal. I didn't know what to do. It was such a shock finding her, I felt like she was a mannequin or it was a prank, I just didn't want to believe it. I couldn't touch her. I called 9-1-1. And then... the police came, and the paramedics, and they all wanted me to tell them about finding her. I had to keep repeating it over and over again."

She stopped talking to wipe and blow again. Her nose was red and raw.

"But they didn't think there was any foul play?" Zachary prompted.

"No. But they didn't ask if there was anyone who wanted her dead or if she had a boyfriend that was violent or she had just broken up with, or anything like that. Not like on a cop show or in a mystery book. They just asked about... when I'd been home last, what time I had found her, when she would have gotten home. The paramedics asked if she had a history of epilepsy or fainting spells. Just... like it was an accident."

Zachary nodded. He sipped his coffee, which was still a bit too hot, but he wanted to give her time to think and to calm down a little. He would get more out of her if she was relaxed and composed than if she got all wound up and couldn't think straight.

"So what was the timing? You said she wasn't usually home during the day?"

"No. She worked really long hours. They were supposed to be at the office before their boss got in, so like six-thirty or seven at the latest. And she would work past dark. She would come home late, sleep for a few hours, and then be back at the office before I even had breakfast. Her hours were crazy."

"How long could she keep up like that? She must have had to take breaks on the weekend at least. Did she get a day off? Sunday?"

"She worked every day. It wasn't a rule that they had to work on weekends, but everybody did. It was so competitive. If the other interns were there on the weekend, then Lauren *had* to be there on the weekend. Otherwise, people would think that she wasn't as dedicated, and when her internship was up, they would just say goodbye and she'd have to find something else. No other investment banking firm was going to take her if she failed her internship there. She'd be... damaged goods. She'd have to find a job in something else, and she really wanted to be in finance. She really did."

"Why was it so cut-throat? Is that normal?"

"For investment banking, I guess it is. They're all like that. And Chase Gold is just a small firm, so if she couldn't make it there, there's no way that some Wall Street or Japanese company would look at her. She had to get a permanent position with Chase and work there for three years before she could go on to look for something else. No one would look at her otherwise."

Zachary shook his head. "Why would anyone want to work like that?"

Barbara pushed tendrils of hair away from her face, making a half-hearted attempt to push them back into the bun. "Lots of professions are like that, not just finance. Look at doctors and nurses. They're the same way. Long-distance trucking. Cab drivers."

"They all have rules now about not being able to work more than a certain number of hours in a row to prevent people from falling asleep at the wheel or cutting off the wrong leg."

"I guess. But this isn't that kind of place. I don't think there are any rules about not being able to work that long. She always worked for hours and hours. She slept at the office on the floor sometimes. Or didn't sleep at all for two or three days. You can't even imagine how bad it was."

Zachary thought about that. He pulled out his notepad and jotted down a few notes to himself. Avenues to pursue. Things not to forget. Barbara's eyes tracked his pencil as he scratched out the lines.

"You look like you've never held a pen before," she commented.

Zachary's cheeks heated. He looked down at his awkward grip on his pencil. Many teachers had tried to correct it during school. He'd moved between a lot of different schools, classrooms, and institutions, and the first thing they always tried to do was correct his grip.

"I have dysgraphia," he said. "That's the only way I can write. I know it looks bad to you, but it's the only thing that feels right to me. It's the only way I can see what I'm doing and form the letters."

She shook her head and didn't make any comment on his chicken scratch. He *could* write neatly. He did when he was filling out forms or writing something down for someone else. But it took two or three times as long if he wanted to make it tidy. When he was writing for himself, he could scrawl it however he wanted to. He could still read it. Usually. Sometimes. He could normally figure out what he had meant, even if he couldn't read every word.

"Lauren had beautiful handwriting," Barbara said, tears starting to make their way down her cheeks. "She should have been a schoolteacher, it looked like something out of a handwriting textbook. But…" she sniffled, "of course, teachers don't make anything, and Lauren wanted to make a lot of money. A lot of money."

"I don't really know what an investment banker does," Zachary said, "but I know it *is* something that I associate with making a lot of money. She was pretty wealthy, then?" He was thinking about motives. If there was anything to Barbara's fears—and he had to assume for the purposes of his investigation that there was—then whoever had killed her needed a motive. And money was always a good motive.

"No, not yet," Barbara said. "She was just starting out, so she wasn't making a whole lot. We rented an apartment together, and it's a nice one, not some little rat's nest, but neither of us could have afforded it on our own. Maybe we could, but only if we didn't need to eat or pay for heating or internet."

Zachary nodded. "And if she was just starting, then she probably still had school loans to worry about too."

"Yeah. All of that stuff. She wanted to get rich, but she wasn't there yet. We are—were—both making good money for our age, but nothing like it would be if she got to be a permanent employee with a few years under her belt."

"That makes sense. What's the name of the place that she worked?"

"I have to look it up…" She pulled out her phone and fiddled with it. "We always just called it 'Chase Gold,' because it was close to that, and that's really what they were trying to do. Chase after the gold and get as much as they could. For themselves and their clients."

Zachary waited while she tapped through a few screens on her phone, searching for it in her contacts or on an internet browser. He made a couple of other short notes while he waited. Things to look into. Questions to ask. Who would want to kill a young woman who spent all of her time working and was still in debt?

"Yeah, here it is," Barbara offered. "Drake, Chase, Gould." She spelled Gould for him to make sure he got it right. "She was really devoted to her job. And I don't just mean that she liked it or put a lot of hours in. She did, but there was more to it than that. She thought they were the best company to work for, and that they were going to get her everything she wanted. She was always saying how good the management was, how well they took care of their employees, how good the other people she worked with were. She thought they were going right to the top. That they would compete with the Goldman

Sachs and Wells Fargos of the world. They just started up a few years ago, and their portfolios were amazing, especially considering how short they had been in business. Or so she told me." Barbara sniffed and rolled her eyes. "Multiple times."

Zachary smiled at that. Nice to hear about someone who liked her job. "That's great."

He leaned back in his seat. The coffee shop didn't have particularly comfortable chairs. He supposed it was to encourage people to have their coffees and to move on, not to just camp there drinking lattes and using the free wifi all day long. He looked at Barbara.

"So what makes you think it wasn't an accident? Tell me about the things that made you concerned."

"You think I'm just crazy, don't you? Everybody just looks at me like I've got two heads. How could a slip in the bathtub *not* be an accident? It's like being hit by a bus, the classic accident that everyone uses as an example."

Zachary waited. He wasn't the one who was doubting her opinion or sanity. He waited for her to stop defending herself and to fill the silence with her concerns. She would, if he just waited.

"It just doesn't fit that Lauren was even home," Barbara said. "Like I said, she was never home during the day. Between ten in the evening and six in the morning, if she was lucky. That's it. No weekends. No days off. No afternoons going home to have a nap. She just shouldn't have been home."

"What was the time of death?"

Barbara looked at him. She shook her head. "I don't know."

"What time had she gotten home? You were out of the apartment from when until when?"

"I was out with a friend overnight. So I didn't get back until... ten or eleven o'clock. That's when I found her. But she was never home at that time of day."

"But if she had been running a bath at six, and hit her head then, that would make sense."

Barbara sighed. "I know. Everybody says it makes perfect sense. But it doesn't. She was young and healthy. She wouldn't just fall down and die. She wasn't drunk or doing drugs. She didn't have any diseases that would have made her pass out. To just step into the tub and fall down and die...? That doesn't make sense either."

"Sure. I understand that. No one expects something like this to happen. But she could have had the flu, or just wasn't paying attention and slipped."

"She wasn't an old lady. Maybe old ladies slip and fall like that, but Lauren never did. If she slipped, she would have caught herself. If she got hurt, she would have called someone to help her."

Zachary made a couple of notes of questions to pursue. He'd have to talk to the medical examiner's office, and he really didn't want to. He would have to psych himself up for it.

"What was the mechanism of death?"

Barbara frowned. "She... fell...?"

"Yeah. Did she drown? Or did she die from the blow to the head? Brain swelling or bleeding?"

"Drowning, I guess. She did hit her head, but then she went into the water. That's where I found her. I guess... she knocked herself out, and then she didn't know that she was drowning, couldn't do anything about it."

"The medical examiner hasn't made a finding yet?"

"I don't know. I guess that's what they're working on right now."

"Okay. We'll need a copy of their report once there is a finding. I'll put in a requisition for it."

Which meant that he would take the elevator down to the basement level at the police station. He would walk up to the desk and fill out one of the forms in his neatest printing, trying his best to avoid an intensely awkward situation with Kenzie.

He wasn't sure how she was going to react. Things had been pretty quiet since they had broken up. He felt horrible about the way everything had ended, but he hadn't called her and begged for her to come back. He hadn't given her excuses for his behavior or followed her around in his car. He had done his best to just back out of her life and forget about what they had shared together.

But going back there, onto her turf, he didn't know how she was going to treat him. Would she yell at him and call him out the way that Bridget did? Would she go all quiet or ignore him? Or just stare at him with her dark, intense eyes boring into him, hating him for the time she had wasted on him?

"Uh... Mr. Goldman?"

Zachary blinked and refocused on Barbara. It was Barbara he had to talk to and interact with. He needed to stay focused on her. "Sorry, just thinking about something. What was that?"

"If the medical examiner says that it was just an accident, that will be the end of it, won't it? The police won't investigate it as a homicide. They won't hold anyone responsible."

"No. But if I find something, we can get them to open an investigation. I've done it before. I'm assuming you already know that. That's probably why you picked me out, isn't it?"

She gave an embarrassed little shrug and nodded.

"I can't guarantee anything," Zachary said. "I don't know whether it was an accident or something else... but it sounds like it's going to be pretty hard to find evidence that it was anything else. I'll look. I'm just warning you... Don't expect miracles. Just because I've been able to prove that other deaths were homicides, that doesn't mean that I can prove any death was. Some of them are going to be just what they look like."

"I know. But… no matter what anyone else says… I want to do everything I can for Lauren. I can't just close my eyes and say 'oh, what a bizarre accident.' I need to know. I need to do everything I can to bring the responsible party to justice. If there is a responsible party."

"You said before that the police hadn't asked you anything about an ex-boyfriend or anyone who might have wanted to harm her."

"Yes. I mean no. They didn't. They didn't want to know anything like that."

"Does that mean that she *did* have an ex-boyfriend who might have wanted to harm her?"

Barbara's eyes widened. "Oh, no. I didn't mean to imply anything like that… She did have ex-boyfriends, of course, but no one who was bitter or anything. No one who ever threatened her or stalked her."

"Was there anyone who was abusive while they were together? She might not have told you that he hit her, but was there ever anyone that you suspected… that you thought might have hurt her? Even someone who was verbally or emotionally abusive. Someone you didn't feel comfortable around or were glad that she broke up with him."

"No… I don't think so… everyone that she was with was pretty casual… it isn't like she had any time for a relationship. She would take someone to a firm event, or sometimes she brought someone home from work… but she didn't really have a life outside of the office."

"She dated people from the office?"

"Yes… she went out for a meal with them, maybe brought one or two back to the apartment to…" she shrugged uncomfortably, "…to sleep it off. Just to crash somewhere before they had to go back to the office again in a few hours. There just was so little time, and she was under so much pressure… it didn't leave time for a real relationship."

"Even if it isn't what you would call a relationship… men can still decide that they want what they can't have. They might think that she should have spent more time with them, given them more attention, maybe not gone on to see someone else so soon… if they went out to eat, or he went home with her, then he might have expected more. He might have thought that it was turning into a committed relationship when it wasn't."

"I guess so. I don't know. I never saw anything like that. The guys that I met from Chase Gold always seemed pretty casual. Not like they were pining after her or acting possessive."

"Do you have the names of some of the men that she dated? Maybe an address list?"

"All of her numbers would be on her phone… I guess it's at the apartment. The police didn't take it, I don't think. They just took a quick look at her electronics, but there wasn't anything that didn't look right to them, so they said they didn't need to take anything with them."

"Who is the detective on the case?"

"I don't think there was a detective. Just… whoever comes out to have a look when someone dies suddenly. They're not really investigating it. Just filling out the forms."

"Someone would have been assigned to it. I'll look into it. See if they have any thoughts."

"They aren't going to. They are just going to think that it was an accident, like a million other accidents that happen every day."

~ ~ ~

Order *Her Work Was Everything*, Zachary Goldman Mysteries #7 by P.D. Workman now!

ABOUT THE AUTHOR

Award-winning and USA Today bestselling author P.D. (Pamela) Workman writes riveting mystery/suspense and young adult books dealing with mental illness, addiction, abuse, and other real-life issues. For as long as she can remember, the blank page has held an incredible allure and from a very young age she was trying to write her own books.

Workman wrote her first complete novel at the age of twelve and continued to write as a hobby for many years. She started publishing in 2015. She has won several literary awards from Library Services for Youth in Custody for her young adult fiction. She currently has over 40 published titles and can be found at pdworkman.com.

Born and raised in Alberta, Workman has been married for over 25 years and has one son.

~ ~ ~

Please visit P.D. Workman at pdworkman.com to see what else she is working on, to join her mailing list, and to link to her social networks.

~ ~ ~

If you enjoyed this book, please take the time to recommend it to other purchasers with a review or star rating and share it with your friends!

Lightning Source UK Ltd.
Milton Keynes UK
UKHW021441090820
367887UK00010B/269